Miss Kwa Kwa

Praise for *Miss Kwa Kwa: Traditional Weapon*

'Laugh out loud with a gem of a book... This novel is better than hilarious; Simm's characterisations of everyone from a rural dorp to a Hillbrow prostitute to a politician are spot on. Male writers who can get into the head and the heart of a woman are thin on the ground and a delight to encounter. You will laugh aloud reading this book.'

– Rehana Rossouw, *Business Day*

'We have definitely reached a stage in our democracy where we can begin to laugh at ourselves, and for the first time a novel has been written which does just that... a great read that will keep you entertained from start to finish.'

– Angelique Serrao, *The Star Tonight*

'An entertaining and neatly crafted romp... Read it for a rollicking, action-packed adventure with a cast of unusual characters.'

– Tumi Makgetla, *Mail & Guardian*

'I almost got stomach cramps, I was laughing so hard. This book gave me hope for South African literature.'

– Itumeleng Motuba, *Sowetan*

'★★★★★ Simm's novel is filled with satire, caricatures and outrageously funny passages that will make you laugh out loud... A novel that is as amusing as thought-provoking... Another reason why local is lekker.'

– Nikki Temkin, *Heat*

'A marvelously witty book. Rainbow nation at its best.'

– *Elle* magazine

'★★★★ This book is hilarious. MK is the most loving, charming, vile, disturbed, ambitious and shameless hussy I have ever encountered in a South African book. I loved her and found myself rooting for her to succeed.'

– *City Press*

'Simm skep oortuigende karikature om die satiriese trant van die roman te verskerp. In Miss Kwa Kwa beeld hy die omstandighede en emosies van die Suid-Afrikaner ná tien jaar van vryheid op skreeusnaakse wyse uit... 'n absolute plesier om te lees.'

– Lydia du Plessis, *Volksblad*

Miss Kwa Kwa

The Dark Side of the Braai

Stephen Simm

JACANA

The content of this novel is a pure product of imagination and not based upon fact. Characters, institutions, corporations and organisations are either products of the imagination, or if real, used fictitiously without any intent to describe their actual conduct, thoughts, intentions or backgrounds.

Miss Kwa Kwa is based on a character created by Stephen Simm and Makgano Mamabolo.

First published by Jacana Media (Pty) Ltd in 2007

10 Orange Street
Sunnyside
Auckland Park 2092
South Africa
+2711 628 3200
www.jacana.co.za

ISBN 978-1-77009-386-7

Cover design by miss sweden
Set in Warnock 12/15pt
Printed by CTP Book Printers, Cape Town
Job No. 000565

See a complete list of Jacana titles at www.jacana.co.za

This book is dedicated to a bunny, two kitties, a jowa,
and mental health professionals everywhere.

Prologue

THE WORLD IS full of strange and perplexing questions, questions that seem not to have satisfactory answers. Questions too big for the limited human brain to grasp. Questions like: Where do we come from? Can the universe really be infinite? What actually goes on in the Oval Office? Why are there so many ads for hair products and cars? How big a concern is global warming? And all the crazy natural disasters, and even crazier fundamentalists? Will we all end up as low-fat, high-fibre, white-teethed, gentle-tanned and even-complexioned ad-bots with shiny hair (great body, multi-dimensional colour, no trace of grey), with agreeable children (get enough calcium, stain-free clothing), who talk in slogans and sound-bites even as the world goes up in flames thanks to some catastrophe courtesy of either Mother Nature or Mister Warmonger?

And what does any of this have to do with Miss Kwa Kwa?

Who the hell is Miss Kwa Kwa? Just what exactly happened the week she cannot remember?

And can there ever truly be innovation in toothbrush technology?

Be warned...

The story you are holding in your hands is dangerous.

The material clutched in your eager little paws at this very moment is flammable, incendiary, nonsensical, ridiculous, grave, cautionary, important and entirely inconsequential.

It's a pack of dirty lies.

It's all true.

So don't say you weren't warned.

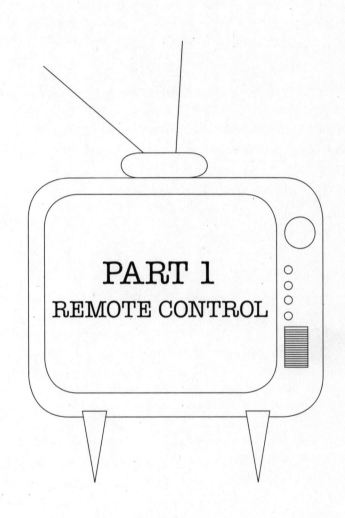

PART 1
REMOTE CONTROL

Someone and a
Bunch of Nobodies

JOHANNESBURG IS CITED as the largest manmade forest in the world. Thus it would be a fair statement to say it is populated with wildlife. Not the kind of wildlife, however, that Africa is famed for.

Nevertheless, the city of Johannesburg is crawling with wildlife. Predators aplenty and massive herds of wide-eyed prey. In Joburg, you're either one or the other; sitting on the fence is not an option (particularly since most fences are fitted with either spikes or barbed or electrified wire).

Johannesburg is also regarded as the 'New York of Africa', i.e. it is the money capital of its fatherland and its continent. For this reason, it is also called iGoli, the 'City of Gold'. This is the reason so many continue to flock here despite its considerable risks.

One such bright-eyed hopeful is a young woman, known to a few as Palesa, to most as Miss Kwa Kwa, and to herself as MK. Her journey into the City of Gold had been an eventful one, to say the least. Frustrated by the limitations of her tiny hometown, she had migrated to Johannesburg in the hopes of using her title, Miss Kwa Kwa, to ensure bigger and brighter fame. As it turned out, the title was not enough. Nor were blackmail, children's television or hijacking (or, as she had dubbed it, 'shejacking'). Several unfortunate parties had fallen prey to MK in an impressively short period of time. In the aftermath of the whole debacle, a romance had bloomed, a friendship was forged, and only one serious injury was sustained (and he'd deserved it).

All in all, she was just a simple country girl.

The aforementioned romance did not include MK. More about that later.

The injury occurred when Pieter Dippenaar fell down a flight of steps and broke his neck. But don't feel sorry for him – he'd been trying to kill our fair heroine, and was a pretty despicable guy all-round.

The friendship forged was between MK and a television producer named Mick, and had sparked on the same fateful night as the other events mentioned. It had also led to Mick producing a television talk show for MK: it traded on MK's alter ego, Miss Kwa Kwa, and was titled *Kwa Kwa Konfidential*. That's all you really need to know right now. The details of the chaos leading to this point are shrouded in secrecy and conjecture and are probably best left in the dark (and the pages of the other book).

In a city that runs on trading, MK traded heavily on concepts prefixed by 'mis': misperception, misinformation, misleading, misrepresentation. She counted on being misread, misinterpreted and misjudged. All of this under the guise of the most important 'mis' – Miss Kwa Kwa.

Miss Kwa Kwa could charm your socks off. Miss Kwa Kwa was loud, endlessly lovable and utterly unforgettable. Unfortunately

Miss Kwa Kwa was not very bright, not at all.

This is where MK differed from her public persona – MK was incredibly intelligent, with a disturbingly brilliant gift for reading people. However, it served MK much better not to let people know this. Who has their guard up when dealing with a rural beauty queen? MK had long since realised that this was key in dealing with people, a species famous for being suckered by first impressions.

Superstardom Lesson No. 38: You don't need to be smart to be famous! I could give you examples here but I don't have that kind of time. Open a magazine or turn on the news.

Mick Emmott was the only person with a fairly accurate picture of these two sides of MK and, as such, was best kept on her good side. Aside from this measure of self-preservation, MK genuinely loved Mick – he was her first real friend. The fact that he was gay didn't really bother her. A middle-aged man, Mick had only had two significant relationships in his life: the first was a disastrous marriage in his youth (the only good outcome of which was his son), and then a long-term partnership with a man who had left him for a younger model, causing Mick to have a life-changing heart attack. These days Mick was single, and MK thought of him more as a spinster than a homosexual. He was a workaholic, which MK admired – especially since he produced *Kwa Kwa Konfidential*.

Miss Kwa Kwa was joined by different guests, mostly famous, and interviewed them. The innocent Miss Kwa Kwa asked seemingly innocent questions, but these were carefully constructed by MK to reveal the hypocrisy or stupidity of the guest. Although these were qualities MK herself deemed necessary, she despised them in others, specifically so-called 'role models'. The difference, as she saw it, was that her actions didn't impact negatively on the public at large. When someone in a very high position displayed them, however, the results could be terrible for many people. While notoriously wary of people,

MK had a secret soft spot for innocents – children. And anyone that threatened their future, either directly or in the tiniest, most insidious way, needed to be rooted out, whether it was a flaky celeb that promoted brainlessness or a politician that abused his power. Hence, *Kwa Kwa Konfidential*, while primarily aimed at boosting her starpower, was subtly underpinned with this drive. The only way she – Miss Kwa Kwa, that is – got away with it was through her enchanting 'naivety'. Everything had been going swimmingly with the show until it had suddenly and unexpectedly drowned. After only three screened episodes the show was cancelled.

Apparently the broadcaster had taken exception to remarks Miss Kwa Kwa had made to her guest, a high-profile politician who had recently made news by drunkenly crashing his car into the wall of someone's house. He had only agreed to do the show on the condition that the incident was not discussed. To MK's credit, she had not specifically mentioned the incident, but rather had 'innocently' offered him a drink, and beamed: 'Go ahead. We've warned the residents in the surrounding areas.'

Although the short-lived show had garnered Miss Kwa Kwa a small cult following, it had not achieved any of her larger objectives, which included, but were not limited to, global adoration and perhaps even domination. And so she found herself unemployed again, and in need of a meal ticket. She decided it was time to set her sights on new prey...

And what better place to hunt than the largest (manmade) forest in the world?

Until the eerie day she'd awoken to discover that perhaps *she* was now prey.

She could taste sand in her mouth, and hear murmuring in a language she didn't understand. Of the many possible ways of waking up, this didn't seem a particularly auspicious one. It seemed unlikely that a wonderful day – or even a normal one – was to follow.

Also, she felt unable to move, and her eyelids seemed exceedingly heavy. She fought to open them, noting groggily that this was much more difficult than it should be. Eventually, with a strain that seemed not unlike pushing a dead rhinoceros up a hill, MK managed to open her eyes a smidge.

At first nothing made sense, but soon her vision had cleared enough for her to realise that she was lying on her side. The vertical sliver of image was as perplexing as her sudden and mysterious physical difficulties: at the bottom was nothing except sand and rocks, which in the middle of the picture met with sky. The sky was a purplish colour and the sand a gold that almost glowed. Sunset.

Where the hell was she?

She decided to get up, and was most unnerved to discover that her body simply would not comply. Or could not. Panic set in, an instant cold front, but still she could not move. Hoping her voice still worked, she tried to call for help. What came out was a hoarse whisper that sounded more like a fingernail scraping over paper.

One of the murmuring voices rose sharply, again in the strange language, and a shadow fell over her.

Two seconds later, the darkness rushed in again.

MK awoke with a fright, and scrambled to her feet.

She glanced around her flat and was relieved to see her bedroom around her. A cream-coloured blur disappeared under the bed, leaving only a bushy tail sticking out. Her kitten, Wiggy. MK looked down at her hands and arms and was thrilled to note that they did exactly what she wanted them to. She wiggled her legs around and was similarly pleased with their compliance.

Just a nightmare, she thought, flooding with the special kind of relief reserved for this scenario. *Thank God.*

'Wiggy,' she cooed, squatting down beside her bed. 'Did I give you a fright, little boy?' The protruding tail swept to one side, agitated. She grabbed it playfully, and he emerged, wide-blue-eyed. 'Oh baby, I'm sorry!' He circled her, and stuck his shaggy tail in her face magnanimously. Apology accepted, apparently. Wiggy had come into MK's life two months prior: she had taken her trash downstairs and nearly fainted at the sight of something moving in the bin. Relieved that it was not a baby, but rather a baby cat, MK almost walked away and left him there. Until he spoke, a squeak of such plaintive desperation that she turned back. One of his eyes looked weepy, and didn't seem able to open all the way. Aside from that he was a cute little bugger. He hopped and shambled over the giant rubbish bags towards her and squeaked again, more insistently this time. Resolving that she would take him to the vet to get fixed up, and then to the nearest animal shelter, MK picked him up. MK had always judged herself to be too selfish for a pet, and hated the idea of something depending on her. No, he'd have to go.

But two months later, here they were: mother and furry, four-legged child.

MK picked him up and rubbed her face in his fluffy belly even though she knew he hated it. She felt his paw batting the top of her head, and chuckled as she put him down. When she headed for the front door, Wiggy darted ahead of her and plonked onto his back outside the kitchen. Like his owner, he was a master manipulator.

'One sec, boy,' she smiled. 'I'm just grabbing the paper.'

The first thing MK noticed when she opened her door was that it was later than she usually rose – the sun was already high in the sky.

Wow, no wonder he's so hungry.

The second thing she noticed was a small pink envelope pinned to her newspaper. Written on it was simply '23' – the number of MK's flat. She sighed – this was no doubt the work of Mrs Siegl, the busybody and self-anointed 'caretaker' of the building, who lived at number 22. The last note had requested that MK please keep her television volume lower. It also implied that perhaps MK should have her hearing checked. That one had arrived in a cheery yellow envelope with a sun-moon-and-stars motif on it. The envelope had proved more offensive to MK than its contents.

Speaking of the strawberry-soap-scented devil... there was Mrs Siegl, peering through the lace curtains of her kitchen window at MK. Their eyes met. Mrs Siegl cursed to herself for being spotted; MK cursed to herself for acknowledging that she had been spotted.

'Hi,' called Mrs Siegl, opting to pretend that she had intended to be seen.

MK winced at her neighbour's chipper falsetto, again amazed at how it belied the evil heart behind it. She waved and hurried to get back inside before Mrs Siegl initiated a 'chat'.

'You're back?' asked Mrs Siegl loudly through her closed window.

MK only smiled, pretended she hadn't heard, waved and retreated into the Siegl-free safety of her own flat.

Back? Back from where? wondered MK as she tossed the note onto the kitchen counter and unwrapped her newspaper. Wiggy flopped against her ankle impatiently.

'Yes, yes, baby, one second.'

She unfolded the paper to read the headlines. As her eyes scanned the page, one tiny detail caught her eye. Attention to detail was, of course, one of MK's great strengths.

The day was wrong.

The paper said 'Thursday' and today was Friday. Although MK was accustomed to sloppiness in South African journalism, she couldn't imagine how *this* could've slipped through the cracks. Especially this publication – it was the best, the reason she had it delivered daily. Her eyes skimmed across to the date.

The date was wrong.

Her quick mind raced overtime to come up with possible explanations: she had somehow woken up a week in the future (unlikely), the editor had been on serious drugs last night (possible), or she had been asleep for a week (not very likely). A cold, creeping panic, not unlike the one from her nightmare, began flooding through her. What was going on?

Her heart had already slowed with dread, when a loud knock on the window set it racing again. Mrs Siegl grinned at her from the corridor outside. MK smashed the window, grabbed Mrs Siegl by the scruff of her hand-knitted jersey and shook her violently.

Well, she wished she could do that, anyway.

Instead she caught her breath and went to the window to open it.

'I've got them all,' said Mrs Siegl through her sparkling false teeth. 'Do you want them now?'

'Want what, Mrs Siegl?' asked MK, keeping her tone polite. Maintaining the mask under pressure was another of MK's infamous gifts.

'You haven't read my note,' said Mrs Siegl, a touch miffed. 'Your newspapers were piling up outside your door the whole week, so I took them into my flat.'

MK's dread deepened. She didn't show it, of course.

'Thank you,' she managed.

'Really, my dear,' said Mrs Siegl in the tones of the kindly old neighbour she really wasn't, 'if you're going to go away, you should make a plan. We can't have dirty old things cluttering up the corridor. It's not that kind of building.'

'Well then, best *you* clear out of the corridor, *my dear*,' retorted MK sharply before slamming shut the window and closing the curtains to Mrs Siegl's shocked face.

MK leaned against the counter to steady herself. The date on the newspaper was correct. Somehow she had lost a week of her life.

'*Mrowr*,' yelped Wiggy from the floor.

She gasped. *Did the cat get fed?* She was both comforted and alarmed by what she saw next: five small bowls were lined up in the corner, empty apart from the odd piece of dried cat food. Beside them was her biggest cooking pot, filled with water.

What the bloody bloody hell is going on?

Cape Town had already been home to indigenous peoples for tens of thousands of years before it was 'discovered' by Portuguese sailors in the fifteenth century, but history is written by the victor, as the saying goes. It is undeniable that things certainly got more eventful after that point. Almost immediately it was given two names: the Cape of Storms and the Cape of Good Hope, and ever since then it has experienced good measures of both.

Table Mountain, glorious beaches and a currency that favours the foreign continue to draw international visitors in droves. Like Joburg, you may hear numerous languages and accents in one day, although many of them are not local.

Lincoln Thomas, far from his home in Yorkshire, was sitting in a beachfront restaurant, nursing two things – one pleasant (a cold beer) and one not (sunburn). He cursed himself for falling asleep in the sun. Like many Brits before him, he had been astounded by true summer heat, the African sun. He had also completely underestimated its power and was now suffering the consequences. His usually pale complexion had become what could only be described as electric red.

So much for getting shagged tonight, he thought miserably.

Lincoln, or 'Link' as his mates back home referred to him, was on holiday in Cape Town alone. The plan had been for said mates and him to travel together, but the plan had been changed the night before their departure by the group's announcement to Link that he was no longer welcome in their circle.

Link had been upset by this.

'You just can't keep your bloody clothes on, Link,' explained Eddie, the apparent spokesperson for Link's supposed friends. 'Every time we go down the pub, you get a few pints down you and wind up starkers.'

'But,' stammered Link, 'it's just for laughs. You guys used to think it was funny.'

'Yeah, Link, when we were twenty.'

Link frowned, bewildered.

'We're forty now.'

Krissie sat by the hotel pool sipping a cocktail, and took a moment to appreciate the fact that the legal drinking age in this country was eighteen. Unlike Lincoln Thomas, Krissie Blaine *was* still twenty and a native of Los Angeles, California, USA; the Greatest Gosh-Darn Nation in the World.

Some people are born with a silver spoon in the mouth – Krissie was born with a whole cutlery set. In solid gold. Encrusted with jewels. Displayed in a priceless cabinet and polished every hour-on-the-hour by a horde of uniformed servants. Being the daughter of an American internet mogul had its perks.

It also had its drawbacks, as Krissie had recently discovered.

Krissie had caught the public's eye a couple of years ago as one of a legion of young, gorgeous, rich LA party girls famous for... well, being famous really. Although they picked and tried different careers occasionally, none of them had any discernible talent apart from the astounding aptitude to patronise every watering hole in LA every night. Just lately, however, it had begun to catch up with them.

Two were in rehab, and another had recently been photographed 'purging' in the bathroom at a banquet for raising awareness of eating disorders. A fourth had just been crucified by the media for her lacklustre feature film debut (one reviewer had even gone so far as to suggest that the film stock might have been better used to 'throttle the dim star' before she 'deprives the world of more oxygen... or worse – acts in another film').

Krissie herself had thus far dodged the bullet. She had recently embarked on an affair with a married Hollywood leading man, which (miraculously) had not yet been discovered. When everything began to go south for her friends, she decided it would be best to get away for a while.

Now she was in Cape Town, staying at the very exclusive Hotel Shmotel, famed amongst the world's glitterati for its privacy and discretion. She had arrived just two days prior, and so far the world press weren't onto her location. Her first two days had been uneventful, mostly consisting of sleeping and room service, but Krissie was beginning to get itchy feet.

What's a party girl without a party?

She sighed to herself and gazed over at Table Mountain. She wondered what the first Americans must've thought when they sailed into the bay and saw it (Krissie had never paid much attention at school, and just assumed that America had discovered the whole world). She had somehow expected it to be bigger. And since her arrival the clouds hadn't yet done the tablecloth thing on top.

She was stirred from her reverie by the approach of a hotel employee – the same one who had been staring at her non-stop since her arrival. A tall girl with short red hair, a pug nose and large hips. As she neared, Krissie peered over her sunglasses (Karl Lagerfeld) at the name badge on the girl's blouse: Jackie.

'Sorry, Miss Blaine,' said the hotel girl, carefully enunciating her words so that the foreigner could understand. Krissie again took note of the strange accent. Krissie had often been at the same events as Charlize Theron. Charlize Theron didn't sound like this. She spoke proper English.

'Sorry?' drawled Krissie. 'Why? What did you do?' And then, a touch alarmed: 'You didn't go through my luggage, did you?'

'No, no, no,' put in Jackie quickly, 'nothing like that.'

'Good.'

'Well, you haven't really been out of your suite until today, and...'

'So what?' snapped Krissie.

'No, it's fine, fine! We want you to have a pleasant stay, and do

15

as you wish. I'm just here to fill you in on some of the interesting places in Cape Town you may want to experience.'

'Oh,' said Krissie, thinking of nightclubs.

'Yes,' said Jackie, sensing a slight thaw in Krissie's demeanour.

'Like what?'

'Well, many of our visitors like to visit Robben Island...'

'That like an amusement park?' asked Krissie.

'Um, no,' replied Jackie, forcing a smile. 'It's an island where many Struggle fighters were imprisoned during apartheid – including Nelson Mandela.'

'Wow,' said Krissie, affecting a moment of solemnity. 'What else?' She slurped the last of her cocktail through the straw.

'Well,' said Jackie, raising her voice, 'there are a number of historical sites.'

'Do you have any amusement parks?'

'We have one,' replied Jackie.

'We have like a million in LA,' sighed Krissie, fast beginning to tire of Jackie.

'Well,' said Jackie, 'that must be fun.'

'I'll have another one of these,' sighed Krissie, shoving her empty glass at the irritating hotel girl. She was bored of her now.

'Certainly, Miss Blaine,' mumbled Jackie, taking the glass. She nodded and hurried back into the hotel.

Krissie turned herself over. The sun here was gorgeously hot and the cocktail had put her on a very pleasant buzz. After the next one she would go up to her suite, call home and then get ready for a night on the town.

Jackie headed into the restaurant and found the nearest pool waiter – Jabu.

'Another Cosmopolitan for the blonde madam,' she barked at him.

'Sure,' replied Jabu wearily. Obviously Jackie was in one of her moods again.

'We *work* here at the Hotel Shmotel; we don't stand around taking in the scenery.'

'I was waiting for you, actually,' said Jabu patiently. 'There's a phone call for you.'

'Make it snappy with that Cosmopolitan,' barked Jackie. She stalked off back to her desk and picked up the phone. She took a deep breath, inhaling all her frustration, and adopted the friendly, professional tone she prided herself on.

'Good day, Jackie de la Rey speaking. How may I help?'

'Hi,' said a very old voice on the other end.

'I told you never to call me at work,' whispered Jackie harshly.

'Are you coming to the meeting tonight?' asked the caller.

'Yes, I'll see you there.' Jackie hung up and took a seat behind the desk. She opened her top drawer and took out her makeup kit. This heat was murder on her face. Looking into the compact mirror, Jackie powdered her face to get rid of the shine. Jackie hated a shiny face. Jackie hated a lot of things. The significant focal points of her hatred were the reason for her weekly W.I.T. meetings.

The Wives in Training club was formed by Jackie in 2004, when she was only twenty-six years old. In the words of its official mission statement, the club's goal was 'to prepare young women for the most important jobs they will ever perform – marriage and motherhood. In these confusing times, women are being pulled in many different directions, and are forgetting the true reason they are here. We aim to return to traditional, conservative values.' Membership was exclusive and solely at Jackie's discretion.

At the time, Jackie's parents were thrilled. They had never really understood her decision to enter the hospitality industry, but now it seemed that her training was finally coming in handy. As far they (or anyone else) knew, the club functioned to train members in housework and cooking skills, as well as other valuable lessons, such as how to respect a husband and keep him happy.

The fact that, three years later, Jackie not only remained

unmarried, but apparently had no prospects in sight, didn't seem to bother the members one bit. In fact, her members were loyal to an almost fanatical degree.

One might notice that the acronym spells 'wit', but this would in no way point to the mental capabilities of the group. One might also notice that 'wit' is Afrikaans for 'white' – this is more relevant.

Jackie was not involved in any established right-wing Afrikaner movement, but she did have some pretty crazy ideas of her own.

Ideas that, if exposed beyond the walls of her secret weekly meetings, would surely jeopardise her job at the Hotel Shmotel.

And Jackie needed to remain in the employ of the Hotel Shmotel.

It was all part of the plan.

Back in Johannesburg, where the summer was as hot as that of Cape Town but without any of the charm, MK was beating on the door of her one and only friend, Mick Emmott.

Eventually the door opened to reveal Mick looking flustered.

'What in God's name is the matter?' he demanded.

'It's Thursday!' exclaimed MK frantically as she pushed past him into the cool respite of the house.

Mick blinked, nonplussed, and closed the door before joining her.

'I've seen people react that way to Monday, but Thursday... people are usually happier,' he said. 'Where have you been anyway? I've been trying to call you all week.'

'I was hoping you could tell me, Mickey. What does a lady have to do to get a drink around here?'

'Right. Um, lemonade?'

'Fine,' said MK, 'except make it tonic. And add gin. Half-and-half.'

'It's two in the afternoon,' said Mick, raising an eyebrow.

MK shot him a look that spoke of short patience and long days of torture.

'Coming right up,' he said. He watched, unnerved, as MK stalked into the kitchen, thrumming with anxiety. Mick had never seen MK like this and it disturbed him. MK *anxious? Scared?* It was like seeing the Pope smoking a cigarette, or Robert Mugabe winning the Nobel Prize – or other things that you thought would never happen.

Ten minutes and two G&Ts later, MK and Mick were sitting in his garden. MK's shivering had subsided enough to relate her tale.

'You're pulling my leg,' he announced decidedly.

'No,' growled MK, 'but I could break your arm.'

'Okay, okay,' Mick muttered, reminding himself that despite MK's fantastic qualities and their friendship, she was essentially a dangerous woman. 'No need to get so angry – I'm just trying to understand.'

'You and me both, my friend,' she sighed, softening. 'If it was one night and I'd had a few of these, I could maybe understand. But last night... last Thursday night, I just read and went to bed early. And someone had been feeding Wiggy – someone's been in my flat!'

Mick winced involuntarily at the mention of MK's cat. They did not get along. Mick still had a scar from their first meeting and a few more recent scratches yet to heal.

'Do you think Dippenaar could have anything to do with it?' she wondered.

'Why?' asked Mick, surprised.

'Well, let's see, Mick... I ruined the guy's life and he wound up paralysed from the neck down.'

'That wasn't your fault. He dove down a flight of steps trying to kill you.'

'He blames me, though,' she said darkly. 'You can count on that.'

'So, what? You think he sent someone after you?'

'To feed my cat and leave me unharmed? Probably not.'

'Well, who else do you think could be behind it?'

'Don't know,' mumbled MK. 'Maybe Gift Yeni? I nearly ruined his political career.'

'Oh please,' scoffed Mick. 'He met the woman of his dreams because of you. If anything, he's grateful.'

'I still can't believe he married Martie,' she chuckled. 'Or rather, that Martie married *him*!'

'Viva Rainbow Nation!' toasted Mick, chuckling. 'Anyway, you didn't ruin his career. You and I both know that a political career in this country is virtually indestructible.'

'I'm not in the mood to talk politics, Mick,' she snapped, the worry returning to her face. 'I need to get out of town for a while.'

'What?' squawked Mick.

'Just until I figure out what's going on. Obviously I'm not safe where I am.'

'Come and stay here,' offered Mick.

'What, and risk having strange men breaking into your room in the middle of the night?'

'I should be so lucky,' said Mick. 'Besides, that's already a risk we all face daily in this godforsaken city.'

MK trailed her finger along the edge of the table, lost in thought.

'MK?'

'I need,' said MK slowly, with certainty, 'to go to the mountains...'

Mick stared.

MK stared back unwaveringly.

'I just never figured you for the... spiritual type,' explained Mick.

'Oh, Mick,' she laughed. 'There's no such thing as a problem – only an opportunity. I've wanted to go there for ages, and now it's time.'

She paused, then leaned in and tapped the table.

'Cape Town.'

'Why Cape Town?' asked Mick.

'Why not? Besides, I may run into a bit of Hollywood action down there.'

Mick laughed doubtfully and then remembered who he was dealing with.

'Good luck,' he said sincerely. 'Just promise me you'll stay out of trouble. No guns.'

'You know me, sweetie,' she beamed, basking in the glow of opportunity. *'Superstardom Lesson No. 24: Promises are like children – if you can't keep them, don't make them.'*

For the first time since his arrival in Cape Town, Link wished for just a moment of the biting cold of his native England. He was clearly not built for this kind of heat. It was after 11pm and still he felt as though he was burning up. His chronic sunburn wasn't helping either. Even his excessive intake of beer had done little to cool him down.

He gazed around the bar: it was a very small, very dark place with very little going for it. It was called the Stumble Inn. He had abandoned the trendier Camps Bay scene much earlier in search of something a little more in line with what he was used to. Eventually, his aimless driving had led him to this side of town. It was a distinctly less glamorous side of town. The patrons propped up around the place were of varying ages, varying walks of life, and varying stages of collapse. The room itself looked to be in a steady state of decline, and the floor appeared to have been touched by nary a cleaning agent in a good long while.

All in all, it bore a heartening resemblance to Link's favourite haunts back home. Camps Bay, with its picture-perfect palm trees, beach views and inconceivably beautiful people was fine for the daytime, but Link felt altogether more comfortable in places like this for nighttime recreation. The drink was cheaper and so were the women.

Link sighed. His options appeared to be a middle-aged woman, singing loudly along to the Jennifer Rush song blaring from the speakers, and a thirty-something coloured woman who wasn't bad-looking, aside from the fact that she had immense hips and zero breasts, and was wearing a pair of running shorts. Link was pretty much convinced that she was a hooker. 'Jennifer Rush' had an air of shrieking desperation that Link could appreciate, but the hooker had the advantage of youth. 'In the land of the blind' and all that jazz.

Link had just drained the last of his pint and was psyching himself up to solicit the running shorts off the tart when the door screeched open. Link's jaw dropped. In walked the fittest young lass he'd ever clapped beady eyes on. She sashayed into the place like she owned it and lit up the room with a sudden grin.

'I love this song!' she squealed in an American accent. (Jennifer Rush beamed at her as though she had just met a kindred spirit.) 'Hey, everybody,' she said to the room.

No one registered. Undeterred, she marched straight up to the bar and ordered a double tequila. Link stared unashamedly. Come on – someone like her had to be used to it. He felt himself blushing and then remembered it wouldn't make any noticeable difference. And besides, what could he do about it? He was frozen.

The Goddess downed her drink and immediately ordered another. She turned and took a moment to absorb her surroundings. When her eyes settled on Link, his breath stopped. She said something else to the bartender and then made her way over to Link's booth and sat down opposite him. He was helpless to stop his gaze drifting down to watch her long legs fold and cross.

'Hey,' she said simply.

'Erm, hi.'

'What's your name?' she asked playfully.

'Lincoln,' he managed, after what seemed like an eternity. A blissful eternity dominated by this blonde godsend.

'Like Abraham,' she giggled.

'Right,' he said, smiling numbly.

'You're not from here,' she said.

'Nah. England.'

'I love London!'

'Right,' he said, deciding not to correct her.

'What are you doing in Cape Town, Lincoln?'

'My friends... call me Link. They couldn't make it. They had to work and stuff. But it's a holiday. I'm on holiday.'

'Me too. But we call it a vacation,' she grinned. 'I love your accent. *Haw-lee-dayeeh*!' she exclaimed in an embarrassingly poor impression.

'Thanks.' With everything this bird had going for her, he was not going to be swayed by an inability to mimic accents.

In the bar, Jennifer Rush was building to a hideous karaoke climax, but between the Yank and the Brit – silence. Link realised he should say something but could not summon a single thought, much less a word. He got the impression she liked talking anyway. A moment later, the bartender arrived and served two double tequilas and two beers.

'I got us some drinks,' she said, 'Link.'

'Aw, cheers. What's your name?'

'Down the hatch!' she said with a wicked grin.

'Cheers,' he returned.

She smiled at him. He smiled back.

'Spent too much time in the sun, I see,' she said.

'Oh, yeah.' He chuckled. His laughter ended abruptly when she leaned over and put her hands on his face.

'You're really hot,' she said.

'So are you,' he said before he could stop himself. The Goddess laughed, tickled pink by this.

'Oh, you meant the...' he trailed off, mortified.

'You don't say much, Link, but you're cute.'

'You look kind of familiar,' said Link, trying to place her.

'So what exactly are you doing in a dive like this, Link? I mean, you do know about places like Camps Bay, right?' asked Krissie, keen to change the subject.

'Nah,' he replied. 'People there are total phonies.'

'I hear ya,' she said wearily. Then she stood up, moved around to Link and sat on his lap. 'I'm also in the mood for some *real* fun.'

Never a very religious man, Link offered a prayer of thanks for the first time in years. He wished the whole world could see him now.

The whole world may not have been watching, but one person was paying close attention. In the furthest, darkest corner of the establishment sat a man, and he was watching. Like a hawk. He blended into the background with the proficiency of years of experience, despite the fact that he was wearing a gaudy, island-style shirt. He watched his target and his target's new acquaintance.

The way people choose to decorate their toilets really says a lot about their personality and level of affluence. In a place like Camps Bay, for instance, one is likely to find a bathroom worthy of a spread in a home décor magazine. Every little detail carefully thought out and exquisitely executed: luxury toilet paper housed in some kind of dispenser you've never seen before, and a matching set of handwash and moisturiser at the kind of basin that you've never seen before. And the fixtures are sculptural artworks made of rock-face found only in the remotest quarries of Papua New Guinea, where the workers have passed down their craft from generation to generation and now benefit from interest in the West, mass-producing so that we may have a waterfall on the wall instead of a basin... It's pristine.

At a place like Stumble Inn, the decor consisted mainly of rust, graffiti and other people's bodily fluids. One was lucky to find any toilet paper at all.

Jackie de la Rey's bathroom was somewhere between these two poles. Always very clean, it was nevertheless unlikely to ever grace the pages of a home décor magazine. The odd tile was cracked and the old-fashioned basin had begun to slowly detach from the wall. Every available surface was adorned with frills, doilies and little ceramics of dogs and cats, and atop the cistern was a Barbie doll with a long, hand-knitted skirt that cascaded down over the spare toilet rolls.

Perhaps the most unusual piece was the tapestry hanging on the back of the door. It had taken Jackie months of hard work to complete and she was immensely proud of it. It depicted Jesus on the cross, which was not something one would ordinarily see in a bathroom, but Jackie had toiled so long and hard on it that she wanted to make sure it was in a place where every visitor would see it.

Most of her visitors were initially startled when they closed the door and were confronted by the piece. Aside from the awkwardness of being watched by the Son of Man while taking care of business, the tapestry itself was frankly quite unsettling. Jackie had been ambitious: determined to put in as much nuance and detail as possible, she had found herself working on a tapestry almost as large as the door itself. The next thing one was struck by, after the tapestry's dimensions, was its vivid colouring. A combination of Jackie's desire for detail and her lack of skill had resulted in a picture that, while indeed vivid, could also be described as frightening.

Rather than a depiction of the event, it seemed more a hallucinatory, nightmarish re-imagining of it. As a passionate believer in the Passion, Jackie had wished to convey the immense level of suffering endured by Christ, because it reminded her that He had done so for her own salvation. If anyone had asked, this would have been her explanation for her liberal use of red. Nobody ever asked.

Frequently, guests had to spend an extra minute or two in the bathroom, bracing themselves before rejoining Jackie, and composing a compliment for her artwork.

Jackie gazed at her masterpiece as she sat on the edge of the bath, smoking a cigarette. This was the only room in the house where Jackie smoked. The room had a big window, and also she felt that smoking under the watchful eye of her Saviour would give her the strength to quit as soon as possible. Nobody knew she smoked.

The ladies had left about half an hour prior, after the end of their weekly W.I.T. meeting. As usual, they had been more interested in discussing recipes and men. Jackie was frustrated. They were never going to achieve any of their objectives unless they became more serious about the whole thing.

Jackie looked to her dear Lord for patience and solace. Jackie had been a devout Christian since she could remember, and her faith was the bedrock upon which she had built her mission. It wasn't going to be easy – she knew that – but with God on her side, she had faith that things would change as they must. The world was such a scary place lately, what with those crazy Arabs blowing things up left, right and centre, and sin becoming the norm thanks to America and its obsession with sex.

While Jackie was a fan of George Bush, she could see that his country was also the world capital of perversion, excess and so-called liberalism. And the worst part was that its influence had begun to infect her own country. Crime levels were unbearable – all because everyone had this idea that they could just do whatever they flippin' well liked because that was the world now.

Not that it was all America's fault. Jackie resented her own government too.

That's why it had to go.

In Jackie's mind, South Africa had lost good governance in 1990 when a certain black man had walked out of the prison in which he actually belonged.

Jackie realised that hers were not popular – or at least *openly* popular – views in South Africa. But Jackie didn't hate black people – she simply believed, as a good Christian, that the black race consisted of sinners who had already burned in hell (hence their dark skins and curly hair) and been given a second chance on earth. Therefore, their place was below the white man – simple.

The tragedy of this was that Jackie was not alone in these beliefs. Jackie had another conviction, however; one that distinguished her from, shall we say, 'garden variety' racists.

Jackie believed that, although black people belonged below white people in the hierarchy, white men belonged beneath white women. To call Jackie a feminist would be inaccurate. In her opinion, women were not to be treated as equal to men, but should rather take over the earth, placing men in their 'rightful' roles as servants to womankind (until the return of Jesus, of course – he was the exception). Divine faith in mere mortals is an endlessly diverse phenomenon. In the same way in which Jackie's earthly experiences had enmeshed her racism with her religion, Jackie's father had developed similar modifications to his own belief system over the years. For example, he viewed it as part of his role as the physical and spiritual leader of the family to discipline them as necessary – sometimes with his fists.

Jackie had watched her father slap her mother around for years. She had also watched her mother accept this with a pitiful resignation and an unshakeable faith in her religion. This had been the seed of Jackie's two obsessions: if Jesus had given her mother the courage to endure such hardship, then he had to be The Way. At the same time, she had begun to despise the traditional versions of man and woman that her parents embodied. (Later Jackie would realise that this did not happen in every home, but the dynamics, whether subtle or brutal, were the same: men do the driving.)

During her shifts at the hotel, the guests, her bosses and most of the staff saw only the sweet Jackie – never too busy to lend a helping hand or provide a gleaming smile. None of them knew the fire that raged inside her. Her parents didn't know. Even the members of W.I.T. didn't really understand how deep it went, and they shared the same ideals as her. Nobody got the full picture.

Jackie's full name was Jacoba de la Rey – she had been named after the famed Boer War general who had attracted a devoted legion of followers in his day, and has ever since. To some he was simply an historic figure, to others a symbol of Afrikaner unity, and to a radical few, a figure that epitomised the old Afrikaner values that they were plotting to restore. When the song 'De la Rey' exploded onto the South African scene amidst a sea of controversy, Jacoba had immediately seen it as a sign. While arguments raged over whether the song could be construed as a call to arms, Jackie had imbibed it as just that.

Clearly, the poor girl was troubled, to say the least. In the bigger picture, one may perhaps have written her off as a middle-class young woman with a nasty mindset born of the unfortunate intersection of faith, bad politics and bad experiences. There were people like her the world over, after all.

She was a nobody.

That didn't mean she wasn't dangerous.

Bodies in Motion

NEWTON'S THIRD LAW of Motion says that every action has an equal, but opposite, reaction... Hey, who's going to argue with Isaac Newton? The guy figured out gravity from a falling fruit. That's mighty impressive when you consider that a more standard reaction would've been something like 'Fucking apples!'

So it is unsurprising that for all the secretive flapping of far right-wing activity, a similar reaction is occurring at the tip of the left wing. Meanwhile, in-between, the bulk of the bird, moderate and fairly balanced, keeps working to get fed and survive another day. Regardless of how progressive and neutral a nation is, there's always going to be some extremist on the periphery trying to 'effect change', and pretty soon thereafter, an extremist on the other side will start effecting back. These 'effectors' are typically people who believe the best way to be heard is 'Kaboom'.

In South Africa's case, the ongoing rumours that the white right-wing was planning a war to seize back 'their' country, were contrasted by stories that the extreme black left were simply waiting for the 2010 Soccer World Cup to be over so that they could kill all the whites and fully seize 'their' country.

Martie Yeni tried not to think about such things. As a white Afrikaans woman, thoughts like that were better left – in her own mental word – 'unthunk'. Denial came comfortably to people like Martie. Besides, she had plenty of other things to keep her mind occupied, like the fact that as a woman approaching fifty she was a newlywed.

Martie had recently married Gift Yeni in a small but wonderful ceremony attended by many of Gift's family and friends and none of hers. Martie's family and friends had been shocked enough when she had divorced Pieter. While they could admit that his actions towards the end had been 'worrying' (insane) and perhaps 'slightly inappropriate' (illegal), at least Pieter was 'fundamentally decent' (white). Martie had pleaded her case – *He held me at gunpoint and tried to kill the black girl* – to no avail. Divorce was frowned upon.

When they learned that Martie was involved with a *black man?*, well, that was just beyond imagining. Despite Martie's insistence that it was no longer illegal, her people would simply not tolerate it, even going so far as to suggest that perhaps *she* belonged in the loony bin instead of Pieter. Not only did they refuse to attend the ceremony, but they also severed all contact with Martie forthwith. Gift had faced similar, if not as severe, recriminations from his own kin upon informing them of his plans. Particularly incensed had been his then-wife Thando, who had focused with typical narrow-mindedness on the fact that he was dumping her while she was at her lowest – undergoing drug rehabilitation in a five-star centre that was much like a hotel (except for the daily nerve-shredding group therapy sessions).

Thus, when the two divorces had been finalised, Martie and

Gift had taken what each hoped was their last trip down the aisle. Gift Yeni had resigned his post in government before they could catch onto his past dubious dealings. Gift was a good guy at heart, but over the years – in the presence of the insatiable Thando and omnipresent Opportunity – he'd allowed his principles to slip. Now, with Martie by his side, he hoped to get them back on track.

The circumstances under which Martie and Gift met would not be categorised under 'romance' or 'fairytale', but rather 'horror'. They sometimes joked that it was just as well that they were too old for children or grandchildren, in case the question 'How did you meet?' was ever asked. Blackmail, violence and attempted murder do not make for cuddly bedtime stories. Despite this, their love had been instantaneous and undeniable. Their union had even been deemed newsworthy by several major publications (and a few minor ones). When a middle-aged white Afrikaans woman marries a middle-aged black politician, people are keen to parade them as a model of reconciliation.

Yes, there had been 'adjustments'. The first time they had made love, for instance. It was their wedding night, of course, and it turned out to be a night of many firsts for Martie. It was the first time Martie had ever been with a man besides her first husband. And it was her first time with a black man. It was also the first time she'd realised that the male anatomy could vary *greatly* in certain respects. Martie had been stunned – and fearful – when she observed that Gift's... 'gift' was a very large package. She had doubted that... she had adequate 'storage room' for it. But to her (pleasant) surprise, this concern had been put to bed, as it were, when Martie had had the most explosive first of her life – her first orgasm (or as her mother had termed it on the eve of her first wedding, a Feeling). Through all her years with Pieter, she'd certainly had 'feelings' when they'd been intimate, but never anything close to the kind of feeling Pieter had seemed to enjoy. On her second wedding night, Martie had finally – gloriously

– realised what all the fuss was about.

But for all of Martie's personal growth and love for Gift, there followed several months where she couldn't help feeling that she was illicitly sleeping with the garden boy, and that at any moment the police would break down the door and arrest her under the Immorality Act.

There were other lifestyle changes to contend with. The language barrier proved frustrating when friends visited. Martie was trying to learn Zulu, but at her age it was a slow process, and she often got the impression that things were being said about her. For his part, Gift always tried to include her, but she could see it was as difficult for him as it was for her.

In their brief time as a model of reconciliation, they weathered some awful experiences together. Martie began to realise that some of Gift's acquaintances were almost as intolerant and hostile as her ex-husband's.

One dinner in particular would live forever in Martie's memory.

An old friend of Gift's had come into town and looked him up. Gift had promptly invited him for dinner. Martie had welcomed the news as a good sport, keen to go to great pains to lay out a fantastic spread for the happy reunion.

She started cooking the day before, even going so far as to hand-paint a set of crockery for the occasion, in bright Ndebele patterns she found in a book.

Gift watched all of this, concerned. Finally, he managed to get a moment of Martie's attention (between checking the marinade and mixing the bread).

'Listen, my dear,' he said, taking her hands in his. 'I really appreciate all the trouble you're going to...'

'It's a wife's duty,' replied Martie, and she meant it.

'Well, that's fine,' he said, again amazed at her resolute traditionalism. 'I just wanted to... uh, explain a little more to you about who Jeremiah is.'

'He's your old friend,' put in Martie, as if no more need be said.

'He was also very active in the Struggle,' said Gift. 'Very.'

'Oh good,' said Martie, 'I'd like to hear all about it. I'm halfway through my book.' Some weeks prior, inspired to educate herself about the side of apartheid she was less familiar with, Martie had purchased and started reading Steve Biko's *I Write What I Like*. She was thoroughly enjoying it. Martie was continually astounded by how bright Biko had been. Her mind was twisted further open on virtually every page. The consummate product of her era, she had never been exposed to this side of the story, and was humbled by her own ignorance. She'd never realised that blacks were clever back then (despite her progress, Martie still held onto many little notions, for example that all black people pre-1994 were illiterate). She still sometimes found herself surprised when Gift used a big word that even she didn't understand.

'I think,' said Gift, 'we should perhaps avoid the subject of apartheid altogether.'

'Oh,' replied Martie, crestfallen.

'It's just that Jeremiah is still quite... politically charged,' Gift explained.

'All right,' said Martie, 'if you say so, Baas.'

Gift winced at this. He and Martie had stumbled upon this nickname during their first physical encounter. At the moment of Martie's first true Feeling, she had screamed it out. Baas! They had stared at each other for a moment, stunned, before erupting into hysterical laughter. Ever since then it had become her affectionate nickname for him.

'Thanks, Fat-cakes,' he smiled, using his nickname for her. He paused for a moment before adding: 'Another thing: I don't imagine you would... but I'd rather you didn't use my nickname in front of Jeremiah.'

'But I'm calling *you* Baas,' she frowned, 'and you're a black.'

'Yes, dear, I realise that. But the word is still quite loaded for some people, and as I said, Jeremiah is quite... sensitive.'

'Okay,' Martie smiled.

'Also,' said Gift in what he hoped was a casual tone, 'you shouldn't take him too seriously. A pinch of salt. Or maybe two.'

'Okay.'

'He may say some things, but don't take it to heart. He likes to shock people.'

'After everything we've been through,' chuckled Martie, 'I don't think anything could shock me.'

Words Martie would reconsider the following night during dinner, the moment Jeremiah threw one of her newly-painted dinner plates at the wall, shattering it and sending the food she had spent many hours preparing all over the wall and carpet. Apparently he had taken exception to the Ndebele patterning, given that he was Zulu.

'Calm down, Jeremiah,' exclaimed Gift. 'Martie was just trying to be nice.'

'It's not about the *plate*,' hissed Jeremiah dramatically, 'although I have to say the food on it was equally offensive.' He then shouted something in Zulu, which Martie didn't follow, although she was quite sure it was not complimentary.

'That's enough,' replied Gift evenly in English.

'Of course,' Jeremiah rolled his eyes. 'She doesn't speak Zulu. Let me repeat it in English for you,' he said, turning to Martie.

'Thank you,' murmured Martie, unsure if she wanted to hear it.

'I told Gift I cannot believe he has married a white, Boer woman.'

'I see,' said Martie, trying to hold back the tears stinging her eyes.

'Martie is a wonderful woman, Jerry,' said Gift.

'I'm sure,' snorted Jeremiah. 'And what was she doing while we were suffering under the horrors of oppression? Probably beating up her maid for not having dinner ready in time for her fat, white husband!'

'I was always very nice to my maid!' cried Martie.

'Ja,' laughed Jeremiah bitterly, 'just like you're nice to your new boy! Because he gets you in the magazines.'

'I don't care about that,' shrieked Martie.

'Let's all stay calm,' said Gift.

'Tell me the truth, Gift,' said Jeremiah quietly, 'when nobody is around, do you call her Madam?'

'No!' yelled Martie. '*I* call *him* Baas!'

Gift sighed, putting his face in his hands.

Jeremiah blinked for a few seconds, then howled with laughter.

'You are not a very nice man,' observed Martie, her cheeks burning.

'Ja, well things are different now, Marrrrrtie,' said Jeremiah scornfully, adding a roll to the R that Martie found unnecessarily long. 'Time is running out for people like you.'

'Enough!' shouted Gift, standing violently. 'I think you should be going, Bra Jerry, before I break *my* plate – on your head.'

'And,' added Martie, basking in the glow of her husband's heroics, 'you'll be missing the nicest milk tart.'

Gift and Martie had long since grown accustomed to curious or downright disapproving stares in public, but this dinner was certainly the most intense blatant adversity they'd yet had to endure as a couple. It had taken Gift hours to calm Martie down after Jeremiah's inelegant departure.

The trauma of the whole affair had obscured any of the finer details, and – as Martie was a woman well versed in denial – the debacle was quickly put away like a jar of pickles. Only much later would one of Jeremiah's remarks re-emerge in Martie's consciousness, like a bitter, knobbly dill.

Time is running out for people like you.

But that would come later. For the time being, Martie moved on, more determined than ever to bridge the gap between herself and her husband, which seemed so significant to everyone else. She had not abandoned the misery of her previous life in favour

Miss Kwa Kwa

of a new, alien (but thrilling) existence, only to run at the first bump in the road. Martie knew that she and Gift had been brought together by the Ultimate Authority... for a Reason. And when things are capitalised, you know it's serious.

For all of their differences, there were a few, vital similarities. Martie had been shocked to discover that some of Gift's traditional Zulu values were strikingly similar to her own: a conservative outlook, an emphasis on family and community, and a strong sense of honour and decency.

They had decided to make a fresh start by moving to the Cape. They enjoyed the idea of a slower pace and generally quieter life, and settled in the quaint seaside town of Kalk Bay, a short distance from Cape Town proper. Small and picturesque, one truly felt 'away from it all' in Kalk Bay, but it was still close enough to Cape Town should one need to go in for business.

Gift was investigating several possible business ventures in Cape Town that took him there frequently, but Martie only went into town occasionally, preferring to do her shopping in Kalk Bay, or nearby Fish Hoek.

Martie also walked daily. She loved the fact that the train tracks ran right in front of the ocean in Kalk Bay and often lunched in one of the ramshackle seafront eateries after exploring the art, antiques and curios the tiny local shops offered.

Martie had dived headfirst into setting up their new home – homemaking was, of course, what she knew best. Gift had been somewhat surprised at Martie's lack of finesse in this department, but could see she always meant well and took great pride in her efforts, so never uttered a word of complaint. Martie continually took on new projects and had recently, while visiting one of her favourite new bakeries, come across a pamphlet for a new club she wished to join.

It seemed that after many trying years, Martie was finally being treated to a new life of love, serenity and peace. She looked forward to making new like-minded friends in this world, starting with this club perhaps. She glanced at the pamphlet.

W.I.T., it read. *Wives in Training. Established 2004.*

To give the wild notions of imminent war between the 'wings' any credence was terrifying, so MK chose to ignore them. In a nation perched on the wall between a legacy of horrific conflict and limitation and a future loaded with possibility, it was preferable – even necessary perhaps – to focus on breaking through to the side that was pure, exhilarating potential.

MK viewed herself as a citizen of the world first, and a citizen of South Africa second. She knew enough about history to realise that borders were transient. The only connotation she wished to attach to her nationality was a positive one.

Now if she could only achieve US citizenship, she would be set. While she understood that borders were transient in a larger perspective, at the present moment only the US borders contained the best chance of achieving global stardom. But how was she to infiltrate these borders? She couldn't believe she hadn't thought of it sooner: Cape Town. Cape Town was South Africa's likeliest access to Hollywood, given that so many feature films were shot there. She had been stupid to try to achieve fame in Joburg, South Africa's television capital. Local television – in her experience as a viewer and more recently on camera – was terrible. Everyone seemed keen to attribute this to lack of funds and avoided the more blatant transgressions. The broadcasters continually compromised quality at every stage, more out of an attempt to sanitise the product than to save money.

In her time on *Kwa Kwa Konfidential*, she had many times heard the phrases 'It may be above our audience' or 'We can't say that,' or, the worst of the lot, 'It's not aspirational.' Surely a vital aspect of aspiration was the *truth*. Surely drama was built on conflict, and that meant bad guys. But no, apparently the broadcasters believed good drama – and worse, good comedy – came from wishy-washy, kinda-nice, 'aspirational' characters.

Her blood boiled just thinking about it.

For all Hollywood's flaws (such as its lack of voluptuous African women like herself), it knew how to tell a great story. And make people rich and famous. Mick often questioned this apparent shallow narrow-mindedness in MK, and her answer was always the same.

'Sweetie,' she'd say, pouting her generous red lips, 'when I have enough money not to worry about working some crummy job, and millions of fans who adore me, *then* I'll worry about being a nice person. I'd rather look back when I'm old and say "I had a lot of fun" than "Well, I worked like a slave my whole life but at least on the weekends I watched some good TV".'

As it turned out, Mick had a holiday flat in Cape Town, which he eventually agreed to let MK use. Mick had purchased it primarily as an investment property and had only been there once. He had held off on leasing it out to tenants in the continued delusion that he would take frequent holidays and weekends there, but his workaholism had never allowed this.

MK stood on the balcony of Mick's flat and stared at the view. It was breathtaking. Cape Town was beautiful, and MK swelled with a sense of promise. Even the mystery of what exactly had befallen her the last week ceased to feel as ominous. Nobody except Mick knew she was here, and until either her memory was restored or something else troubling happened, there was no need for concern. A new chapter was beginning and MK still counted on a happy ending. MK knew nothing about W.I.T. or its formidable leader. She had never laid eyes on the man in the island shirt, and could never have predicted the part he would soon play in her tale. She had never had the dubious pleasure of meeting Yorkshire's own Lincoln Thomas, and, while she knew who Krissie Blaine was from endless tabloid exposure, she had no idea that she was in town right now, mere kilometres away.

Presented with all this information, MK would still not have been able to see their relevance to her life. The standout event in

MK's life last year (with stiff competition) had been the attempt on her life by Pieter Dippenaar.

MK could never have imagined that these ostensibly unrelated bits and pieces would result in her life being endangered for the second time in as many years.

She *definitely* could not have guessed that this would happen twice in the space of five minutes.

Nearby, in Cape Town's most exclusive hotel, another young woman was unaware that her life would shortly be in danger.

Krissie Blaine was too hungover to be considering issues of mortality. Also, there was an OUG in her bed. OUG, in the jargon exclusive to Krissie's inner circle, stood for Old Ugly Guy, i.e. any man over thirty-five who wasn't famous. This guy had the unfortunate added quality of being hideously sunburned. If there was one thing worse than old and ugly, it was old and ugly overdone. He was clearly not the type who belonged in the sun. His hair was white-blonde and curly – in the bad way. He had an underbite and a round face with little ears protruding from the sides. Altogether he looked like an albino Shrek. Krissie couldn't quite remember how he had gotten here. Her memory blurred at the point where she had met him in that shitty bar and started doing tequila shots.

Damn it. Never tequila. Never tequila.

He was unconscious, his mouth slack and open wide enough that she could see how terrible his teeth were. Around his mouth the pillow was damp with his saliva.

'Eeuuuw,' she whined to herself in disgust. She poked his large flabby arm and noted that in the few areas where he wasn't bright red he was brilliant white. He didn't respond. Krissie hopped out of the bed, deciding to get dressed before she woke him. She was relieved to discover that she already had underwear and a vest on. She threw her gown on and fastened the belt.

'Hey!' she shouted at him.

Nothing.

With a frustrated groan, she gave him a little kick. His only response was to flop onto his back and start snoring. Krissie noticed with horror that he had what she'd heard called a 'morning glory'. From where she stood there was nothing glorious about it. A moan escaped her lips. He was truly revolting.

'Hey –' she began, suddenly realising she couldn't remember his name, 'you! *Get up! Geddup-geddup-geddup!*'

His answer came in the form of a snore that sounded like a pig making an obscene phone call. The answer struck Krissie like tinfoil hitting a filling. But then she was hit by an unfamiliar sensation... a good idea. She sat back down on the bed and leaned in close. His nose was particularly burnt and looked especially tender. She grabbed it between two fingers and twisted as hard as she could. The effect was immediate. He leaped into the air, howling, and fled the bed like a shot.

'What the bloody hell are you doin'?' he screeched.

'Morning sunshine,' she said sweetly. 'Time for you to get lost.'

Link glanced around the suite, piecing together the journey that had brought him here. Oh, yeah. He had met the hottest piece of arse in the world... and somehow between then and now she had morphed into a demonic nose-tweaking bitch. Gingerly he put his hand to his throbbing nose.

'Did you hear me, sweetheart?' she barked. 'Get dressed and then get lost.'

'Erm, alright.' Link grabbed a cushion to cover his shame and began slowly moving around the room, collecting his scattered clothes. It was awkward.

'What happened last night?' she asked suddenly. 'I can't remember.'

'Oh... uh...' This was when Link had a great idea of his own. 'We bumped uglies.'

'*Bumped uglies?*' Krissie grimaced incredulously.

'Did it,' he explained. 'Had sex.'

'Urgh,' she spat. 'You are charming.'

'You said it was the best you'd ever had,' he sighed.

Krissie frowned. This couldn't be true... could it?

'Hurry up,' she snapped.

'Fine,' he said, pulling on his trousers. 'At least I've got the memories. And the photos...'

Krissie paled, despite her carefully nurtured tan.

'Huh?' she squeaked. But she was thinking: *Stay calm, just stay calm.*

'On my mobile phone. It was your idea, darlin'. You were posing like there was no tomorrow.'

'*Give me that phone!*' screamed Krissie, unable to stick with calm.

'Relax,' said Link amiably. 'It's not like I'm going to sell them to a tabloid for a small fortune that will set me up for life and make all my dreams come true...' Krissie looked ready to vomit. Link finished with: 'Well, one of them came true last night – scoring with Krissie Blaine.' There followed a long moment of silence.

'You British asshole,' was the best that Krissie could manage, given that she was facing the scandal of her life.

'You American brat,' countered Link, smiling.

'What do you want?' she asked. 'Money?'

'Nah,' said Link. He paused, rubbing his chin for effect. 'How long are you in town for?'

'I don't know. I haven't decided yet,' she answered, bewildered.

'I'm only here for a few more days,' he said. 'I want to spend them with you.'

'Gross,' blurted Krissie before she could stop herself.

'Those are my terms. We don't have to fool around or anything – I just want to spend the time with you. It'll be fun.'

'I doubt it.'

'And then I'll delete the pictures,' he promised. 'They're really dirty.'

Krissie didn't see any other choice. She would have to agree to this. For now. At least until she could get his phone off him and delete the pictures herself. Then she would call security and get them to kick his overweight, dimpled ass.

'Fine,' she clipped. 'But there'll be no humping of uglies.'

'Bumping.'

'That neither,' she said darkly. 'I'm going to shower. You stay right here – order breakfast or something.' Link grinned. Krissie clutched her gown around her and swanned into the bathroom, slamming the door behind her.

Link laughed to himself victoriously and charged the air with his fist. He couldn't believe his luck! That was the quickest thinking he'd ever done. Of course, he and Krissie had not slept together (he'd tried but she'd refused) but she didn't need to know that. The incriminating photographs were also a fabrication – but she had bought it! She was obviously just as daft as she appeared on television. Link sat back down on the amazingly comfortable bed and imagined a sea of spectators, cheering him on.

Wait till the lads hear about this! Then we'll see who wants to be mates with good old Link!

Lincoln Thomas enjoyed his moment in the sun. Just as well. It wouldn't last.

Soon Lincoln Thomas would be wishing he'd never met Krissie Blaine.

At a substantially less impressive hotel a few blocks away, through a powerful telescope, the man in the island shirt watched Lincoln Thomas jumping around alone in Krissie Blaine's bedroom. He frowned. The man in the island shirt frowned a lot. He was a dreadfully serious individual.

In another country at another time, he was known by a different name. In fact, before he'd arrived in South Africa he had never worn an island shirt (just for posterity, he was wearing a *different* island shirt to the one he'd been wearing the previous night when he'd tailed Krissie Blaine and the Brit). But his other name, his given name, was not known to anyone except his parents (backwater hermits who never saw outsiders, much less talked to them), and a few highly placed superiors at the agency. That name didn't matter now; it served no purpose.

The man sipped his coffee. It was another hot day, but that didn't put him off his drink. The man drank coffee rain or shine, day or night. To his mind it was one of man's most spectacular discoveries. He knew that coffee's origin was Africa, and he'd once read that because it was imported to Europe by Arabic traders it had initially been dubbed the 'Muslim drink' there, even drawing protests from Christians who wished it banned. It seemed silly now. As far as he was concerned, coffee was one of the foundations of modern civilisation, and modern civilisation was something people like him had sworn to protect. Any threat to it was his business. Just the kind of business he was here on. The reason he was spying on Krissie Blaine's suite.

He frowned again. New developments just kept emerging in this case, and he was the only person who could put them all together – who *had* to put them all together. The fact that the Brit was fraternising with Krissie Blaine was especially startling. It seemed almost impossible that a girl like her would associate with a man like the Brit for purely social reasons. He had to be involved.

And if he were involved, he would have to be taken down with the rest of them.

The man finished his coffee and placed the cup in the saucer. He turned the cup so that its handle was facing a northerly direction. He then observed that his gun was not quite in line with the edge of the table. Must've been nudged by the movement of the telescope. He fixed it.

Problem fixer. That was the man in the island shirt.

Mick Emmott was also accustomed to fixing problems – sometimes it seemed that was all he ever did in his job as a television producer. The problems Mick fixed on a daily basis, however, were nowhere near as dramatic as those of the man in the island shirt. No, Mick's problems revolved almost exclusively around budgets, locations, and of course dealing with the Talent.

In his personal life, Mick's only concern was avoiding another heart attack. The moments he felt closest to failing at this were those spent dealing with Talent.

Mick had long ago accepted the fact that Talent was inextricably linked with varying levels of Trauma, it still sometimes proved quite... well, traumatic. Particularly when the so-called 'talent' didn't offer much talent in exchange for the trauma they dished out. In fact, Mick had noticed a distressing trend developing in the last few years: more and more talentless people were finding their way into show business, and despite a lack of any discernible ability, were answering this good fortune by becoming complete divas.

Like the one sitting before him right now, slamming her fist repeatedly on his desk.

'It's just not funny!' bawled the pretty young thing (you don't need to know her name, as she'll soon be leaving our tale, never to return). She was indeed attractive, and also untrained, a combination that saw her get jobs over superior actors fairly regularly. Trained actors are (rightfully) more expensive, but budgets are (notoriously) tight, so unfortunately compromises are frequently made – a fact Mick hated but had to try to manage. To his credit, he always tried to ensure that at least his lead characters were real actors, a step certain other productions didn't bother taking. The result was that you wound up with people like this pretty young thing: a normal person off the street who really believed she could act (untrue) and looked good on camera (true). They always started out sweet, humble and willing to learn, but all it took was five minutes on the set and a little bit of attention from the public before those qualities made a gruesome transformation into sulky know-it-alls who were never happy. Mick called it the

Popcorn Effect: the fresh kernels are warm, and bask in the butter lavished on them. They are eager to grow. Once they pop, they're at the top. They're hot and everybody wants some. In the cinema, popcorn reigns supreme. But popcorn gets stale fast. And what popcorn doesn't realise is that its moment will be brief – there are always thousands waiting to take its place.

'You're not even listening to me!' she squealed, wrenching Mick from his reverie. 'I cannot work with this script. It's just not funny!'

Mick chose his words carefully.

'Well,' he said, 'maybe not at first glance. But there's lots of stuff happening in the script.' And then with some deft ego-fanning: 'I think you could make it really special.'

'I'm not that good,' she grunted. That had to be the truest thing he'd ever heard her say. She went on. 'The script is shit, Mick.'

'O-kaay...' said Mick. 'What specifically would you like to see changed?'

'I dunno,' she said. 'It must just be funnier.'

'Why don't we leave it until rehearsals and see what the director can bring out?'

'It's shit,' she repeated as though Mick was slow.

'I hear you,' he said. 'Thanks for coming in. We'll chat to the director when he comes in. For now, the script stays as it is.' Mick picked up his telephone to indicate the end of their meeting.

'Has it ever occurred to you,' began the PYT darkly, 'that maybe you don't know what's actually funny? You are only the producer, you know. Maybe you should leave the creative stuff to the creative people.'

Mick felt his pulse accelerate dangerously. As he saw it, he had only two options: tell her what she wanted to hear, or risk some kind of heart-related trauma. Slowly, he lowered his telephone and replaced it on the receiver. A big smile forced its way across his face.

'You're right,' he said, trying to unclench his teeth. 'I'm not one of the creatives...'

She grinned back malevolently, Demon Mistress of All She Surveyed.

'But then neither are you,' he finished, choosing the cardiac risk.

'Excuse me?' Incredulous.

'The most creative you've ever been was when you forged a doctor's note to excuse the extra-long weekend you took while the rest of us were working,' said Mick, his voice raising. 'Oh, yes – we knew! But we gave you a chance. You get *one* chance, and that was yours. Remember that. You've had your chance, so there are none left.'

'I just wanted to discuss the script,' whined PYT, now adopting a victimised air.

'Oh yes, the script!' exclaimed Mick, his words expelled in a wave of sarcasm. 'You think it's not funny! *You*, with your *extensive* expertise – no training, limited experience – are judging this script? You wouldn't know good writing if it jumped off the page and slapped you in the face.'

PYT stood up quickly, and retreated towards the door.

'No,' cried Mick, 'we're not done. The reason you know nothing about writing is that, in fact, you know nothing about this business. You don't even appear to know much about *acting – your job!* You have no respect for the people that have gotten you here, and apparently no idea just how lucky you are. *No!* Because you're a star! Well, let me just tell you that you are not only a *dreadful* actress, but you are one of the dullest, most charmless, most offensive and *talentless* people I have ever met in my life on this planet!'

'*Howdareyou?*' shrieked the PYT.

'How dare I? I'll tell you,' boomed Mick, his smile now wholly genuine. 'Because, as you pointed out, I am the producer! I am the boss, and you... are *fired!*'

'I'm going to the channel,' she cried. 'I'll go over your head!'

'Good luck,' spat Mick. 'I've been working with them for twenty years, while you are a nameless nobody to them, who is replaceable at a moment's notice. Which is precisely what is about to happen. *Now get out!'*

The pretty young thing fled the room – and our tale – howling. Mick took a moment to catch his breath then sat back down. He had never lost it like that before. He tried to decide if he should feel guilty, but quickly came to the conclusion that he could not create an emotion that was simply not there. Mick had always prided himself on diplomacy and professionalism, especially in tense situations, but everybody has to break some time. And besides, that particular PYT deserved it – she'd been downright abusive to some of the crew.

The sigh that escaped Mick felt big enough to fill a zeppelin. He's made the right decision. The downside was that, mere days from beginning production on this sitcom, he was short an actor. To complicate the matter, it was shooting in Cape Town, which would make casting a logistical nightmare.

Hang on.

Mick had a friend in Cape Town. A friend hungry for fame and currently unemployed. MK had resolved ages ago never to do sitcom (viewing it as 'common'), but perhaps she could be persuaded. Mick might have to play the friendship card and hope like hell he could reach her deeply concealed soft spot – it was an emergency – but he could add some spin that MK would respond to: *comedy characters are very well-loved by the audience, it will show your versatility, it's paying work, in Cape Town, while you're waiting for bigger things to happen.*

The disturbing thought that this could backfire horribly on their friendship crossed Mick's mind, but he pushed it aside. He comforted himself with the knowledge that MK would be great at comedy – that amount of talent was usually worth a truckload of trauma. Picking up the phone, he decided to start by telling MK what had just happened in his office – that'd get her laughing.

He dialled the number.

Martie dialled the number on the W.I.T. pamphlet nervously. She was excited about the possibility of making new friends, especially female ones. Once upon a time, Martie had been married to the most important man in the small mountain town of Kwa Kwa, and had thus spent her days associating with the other farmers' wives in the area. Lily-white days of bridge, recipe-swapping and church fêtes. Conversation limited to talk of children, husbands and the blight of the country's new political situation. Martie looked forward to meeting Cape Town ladies, whom she imagined would be more interesting and open-minded, and discussing recipes and husbands with them.

After several rings, the line clicked to a voicemail message.

'Hi,' said the voice, 'you've reached Jackie.'

Although the woman was very well-spoken, Martie could detect the traces of an Afrikaans accent. Martie's first response was a warm feeling of familiarity, followed quickly by guilt. She wondered if it was wrong to feel happy to hear another Afrikaner – Martie was never sure, the way things were these days. But she shook off her concern, putting it down to a matter of heritage. Martie had barely spoken her mother tongue in what seemed like forever.

'I am unavailable at the moment,' said the voice cheerily. 'Please leave your name and number, and I will get back to you soon. Have a good day.'

Martie liked the sound of this girl. Her voice was warm, friendly and totally genuine. Martie decided she liked Jackie already.

Beep.

'Erm,' began Martie, and then in Afrikaans, 'hello, my name is Martie. I'd like to find out about your club...' Martie recited her telephone number into the phone, and then, smiling, finished with: 'I must just say it's wonderful to be speaking Afrikaans! These days I don't get much opportunity to. Good day.'

Martie hung up.

Jackie was oblivious to the fact that anyone had called her cellphone. This was because her cellphone was in her desk drawer, while Jackie was in a janitorial closet three floors up, having her third orgasm in ten minutes. This was because Jackie was engaged in violent but immensely pleasurable sex with one of the hotel kitchen staff. This was because... well, we all know why people do such things.

To mark her special moment, Jackie sent a flying fist into the chest of her male companion. He tried to yelp out in pain, but discovered with some dismay that he couldn't. This was because, as a result of the well-placed wallop, he was struggling to breathe.

'Eurgh,' he gurgled instead, flopping off Jackie onto the floor.

Jackie hurried to put herself back together, oblivious to the difficulties her lover was experiencing. She straightened her blouse and fixed her skirt. Jackie and her friend never disrobed entirely – this was because they had only ten minutes between shift change in which to take care of business without anyone noticing. She whipped out her compact and began to reapply her lipstick. At her feet, the young man was paling by the second, unable to draw breath. Completely unaware of this emergency, Jackie slid the lipstick carefully across her upper lip.

Panicked, he grabbed Jackie's leg to get her attention. This was because his vision had begun to swim dangerously, and while he wasn't sure if it was real or simply a hallucination induced by popular culture/lack of oxygen, he could see a light that he was quite certain he wanted to avoid.

His desperate grasp had bumped Jackie, who now had a lipstick lightning rod down her chin.

'Man!' she whispered harshly, staring into her mirror. 'Look what you made me do!' She kicked him. The man had only a moment to consider the cruelty of this action – that he should be kicked as he lay dying – before he realised that the boot had restarted his breathing. Rebooted him, as it were. He sat up, breathing shallowly and painfully, but breathing nonetheless, and experienced a moment of immense gratitude for the simple but oft-unacknowledged gift of life.

'Oh my word!' he squeaked.

'I know,' purred Jackie, assuming he was referring to the lovemaking. And then, switching with startling suddenness to Ice Queen, 'Now get back to work.' She turned to leave just as suddenly, and the youth grabbed her ankle again before he could stop himself. When she spun back round to face him, he recoiled like an over-kicked dog.

'What?' she snapped.

'Don't I even get a goodbye kiss, Jackie?' he whimpered, opting to leave alone the subject of his near death.

'Don't be stupid,' she said. 'And remember to wait at least five minutes before you come out.'

He nodded miserably, but Jackie had already slipped out. He stood slowly and looked down at his chest. There was a deep red mark where he'd been socked. The kind that would be fairly painful and change colours frequently over the next few days. He savoured the ability to take in and expel breath, with the kind of awe and gratitude usually reserved for asthmatics and shipwreck survivors.

He really wished that Jackie would lighten up about their relationship, but she was very clear on the rules: only in the closet, only when she said so, and only on the condition that *nobody ever found out*. Sometimes he wondered if Jackie actually had any feelings for him beyond the closet. He sighed, lovesick and bruised, and fixed himself up.

In the elevator, Jackie felt the mixed bag of emotions that usually surfaced after a closet romp: satisfaction, the glee of naughtiness, shame and absolute dread at the thought of someone finding out about it.

Nobody could ever find out about her and Fahiem. This was because he was coloured.

It was also because he was Muslim.

But mainly it was the coloured thing.

Reality is so much more fascinating than television. Perhaps that's why it was inevitable that the two would collide with such dramatic success. MK loved watching reality television. Although she had reservations about *doing* television, she loved *watching* it. Good TV, bad TV – there was always something to be learned about the craft. She studied it, she consumed it, sucked it all in like so much fresh, vital air.

Some people think that television is evil. Others merely proclaim it as too passive, or go a little further and charge it with numbing minds and fuelling apathy. It's the idiot box, the boob tube, the goggle box, the telly, the babysitter, the small screen. It showed the world man taking his first step on the moon and, more recently, caused a bunch of Japanese children to collapse into seizures. Noël Coward once declared that television was only for appearing on, not looking at.

MK enjoyed both, but would happily give up the latter for the former.

But she had standards. Never soap and never sitcom. In her opinion, they shared a significant quality – they were laughable. And, in both cases, not for the right reasons.

Superstardom Lesson No. 48: Fans are just like junkies – always leave them wanting more. Television is a powerful drug with millions of users worldwide. Give them a taste, but don't stay in one place too long, or they'll turn on you.

It was this lesson that MK used as a guiding principle. Soap required way too much time, and seemed to suck actors in forever. Also, actors battled to escape the character upon leaving said soapie. Most importantly, one was kept too busy to pursue bigger game.

As for sitcom, MK had watched local offerings over the years with a mixture of incredulity and pity. Incredulity that such drivel was not only commissioned, but also developed and then produced *for broadcast* to *actual people* who were expected to find it *funny*, and pity for anyone who should have the misfortune of witnessing the embarrassment that was local comedy. Beyond that, she found it insulting. Apparently the makers of such shows believed their audience to be stupid. Generally, MK aimed to be perceived just so, but in her anonymous capacity as a viewer with at least half a brain, she found their 'comedy' offerings basically intolerable.

The way MK saw it, if there was to be any performance expected from her (apart from that of international star), it would only be one that would further her agenda (becoming a bigger international star).

MK had been working on a reality show featuring herself as the star. Although Mick was smart enough to realise it would probably be highly entertaining viewing, he had expressed some reservations about being able to sell it anywhere. MK was, after all, still pretty much a nobody. (Mick had not used this word, of course.)

Since the premature cancellation of *Kwa Kwa Konfidential*, MK had felt lost. She found uncomfortable questions surfacing in her mind. Questions like: *Fine, so you want to be famous, but what do you want to be famous for, exactly? What are you going to do next? Are you even in the right place for this?* MK hated this internal cross-examination. She had focused with such narrow fixation on these goals that she had rarely stopped to wonder why she so badly wanted to be famous. Somewhere in the background lingered a possible answer – *because then I'll be happy* – but MK always pushed it away, afraid to consider the potentially disturbing flaws implicit in it.

The truth was, she didn't know where to go next. She had pinned so much on her talk show, that its collapse had proved a burden almost unbearable. A burden she had shouldered – as always – alone. Mick Emmott was probably the person closest to her, but he was still miles off. Nobody saw this side of her. For a woman who had built her entire adult life on masks, the oldest ones were virtually impenetrable.

I'm in Cape Town, she thought to herself. *That's a start.*

Surely the Mother City would provide.

MK would never have guessed that her first offer would have come from Mick, much less for a supporting role in a sitcom.

Superstardom Lesson No. 21: Always get the lead. A 'supporting role' is best used for chicken mayonnaise, cheese & tomato, or Mary Kate & Ashley Olsen. Even better, give them *the sandwiches – they look like they need a snack.*

MK had spent two hours on the phone with Mick discussing the sitcom. Voices were raised, promises were made, and a few hang-ups were traded. Ultimately MK had agreed to do it. To Mick's credit, he had done an admirable job of trying to sell it to her – comedy characters are well-loved, yackety-shmackety, blah-blah-blurgh – but in the end it was the income that had spoken to her. She needed the money to keep her going while she waited for something better to come along. Also, she supposed she kind of owed Mick a favour – he had fought for *Kwa Kwa Konfidential* and wanted her to find fame almost as much as she did. And he was desperate. This was potentially something she could exploit.

He had met her conditions: her role was to be expanded from 'supporting' to 'lead' and she would be allowed to give 'input' on her dialogue. MK had wanted full script approval, but Mick had argued her down to just her own character.

Shooting was to begin in two days, so Mick was having the first episode's script couriered to her from his Cape Town office first thing in the morning. (Mick had shuffled the schedule so that the existing episodes, which featured the character more prominently, were shot first. He now faced the crisis of getting the remaining episodes rewritten very quickly.) After a deal had been struck, Mick had briefly outlined the show to MK.

Her character owned a shebeen frequented by the other characters.

How original.

The show was entitled *The Rainbow Hotel* and seemed to be about the motley staff of a high-end Cape Town hotel and the hi-jinks they got up to while trying to deal with demanding guests – and each other. How original. In contrast to their pristine workplace, the gang let off steam after hours at the aforementioned shebeen run by Thembi – MK's character. MK had immediately demanded her character's name be changed, partly because it was Zulu and she was Sotho, but mainly because it was overused. It was like naming a cat Whiskers. Lazy.

MK felt a pang of longing for Wiggy, her gorgeous little feline fluffball. The upside of this sitcom debacle was that Mick would now be coming down to Cape Town to oversee the production personally – and he would bring Wiggy. MK had left the kitten with him when she left, and had been surprised by the depth of her sadness on parting with him. Wiggy had not been too thrilled himself, and had marked the occasion by attacking Mick's ankles in savage protest. MK looked forward to seeing him again; she longed for the warmth of something familiar.

Not that she was afraid.

MK did not believe in fear.

Superstardom Lesson No. 32: Some people say there is nothing to fear except fear itself. These people have obviously never heard of corporate America. But aside from that, there is nothing to fear except bad hair days and the health minister.

MK sighed, giving herself over to the new flow of events, and turned the television back up. She was just settling in to watch some brainless-but-strangely-gripping show about the 50 Dumbest Celebrities in Hollywood when there was a melodic but insistent knock at the door. MK decided to ignore it. The next knock became less melodic and more insistent. An irked MK got up and went to it.

'Yes?' she barked through the closed door.

'It's your neighbour,' chimed a voice too sweet to be on the side of Good.

MK's jaw dropped. *No...*

Yes. There stood Mrs Siegl, the nosy cow who lived next door to her in Johannesburg.

'Well,' said Mrs Siegl, forcing a smile.

'What,' asked MK, 'are you doing here?'

'Your television is very loud,' muttered Siegl, coming straight to the point.

'And, what? You heard it all the way from Joburg?'

'No,' said Mrs Siegl with an indulgent laugh. 'I have a holiday flat here. Right next door. And I can hear your television *quite* clearly from there.'

MK's hand, with remote control, whipped out behind her and lowered the volume. Her stare never left Mrs Siegl's face.

'Thank you,' said Mrs Siegl, a touch disturbed. After a moment's hesitation, where she looked as though she felt she should say something else, Mrs Siegl opted instead to turn and beat a hasty retreat.

MK closed the door, and looked up to the sky. Well, the ceiling, but you get the drift. While generally able to appreciate the universe's twisted sense of humour, right now MK was not amused. In fact she felt rather like she was being kicked while she was down. An elderly, feeble kick, but it was the thought that counted. Trying to find a positive, MK decided that, while irksome, Mrs Siegl's presence was some kind of sign that she was precisely where she was meant to be.

Crudely put, Newton's First Law of Motion states that an object at rest will stay at rest and an object in motion will remain in motion unless acted upon by an external and unbalanced force. Well, whether MK was at rest or in motion, physically or mentally, is a debate for another time and place. What is certain is that, mentally, she had been 'acted upon' by an external force that was in many ways 'unbalanced'...

MK could still not remember anything about the week she had lost, and could also not find any residual effects on her body or soul. As far as she could tell, her mind was pretty much as it had been before the mysterious incident. But the mind is a strange, dark place. It's often said that we only use a fraction of it, and while some may relish in theories to explain the remainder – telepathy, telekinesis, time travel, or the ability to fly to work when the traffic is just too terrible – others have found ways to exploit this vast, unconscious area.

Like the people who took MK to the desert.

The people who enacted a force on her subconscious, who stuck their metaphorical fingers into her busy brain and not only shuffled a few things around, but implanted a few new things for good measure.

Dangerous things.

Things that were only waiting for the right trigger.

AD BREAK

HAS LIFE BECOME A TIGHT FIT?
Clothes, plane seats, movie theatres...
The world is made for thin people.

LOOK NO FURTHER!

The weight-loss sensation that's taking the world by storm!

Used for centuries by the San, who needed to suppress their appetites during long periods without food. We've taken advantage of their dwindling numbers to bring you the benefits of their knowledge!

If they can survive desolation, you can survive the city! Made from natural* ingredients, GOODIA is totally safe.**

MOST IMPORTANTLY, we guarantee you it will help you lose weight *without having to get off your couch!****

**Get one month's supply today,
and we'll include another month's supply FREE!******

DO IT TODAY! THIN PEOPLE ARE HAPPIER
AND NEVER STAY SINGLE LONG.

GOODIA is not to be substituted for food. Consult your doctor while making any major lifestyle changes.
* May also contain traces of ephedrine, chlorine and succinylcholine.
** Has been shown to cause brain damage in test mice, which is probably reversible.
*** Except to exercise, prepare balanced meals and make regular trips to the doctor.
**** We recommend not taking GOODIA for longer than a week. We also strongly advise frequent visits to a doctor and/or neurologist.

The Light of a Pale Blue Sun

AND NOW BEGINS the third chapter of the second book of Miss Kwa Kwa the one and only, now known as Palesa Moshesh. Here lies the second sentence of the third chapter of the second book... okay, okay, you get it. Now, on the count of three, squeal with glee. 1... 2...

Glee was something Fahiem Abdul knew all about. Fahiem was one of those fortunate souls who are blessed with a perennially sunny disposition. Nothing got him down. He appreciated the small things. He epitomised the flow of water as it relates to a duck's back. He greeted the world with a smile, and so was frequently met with one. People around him just couldn't understand it. They speculated that there had to be *something* that got him down – he was just apparently very good at hiding it. This was not true. Fahiem was pretty much the happiest person you'd never met.

Until Jackie de la Rey came into his life.

When Fahiem had gotten his job in the kitchen of the prestigious Hotel Shmotel, his parents were thrilled. Fahiem had accepted the news the same way he would react if told his car had just been stolen – with a smile and a nod. Unlike so many people around him, Fahiem had no expectations of life, nor any sense of entitlement. He simply went with the flow, whichever way it took him, with the serene sense that life would unfold as it must. In his humble opinion, people's problems usually worsened (or began) when they tried to control things. So, while Fahiem's family cheered and celebrated and made a fuss, Fahiem just went along with it. He was just happy to have a job after hotel school, since his parents had spent so much on his studies. And so Fahiem began his employ with characteristic friendliness, willingness and a lack of expectations.

He had certainly not expected to meet the woman of his dreams. And he could never have imagined that the woman of his dreams would, in her handling of him, alternate between fiery hot and cruelly cold.

True, they had nothing in common. For one thing, Jackie was much older and clearly more experienced; Fahiem was twenty-one and a virgin. Although they had never discussed it, it was clear from the gold cross she wore around her neck that Jackie was a Christian. Fahiem was Muslim, but didn't see this difference between them as an impediment. He was quite sure his parents would disagree, which was one reason he had not yet told them about Jackie. The main reason was that Jackie had insisted that *nobody* find out about them. This hurt Fahiem, who could only surmise it was the religion issue.

Whatever the cause, its effect was wearing Fahiem down. Being with Jackie was a rollercoaster ride. One minute she was pawing at him like a weight-watcher on a doughnut, the next she was tossing him aside like a stale rice cake. There was just no middle ground. He would even settle for slightly cold toast. He was sick. Lovesick.

No one had ever told him that love was so difficult. Every now and then a nasty suspicion would float to the surface of his mind: that Jackie did not return his love. But Fahiem always pushed these thoughts aside –she was just *complicated*. Clearly she functioned in a unique way, and Fahiem had been working overtime to crack her code. So far, what he had gathered was that Jackie needed to be in control – and if she felt she wasn't, she got angry. That was fine – Fahiem had no interest in control. The tricky part was that, even when Jackie had control, she was *still* angry. In fact, Jackie was angry a lot. This led Fahiem to conclude that anger was how Jackie expressed affection. She wouldn't get so angry if she didn't care, right?

Still, it was taxing – even for someone as easy-going as Fahiem.

Jackie never wanted to talk. Fahiem knew this was only because their connection went beyond words, but still, he wished that their communion would *occasionally* make the transformation into actual dialogue. Not that the other things they did weren't nice. They were very nice. Fahiem enjoyed them very much. Some of the things Jackie had taught him he'd never even heard of before. Very nice, enjoyable things.

And yet he longed for more – like walking on the beach together, laughing and holding hands; arriving at her front door with flowers, in the rain. All the stuff you always see on TV. Fahiem wanted that. He had learned, however, not to suggest such things to Jackie. It made her angry, and although Fahiem chose to interpret her anger as affection, there were degrees to her anger that were best avoided.

Fahiem was a Good Guy.

Poor guy.

Little did poor Fahiem know how long it would take before the forecast of his disposition would return to sunny. Or what storms would rage in the interim.

Martie's exuberance was not to be dampened – even by a fairly painful penguin bite. She'd had such a wonderful lunch with the young lady who ran Wives in Training. Jackie was polite, friendly and extremely interested in Martie. Martie also loved her full name – Jacoba. It hinted at a family bred on sound traditions. She asked Martie quite a bit about her own family background. Martie was very honest, except about the fact that she and her family were no longer speaking. Jackie seemed impressed by Martie's account of her family, and Martie was keen to impress, so she didn't feel it was necessary to include the recent fall-out. It was only a woman's club, after all.

'And you're married?' asked Jackie.

'Yes,' said Martie.

'What's your husband like?' asked Jackie, the beaming picture of amity.

Martie thought for a moment about the trauma that had precipitated her meeting Gift, and all the hoopla surrounding their union, and decided to stick to Gift's personal qualities.

'Well,' she said. 'He's lovely.'

Jackie saw this hesitation, but did not show it. It seemed to conceal something more, another story. If this woman's husband was 'lovely' in the way Jackie's father was lovely to her mother, then Jackie felt for Martie. Jackie nodded sweetly, urging Martie to continue.

'He's very traditional,' said Martie, then added, 'Like us!' She winked at Jackie here, another teensy moment that would set in motion a chain of events far from teensy. Martie meant the wink to say: *conservative, wholesome family values*. Jackie interpreted the wink as: *conservative, white and more than that I don't want to come right out and say, which is why I'm winking*.

'Conservative?' ventured Jackie, trying to delve a little deeper.

'Yes, definitely!' chirped Martie. 'We often watch the news together and just can't believe what's going on in this country today.'

Jackie nodded, pleased. Once again, she was interpreting Martie through her ivory-framed glasses – Martie was actually referring to things like crime and the ever-growing corruption of today's youth.

'They *are* unbelievable,' said Jackie quietly, with a knowing grin.

'Ja,' said Martie, deciding that Jackie was referring to today's youth. 'It's disgusting!' she added, sensing this was going well.

Jackie chuckled, genuinely pleased. Martie was looking like a promising prospect for inclusion in W.I.T. She didn't have any striking abilities that Jackie could discern, but a body was a body and in big enough groups, bodies were useful. It was at this point that Martie tried to pet the penguin. After a leisurely lunch at the restaurant adjoining Boulder's Beach, the two ladies decided to go for a walk along the shore. Martie was very excited to see all the penguins, and Jackie deemed it an appropriately secluded spot for her more sensitive questions.

Jackie was momentarily lost in her train of thought when Martie approached the penguin, cooing softly. Jackie called out, but a moment too late...

'Oh, Martie, you're not supposed to...'

'AAAAAARGGHHHHH!' howled Martie. '*Bliksem!*' she yelped, retracting her newly-bitten hand while the offender waddled off as quickly as its little land-legs would carry it. A moment later, her pain was eclipsed by red-faced embarrassment.

'It's okay!' she sang brightly, trying to disguise her discomfiture, but the attempt was in vain when, trying to march back to Jackie in a breezy fashion, she tripped and came crashing onto her backside.

'Oh my God,' said Jackie, rushing to help her.

'Goodness!' said Martie before erupting into peals of shrill laughter. As she allowed herself to be helped up by a heaving Jackie, she prayed her cheeks weren't as scarlet as they felt. 'Thank you,' she sighed, trying her utmost to dust the sand off her posterior in a dignified manner. 'It's bumpy on the beach.'

Not very bright either, Jackie surmised. *Perfect.*

'I'm not used to it,' said Martie, trying to elaborate in the hope that Jackie wouldn't think her dim. 'I'm from the mountains... Well, they're bumpy too... but I was used to that. The beach... is a different *kind* of bumpy.' Martie's heart sank: what had begun as such a wonderful meeting was now completely unravelling.

'How's your hand?' asked Jackie sincerely.

'Oh, it's fine!' sang Martie. It wasn't. It was throbbing obscenely. But to prove her statement, she waved the hand quickly past Jackie's face. A little droplet of blood landed on Jackie's cheek.

Both women froze. This was like the awkward moment when one accidentally spits on someone else while talking. Neither party wants to acknowledge it, and the spitee has to wait long, excruciating seconds for the spitter's gaze to drift elsewhere before swiftly wiping it off. Except this time it was not spit. This was worse. Jackie broke the moment first.

'You're bleeding,' she said, casually extracting a tissue from her bag and handing it to Martie. She then took one for herself and wiped the blood splat away as though as it were nothing but a drop of rain. In her job at the hotel, Jackie had mastered the art of remaining gracious at all times.

'I'm so sorry,' said Martie, losing her restraint. 'I'm sorry.'

'Martie,' said Jackie with a beatific smile, 'it's fine.'

'I should go. I need to start dinner.'

My God, thought Jackie, *look at this woman. She's a wreck. Her husband obviously rules with an iron fist. She needs me.*

'Thank you for your time,' said Martie, with the air of one who has just lost a friend mere hours after finding her. 'I'm sorry.' She turned to leave, forlorn.

'Martie,' said Jackie, taking her arm. 'I had fun. I'd like you to come to a meeting with us.'

'Really?'

'Yes.'

'Oh, thank you!'

'On one condition: go to a doctor and get your hand sorted out.'

Martie nodded feverishly. She was in.

She walked back to the parking lot with her new friend, giddy with glee.

Glee was probably the furthest thing from Krissie Blaine's mind, ever since she had gotten a certain something stuck on her shoe that she couldn't shake off – Lincoln Thomas. He had been her 'NBF' (New Best Friend) for nearly twenty-four hours now and Krissie felt ready to resort to bloody violence.

Since striking their little deal the previous morning, Link had done nothing but... hang around. And stare. And ask nosy questions about her and her Hollywood life. He also had a predilection for picking his nose when he thought she wasn't looking. She vowed to change rooms as soon as he was gone.

Unfortunately for Krissie, Link wasn't as stupid as he looked: he kept close watch over his phone at all times, and refused to afford her even a glimpse of the incriminating pictures he had taken of her. And he made further demands, forcing her to pose for 'normal holiday snaps' with him, and sign endless numbers of autographs, ostensibly to sell online upon his return home.

'When exactly are you going home?' she asked, unable to keep an even tone.

'Aw, come on, luv,' he said with a lascivious wink. 'Aren't you having fun?'

She glared, transmitting waves of hatred and resentment at him.

'Ooh,' he said, lightly trailing a hand over his sunburned arm. 'Cream time.'

Krissie wilted. Not again. She had put cream on him only an hour ago. In tones not usually reserved for an NBF, she pointed this out.

'Cream time,' he repeated emphatically, handing her the after-sun lotion.

Krissie snatched the bottle from him and sat down behind his freckled back, which had now started to peel. Swallowing hard, she gazed out the window, silently screaming for help. It came, in the form of an idea.

'I want to go and get some sun,' she purred.

'Can't,' he grunted. 'I've had enough.'

'Well, you can sit in the shade.'

'Nah,' he said simply.

'Fine,' she sighed deliberately. 'I really wanted to try on my new bikini. Well, it's not really a bikini – it's more like a few pieces of string,' she chuckled.

'Let's go!' said Link, experiencing an abrupt change of heart (accompanied by stirrings in a different organ).

'I'll fix us a quick drink first,' she smiled.

Link liked this girl more and more each minute.

After a quick trip to the bathroom to change, Krissie re-emerged and hurried over to the counter to prepare their drinks. For Link, she prepared a special cocktail, one her mother often consumed after a tough day: a cold beer with a crushed sleeping tablet. She kicked herself for not thinking of it sooner.

'Down the hatch!' said Krissie.

'What's the rush?' asked Link.

'We can't carry drinks in the elevator – it's trashy.'

'I am trash, luv.'

'You're telling me a guy like you can't down a whole beer in one go?'

'Watch me!' he said, accepting the challenge.

It's so easy with men, thought Krissie.

Twenty minutes later, Krissie and Link lay by the hotel pool. Beside her, Link slept the sleep of benzodiazepines. She knew he was still breathing because he was snoring his famous snore. Krissie resisted the urge to throw him into the pool: she doubted she had the strength, but, more importantly, she didn't want to risk waking him. It had been difficult enough dragging his deck chair into the sun, which now flooded him. He'd not had a chance to put any sun-block on before passing out, but that was okay – Krissie had very kindly taken the trouble to apply some for him.

After careful consideration, she had decided to use the sun-block to spell out a word across his forehead – GAY – and render a crude depiction of a male member across his chest. A couple of hours in this heat, and her work would bear semi-permanent results on his skin, by which time Krissie planned to be out on the town. Alone.

Unfortunately, Link had locked his phone in the safe in Krissie's room, creating a new combination, which she did not know, as part of their deal. So, while Krissie would not be able to take advantage of his drug-induced nap to destroy his sordid little snaps, at least she would be able to get away from him for a while and, as an added bonus, crisp his bacon.

Krissie sighed. Sometimes it proved very difficult being so rich, beautiful and famous.

On the other side of Signal Hill, Krissie's STBNBF (Soon To Be New Best Friend) was being introduced to a bunch of new faces. It was the day before production was to begin and MK was visiting the studios that would soon become 'home' for the next three months. The word 'home' had been used by the production manager, a squat man in dungarees who looked like he belonged in plumbing. He was very polite, but MK's special people-reading gifts told her he was the type who would probably turn nasty after about a week. His name was Wimpie (pronounced 'Vimpy' in Afrikaans, although MK had already made a mental note to 'innocently' keep calling him 'Wimpy').

Superstardom Lesson No. 26: NEVER wear dungarees. EVER. Not for ANY reason. Life is not a cartoon.

Wimpie led her through a tiny office and a pokey corridor to the studio door. He heaved it open, and they stepped inside. It looked like a warehouse where giant thieves stashed stolen pieces of rooms. To her left and to her right, MK saw that the various sets were simply lined up beside each other, leaving the centre area free for the cameras. Everything looked dreadfully cheap, but MK forced herself to keep smiling.

'Cool, hey?' asked Wimpie.

'Mmm,' said MK, adopting her new public persona, Palesa. Her Miss Kwa Kwa title was simply not practical in daily life and work, so MK had settled on her given name, Palesa. The character of Palesa was not very different from Miss Kwa Kwa: rural, not too bright, but very charming. Important qualities if one was to surprise and impress others. She glanced around. 'Gorgeous.'

She followed Wimpie through and out another door, which lead onto a courtyard populated by plastic tables and chairs.

'This is the canteen,' he explained.

'Where's my dressing room, sweetie?' she tinkled.

'Oh, back inside,' he said. 'You'll be sharing with Saartjie.'

'Sharing?' asked MK, taken aback.

'With Saartjie,' repeated Wimpie, and, as though this more than made up for it, 'the star of the show.'

MK's back instantly went up at the use of the word 'star' in reference to someone other than herself. Palesa, however, smiled broadly.

'Lucky me!' she cried, so sincerely that Wimpie found himself almost feeling sorry for her. Clearly she was just another wide-eyed rural in over her head.

'Did I hear my name?' asked a voice behind them loudly.

MK turned to see said star standing before her. Saartjie Williams. The heroine of countless local television series, mostly sitcoms, Saartjie Williams was probably as recognisable a face as you could get in South Africa (even if people weren't entirely sure where exactly they knew her from). Now here she stood before MK in a pink and white tracksuit with messy hair and no makeup. 'Star' was not the word MK would've used.

'Saartjie Williams,' said the woman, holding out her hand.

'Like Baartman,' said MK before she could stop herself. Saartjie's smile faltered. She withdrew her hand. 'Of course I know who you are, sweetie,' MK added quickly. 'I'm such a fan.'

'That's nice,' said Saartjie, sounding like she meant the opposite. 'And you are?'

'This is Palesa Moshesh,' said Wimpie. 'She'll be playing Thembi.'

'No,' corrected MK gently, 'that'll be changing.'

'Hah,' scoffed Saartjie humourlessly, 'Seems like a lot is being changed for you. Scripts being rewritten, *nogal*. You must be very good, hey? What have you done?'

'You may have heard of *Kwa Kwa Konfidential*?' MK answered grandly. Saartjie looked her up and down once, saying nothing for a moment but speaking volumes.

'No,' she said. 'But welcome. I'm sure we'll do some wonderful things together.' She smiled at MK with exaggerated warmth.

'See you in the dressing room!' replied MK with equal enthusiasm. Saartjie chuckled and gave an amiable wave before she left.

'Wow, said Wimpie, 'she really likes you.'

'Good,' enthused MK. But she had another word flashing at the front of her mind...

War.

How was poor Wimpie to know that in the world of female battle, blows and parries could be exchanged in a moment as simple as passing the salad? And that frequently, war was waged during just such moments. One thing was for sure, though: war *had* just been declared. Saartjie Williams and MK had, in a heartbeat, sniffed each other out – and smelled threat.

However, while Saartjie had the good instincts to detect a creature similar to herself in many ways, she could not have known what she was *actually* dealing with. On any given day, MK was unlike anyone most people had ever encountered, but since her lost week, she'd gone beyond being a threat. She was dangerous.

Potentially deadly.

Lincoln Thomas was running as fast as he could, which was not very fast at all given that his legs had been replaced by what appeared to be two mounds of red jelly. He realised he could no longer run – he was staying right where he was. He noted with mounting terror that the ground was shuddering in loud, rhythmic crashes. Something exceedingly large was coming this way, and its thundering footsteps were causing his jelly legs to wobble violently.

'Wherrrrrre the hell arrrrrrre ya, ya Brrritish aaaaaasshole?' shrieked an immense voice with a distinctly American accent.

Link turned to see a fifty-foot Krissie Blaine heading towards him. Her platinum hair lashed about her shoulders like thick jungle vines. Her bronzed limbs stretched into a sublime infinity. Her eyes burned with gigantic sparkle. He was in equal parts terrified and turned on. She slid down onto her knees smoothly, but still he felt the tremor.

'Is this what you want, baby?' she cooed, untying the knot of her flimsy blouse seductively. The entire otherworldly landscape became flooded with crimson light. Link realised it was coming from him – his sunburn was glowing like a newborn sun. He nodded numbly at the creature.

Krissie's eyes widened with a relish that struck him as slightly diabolical. A dangerous smile played at the corners of her gleaming, generous lips.

'Shit,' he murmured.

With a grand flourish she ripped open the blouse. The gesture sent a shockwave through the air that nearly knocked Link off his feet. As soon as he had righted himself, his eyes shot up, ready for the IMAX version of his fantasy. He recoiled in horror at what he saw...

Where he was quite sure a pair of breasts ought to be, were instead two heads. Link blinked in horror. One was Eddie and the other was Rob – two of his mates from home. Eddie raised an eyebrow at Link in an expression that Link had only seen on his face once before.

'We're forty now, Link,' he said.

'Yeah,' chimed in Rob. 'When are you going to grow up, mate?'

The giant Krissie head lowered so that her face was in front of his. She made a thick, glugging sound as though she were about to spit in his face. He closed his eyes and tensed, petrified at the thought of its volume.

SPLASH.

Everything swam in Link's head, now total darkness. He tried to pull himself out of the dream. Boy, that was one for the record books, under 'Fecking Weird', but it was just a dream nonetheless.

The sensation that his face was wet lingered, however... He battled to drag his eyes open, but it felt very, very difficult. The only other time he had struggled to wake up like this was after foolishly smoking a Jamaican's grass. This wasn't normal.

'Wakey-wakey,' said a voice out there in the conscious world.

Link groaned. His head ached. His eyes refused to open.

Suddenly he felt a slap on his cheek – not a very hard one, but it smarted badly. Damn sunburn. It felt *worse*, if that was possible. Maybe he'd fallen asleep in the sun when he was by the pool with Krissie...

'Open your eyes, champ,' said the voice again. American accent... Male...

With all the energy he could muster (frustratingly little) he cracked open his eyes. It took a moment for a picture to form, and when it did it was most baffling: a man sat before him. In a brightly coloured shirt with palm tree patterns on it, the kind of shirt people always seemed to be wearing in movies set in Hawaii. The man, dark hair and solid build, was smiling a smile full of teeth so perfect and white they affirmed the American cliché.

'Water,' croaked Link with a tongue that felt as though it had been dragged through a sand pit.

'In a glass this time?' asked the Yank, with a friendly chuckle.

'You thwoo wa'ah immah faysh?' said Link, courtesy of the driest mouth he'd ever had. The Yank poured a glass of water.

'I threw water in your face, yeah. You wouldn't wake up. I think she drugged you.' The Yank brought the glass towards Link, but to his dismay Link discovered he couldn't move his arms.

Jelly legs flashed through his addled mind, a bizarre detail from a bizarre dream, the memory of which hovered vaguely in his consciousness. Link looked down, confused, and saw that he was tied up. A long section of thin but clearly strong cord bound him to the chair he was slumped in. When he looked up again, the glass forced its way into his lips, and he allowed it. The Yank carefully gave him one sip, and then another. It was so good.

'Thirsty, are ya?' asked the Yank with a grin.

Many of Link's forty years on the planet had been spent slouched in front of the tube, watching a vast assortment of things. He was the type that watched television for the sake of it, regardless of what was on. Game shows, infomercials, wildlife documentaries, soaps, and countless movies. One that sprang to mind now, looking at the American's grin, was *Deliverance*. Hello panic.

'What's going on?' he bleated.

'Keep it down, pal,' hissed the man, his charm evaporating. 'You know the game. So let's just keep things professional, right?'

Link's eyes darted around the room, trying to get a sense of where he was. The man was sitting on the corner of a bed. He noted a floral bedspread, and nondescript pastel curtains that didn't match the linen. There was a tiny en-suite bathroom. And a table with a chair that Link was tied to.

He screamed. Surely somebody would hear him. Unfortunately his new acquaintance was quick on the draw, and silenced him with a big, warm hand. He followed this quickly with a sharp jab in Link's ribs that instantly took the wind out of him. Link had been in his fair share of bar-fights – enough for him to know that the Yank knew what he was doing. Link gasped, trying to restart his breath. The sound that came out was thin and raspy and every time he inhaled he heard a moist click.

'I warned you,' said the Yank evenly.

Link nodded furiously to indicate his compliance.

'I've gotta say, you're good,' said the man. 'Very convincing.'

Link was lost.

'But after watching you for ten minutes, I knew. Nobody is really that stupid.'

Link frowned at him.

'You're doing it now,' smiled the Yank. 'The whole "clueless British lout" thing. You must've been in deep cover for years. What are you, about forty-five?'

'Forty,' said Link, his ego momentarily overcoming the battle to breathe.

'The sunburn's a nice touch,' said the man.

'What are you going on about?' asked Link in a pathetic tone.

'Drop the act, champ. I told you: I'm onto you, I don't have time for games – now start talking.'

Link stared, utterly bewildered. The man waited. After what seemed like hours but was really five minutes, the man stood, a dark look shadowing his face.

'If that's the way you want it, fine.' He grabbed Link's badly burned nipples and tweaked them hard. Link howled in agony. As if from nowhere, the Yank produced a balled up sock and stuffed it in Link's mouth. It tasted used. Dizziness came over Link and his head slumped back.

'I know lots of ways to get a conversation going, buddy,' said the American freak show. 'Lots of ways to loosen the tongue. And you're about to get a demonstration. I'll need my tools though...'

Link sobbed quietly as the man moved away to open a drawer. Link opened his eyes and looked up at the ceiling. There was a mirror on it. He didn't speculate about the possible reasons for this because something else caught his eye: in his reflection, he could see something on his forehead. It looked like white marks on his skin, or places where the skin was paler. A word... it said: GAY. He wondered briefly how it had gotten there.

This would cease to be of relevance when the man in the island shirt turned and came back towards Link carrying some of his 'tools'. The most disturbing thing was the Yank's expression.

It was one of unadulterated glee.

Six o' clock in the morning is not a time when the average person experiences glee. Generally speaking, those who are awake at this time have either just gotten out of bed, or not yet gotten into it. In Krissie's case, the latter was true: having left the British OUG unconscious by the pool yesterday afternoon, she had gotten dolled up, called a cab and proceeded to get very wasted all around the town.

Now, as the sky to the east was just beginning to pale, she was exiting a local taxi. Krissie had discovered to her delight that taxis in this country showed little respect for the rules, and preferred to move at breakneck speed. Not unlike her. She had somehow managed to find her way to the taxi rank and boarded one of the local minibus taxis. She had so enjoyed the crazy ride that, instead of getting off at the hotel, she'd handed the driver a R100 note and told him to give her a private ride around town. Who needed an amusement park when you had these giant bumper cars? Eventually the bumpy ride had begun to take its toll, however, and Krissie had directed him to her hotel – nausea had started billowing up from her core. She regretted the hot dog she had bought the night before in Long Street, a raucous street in town overflowing with nightlife. Some of her FFTs (Friends For Tonight) had insisted she try one, claiming it was a local speciality (although they had called it something else – a boerewors roll). Despite the fact that they were being cooked in a cart on the curb, under what looked like less-than-hygienic conditions, the hot dog was *delicious*, in the way that hot, greasy fat can be when intoxicated. Now she was regretting her choice.

The driver hooted cheerfully as he drove off, and Krissie waved and blew him a kiss. She turned to the hotel and began a slow, unsteady ascent towards it. The entrance looked very brightly lit, and Krissie felt the need for some fresh air, so she changed course and circled around to the side of the building. The security guard let her pass with an amused smile.

'Hi, gorgeous,' said Krissie, somewhat less brightly than usual. The distraction cost her: she stumbled as her heel came down into a grate, twisting her ankle and nearly bringing her to the ground.

'Gawd,' she exclaimed, before turning back to the guard. 'The ground here is, like, really uneven...' The security guard only grinned. 'Thanks for nothin',' she muttered, removing the shoes. Barefoot, she walked towards what appeared to be a staff entrance. In front of a small door stood two young guys. One was smoking a cigarette.

'Hey,' she called to the smoker. 'Can I get one of those?'

'Uh,' said the smoker, unaccustomed to seeing guests here. He handed her a cigarette from his pack. She nodded her head unsteadily in thanks and put it in her mouth. She seemed unable to keep the end in one place for too long, but eventually he managed to get the flame of his lighter underneath it. The cigarette tip lit up in a colour similar to the brightening sky.

'Pleasure, ma'am,' said the guy, hurriedly putting his out. He disappeared inside quickly. The other one was about to follow when Krissie grabbed his arm.

'You're not gonna leave a girl to smoke alone, are ya?'

'Well,' he said hesitantly, deciding that attending to a VIP guest was more important than getting to the kitchen five minutes early. 'I don't smoke, ma'am.'

'Me neither,' she said, throwing her smoke away with a grimace.

It was not helping her nausea. Her skinny arms drew up in front of her. The chill that sets in just before the sun appears.

'Oh,' mumbled the boy. Swiftly, he removed his jacket and put it around her shoulders. She seemed very underdressed for this time of day, in what may (ambitiously) have been described a dress: a garment which left her arms, shoulders and most of her legs exposed. Her eyes were framed in smudged black makeup and her lips retained sticky traces of bright red lipstick. There was something stuck in her tousled hair that looked like a beer label.

'You have something...' he began. Krissie reached up and fingered through her hair, plucking it out.

'Thanks,' she said softly. She looked at him with a frail smile of gratitude. Then she doubled over and vomited on his shoes.

Krissie lowered herself to her knees. Two seconds later, she noticed that the hotel employee was holding her hair back for her, but the worst was over. Without thinking, she wiped her mouth on her sleeve. Well, his sleeve.

'I ate a bad hot dog,' she explained.

'Oh,' said the boy, helping her up. He noticed that her knees were fairly battered. 'Can I help you to your room?'

'Yeah,' she replied. 'But not through the front. Do you have, like a service elevator or something?' He nodded. Krissie noticed his face, as if for the first time. It was sweet, open and a gorgeous colour – like a latte. 'You're hot,' she said. 'And sweet.' This was not the first time Krissie Blaine had thrown up outdoors in the wee hours. The guys she usually hung with in LA, however, were rarely chivalrous enough to hold her hair back for her. In fact, a typical response from one of them would've been to scold her for ruining his shoes.

'Er, thank you, ma'am,' said the hotel guy. Blushing.

'What's your name?'

'Fahiem,' he answered.

'Hmm,' she responded, deciding she wouldn't try to pronounce that. 'If I didn't have dog-breath right now, I'd kiss you.' Fahiem laughed uncomfortably. 'I need to go and get some beauty sleep, but what time do you get off work? We should go out.'

'Um...'

'Just come up to my room.'

'Uh...'

'I'm holding your jacket hostage.' She grinned wickedly, kissed his cheek, and disappeared inside.

Fahiem gulped. It seemed that the magazines were right about her. He hurried back to the kitchen, and tried to pretend that the knot in his stomach was nothing but the consequence of being star-struck.

A few hours later, MK arrived at the studio with her own stomach knot. It was the first day of rehearsal and she still hadn't met everyone yet. She was expecting to be cast immediately as The Outsider, the one that the cast decides to dislike and blame for anything that goes wrong. After all, she was the Johnny-come-lately, the one who had insisted her role be fleshed out. That was fine: she would kill them with kindness. She was ready for them.

What she didn't expect was to find a bunch of flowers in her dressing room – from Saartjie Williams, her NWE (New Worst Enemy). The bouquet included roses, lilies, carnations and even a protea. It was breathtakingly beautiful, and massive – it filled a basket that took up practically the whole dressing table.

The bitch.

Obviously Saartjie Williams favoured similar warfare tactics. MK kicked herself for arriving empty-handed: Saartjie – 1; MK – 0. She tossed aside her bag, and picked up the card. On the front was a cutesy drawing of a dog with a sunflower in its mouth. MK snorted in contempt and opened it up to read the message.

> **Dearest Palessa,**
>
> **Welcome to the family!**
> **Here's to laughter.**
>
> **Light & luv,**
> **Saartjie Williams x**

The name was signed with such dramatic flair it made MK's fillings ache. She took a moment to read between the lines...

'Dearest Palessa: Unless you're a pensioner, using 'dearest' when you have only just met someone is so patronising and fake. She knows I know that. And misspelling Palesa – a subtle undermining.

'Welcome to the family!' Using the word 'family' in a professional context is, again, false and too ridiculous to be taken seriously. The exclamation mark is just plain offensive. And false.

'Here's to laughter': Right. At my expense, you mean.

'Light & luv': totally pretentious and false. And the spelling of love, intended to be cutesy, is just another insult.

'Saartjie Williams': She signs her full name to remind me that she is in fact a name. A big name. Around here, the biggest name. Just in case I'd forgotten.

MK delighted in tearing the already-small card into as many pieces as she could. As she was thus occupied, the door opened. Without thinking, MK shoved the pieces of card into her mouth. It was Saartjie, with the biggest, fakest smile MK had seen since Tony Blair resigned.

'Good morning, my dear!' chirped Saartjie. 'Are you excited? Big day!'

'Mmmm!' MK affirmed, pursing her lips to disguise the contents in her mouth.

'Do you like the flowers?' asked Saartjie.

'Mmm!' moaned MK, nodding vigorously.

'Well, don't let me keep you from your breakfast...'

'Mm-hmm,' smiled MK, arching her eyebrows guiltily. For further authenticity, she chewed. The taste was bitter.

'We're all in the studio,' said Saartjie casually, 'when you're ready...' She favoured MK with another bloodcurdling smile then exited, closing the door behind her.

MK spat out the soggy balls of greeting card and picked the remainder out of her teeth. She couldn't believe the gall of that woman. *When you're ready...* implying that MK was holding them all up! Her eyes settled on the bouquet-in-a-basket...

Two minutes (and a rinse of mouthwash later), MK entered the studio, bearing a basket full of flowers.

'Hello, everybody!' she sang dazzlingly. 'So lovely to meet you all! These were given to me by Saartjie to wish me luck. And I felt so guilty I didn't bring anything, that I thought I must share the love with you. I can't afford such pretty flowers... yet!' A few people lit up, swept away by her energetic charisma.

Saartjie looked on with a face meant to express how touched she was. But MK could see the anger in her eyes.

'Besides,' said MK, glancing at Saartjie, 'I don't need luck.' MK went around, handing each person a flower and a kiss on the cheek. She chose the flowers based on her impressions of the individuals, or simply to match their outfits. 'I think we should all rehearse with our flowers in our hair today!' Everybody laughed, including Saartjie (although hers was somewhat brittle).

MK made bits of small talk as she went, learning and mentally noting minor details about each person. She cracked jokes. The others gathered that, while she wasn't the brightest crayon in the box, she was definitely fun to be around. She was loud and you couldn't help liking her.

Saartjie watched all of this with mounting alarm. Although she didn't fully grasp how smart MK was, she could sense that she wasn't as stupid as she pretended to be. She was definitely gifted in the People department, and in this business sometimes that was more important than anything else. If half of this girl's charisma translated to the screen, she would steal the show. Saartjie couldn't let that happen. Not on *her* show.

She was pulled out of these disturbing ruminations when MK touched her arm. Saartjie met her gaze. The battle was in full swing now. MK grinned innocently and glanced down at the remaining flowers in her basket. Saartjie's eyes followed. There were a few roses, a sunflower and the protea left. MK's hand floated around for a moment and then chose the protea.

'This one,' she said enthusiastically, twirling the dried-up flower, 'is a bit big to put in your hair.' She appeared genuinely perplexed. 'Maybe we can tie it onto your head with some ribbon.' The others laughed, and MK feigned surprise.

'Thanks, my dear,' said Saartjie, keeping her smile in place. 'I'll put it my dressing room.'

'*Our* dressing room,' corrected MK cheerfully. 'Now, for me, I choose the sunflower...' And then, with a little wink at Saartjie: 'It's a new day.' Saartjie's smile faltered ever so slightly. MK then scanned around the studio, and spotted a vase in one of the sets. She tottered over and placed her sunflower in it. Now, it would stand there all day, big and pretty, reminding everyone – especially Saartjie – where it had come from.

'You can't put it on the set, dear,' said Saartjie through slightly gritted teeth.

'We're not shooting today,' said Wimpie. 'It's fine.'

MK beamed.

Saartjie shot a blight-inflicting look at Wimpie, which went unnoticed, however, as everyone was called to attention by the director. Saartjie dumped the offensive plant into Wimpie's hands.

'Get rid of this,' she hissed before putting on her game face and joining the others. MK allowed herself a moment of celebration – *one all!* – before switching her focus to the task at hand. Acting.

Something she had been doing (masterfully) for years already, but never when people knew she was doing it. And while in her opinion the genre of comedy left much to be desired, that was no excuse not to give it her best. Besides, now she had Motivation: to act the tracksuit pants off Saartjie Williams.

'Wakey-wakey.'

The smell of coffee.

Link was afraid to open his eyes. He didn't want to see the crazy American, or have to tolerate any more of his nefarious torture. Then... the feel of silk on his skin. He was in a bed, a comfortable one.

It was the happiest sight of his life: Krissie Blaine bearing a fresh cup of coffee – in her brilliant hotel suite. He laughed, almost wept, in the throes of the sweetest relief he had ever known. Krissie smiled at him in a most pleasant manner: where there had once been a sulky pout was now an expression so warm, so affectionate, so *caring* that...

It had to be a dream.

No...

'Wake up!' Link's eyes snapped open to reveal the stuff of his worst nightmares. He was still in the shitty hotel room with the demonic grinning Yank. There *was* coffee – in the Yank's hands – but this did not comfort Link. It seemed more likely that the Yank would scald Link with it than let him drink it.

'Good morning, sunshine!' chirped the Yank. 'How did you sleep?'

'Fine,' replied Link meekly. This was a lie, and they both knew it. After hours of interrogation broken by seemingly endless periods of torture, Link had finally passed out. However, the Yank had woken him every hour or so to continue his 'work'. Link had bruises all over his body, as well as several burns of varying levels of severity. Also, he no longer had eyebrows – having had them extracted, one hair at a time.

'You look surprised,' chortled the Yank. This was meant as a joke, but under the present circumstances, Link was not amused. 'Coffee?' Link said nothing. He'd learned that if he kept quiet, he stood less chance of saying the wrong thing. The problem was that Link could not discern what the *right* thing was. The Yank seemed to have some warped reality in his head that Link could not decipher. 'You're tough, Lincoln Thomas,' said the man, 'I'll give ya that.' He flicked open a pocket knife and brought it towards Link. Link squealed, but was shocked to discover that the man had cut loose one of his hands. Now he handed Link the cup of coffee. Link took it but only stared at it miserably.

'Is it poisoned?' he asked.

'Of course not!' laughed the Yank. 'Now, listen, Link – can I call ya Link? I know your friends call you that. Anyway. Link, I'm running outta time, so we need to get this to the next level...'

Link shuddered. Quickly he gulped some coffee, hoping it *was* poison so that he would not survive to find out exactly what the 'next level' entailed. To his dismay, it tasted like normal coffee.

'Now,' said the Yank. 'I know you're MI5.'

Link's eyes widened. As far as the swelling would allow.

'Correct?' pressed the Yank.

'Wha'?' asked Link, incredulous. The man slapped him across the face, just hard enough to cause Link's existing pains to flare up. 'No!' he yelped. 'Nonononononono! I'm not MI5!'

'MI6?' ventured the Yank.

'No! I'm just a yob from Yorkshire who came here on holiday to get some sun, drink some beer and meet birds! I don't know nothing about nothing – *ifIdidIwouldtellyapleasebelievemeplease!*'

The man in the island shirt frowned. Slowly, he sat down on the edge of the bed, facing Link, and stared into his eyes. This was very troubling. His instincts were telling him that the Brit was telling the truth. Still, one heard tales of people who took days to break, and he'd only been working Lincoln Thomas since the day before. He opted to take a different tack.

'Lincoln,' he said gravely, 'I'm here on information that terrorist cells have planted an agent in this country. Someone who is going to cause a lot of trouble for the free world. Now, I'm going to do everything in my power to stop that from happening.'

Link wondered if this bloke was for real or simply a nutter who had watched too many spy movies. Either way, he seemed to have a flair for the dramatic. Link sensed that he was expected to say something.

'Right,' he said.

'What is your connection to Krissie Blaine?' asked the Yank.

'I just met her.'

'How did you come to be staying with her at her hotel?'

'Er,' mumbled Link, trying to decide if the embarrassing truth would be the best answer. 'I met her in a bar, and she invited me back to her hotel.'

The Yank's eyebrow raised in disbelief.

'Nothing happened,' put in Link quickly. 'I'm not her type. We just had a few laughs together, that's all. What's she got to do with the terrorism thing?'

'It's all about stupidity, Link,' said the Yank gravely. 'It's about numbing minds. There's a plot to numb American minds by force-feeding them a never-ending stream of brainless garbage. And you know why, Link?'

Link should his head. He hadn't the foggiest.

'Because,' explained the man grimly, 'the terrorists think stupid people are easy to control. They are the ones who are behind this whole obsession with celebrity. They're smart enough to know that in dark times like these, people would rather hear more about Britney's breakdown and Lindsay's drinking than the latest crisis in Darfur. They want Americans to be stupid so that they can take control of us.'

'So,' said Link, curious now, 'you're saying that terrorists are behind the tabloids?'

'Oh, it goes deeper than that,' growled the man, 'but essentially, yeah, they're involved. And once we're stupid enough, they'll just swoop in and take over!' The man was clearly getting angry now. 'But they're underestimating us! *Do you know how dangerous a nation full of stupid people can be?*' He charged the air with his fist emphatically, as if to underline his point.

'Are you going to kill me?' asked Link.

'What?' asked the man, laughing now. 'Why?'

'Because I know too much...' said Link.

'One of our greatest presidents in America was Abraham Lincoln – did you know that, Link?'

'Um, yeah.'

'Like you – Lincoln. I like you, Link. I may need some help down here, and I think you're the man for the job.'

'I don't think so, mate.'

'C'mon! You'll be working with an agent of one of the most powerful organisations in the world. You'll enjoy it. And if you don't, *then* I'll kill you. Or if you try any funny business, I'll kill you. Do you believe me?'

Link nodded furiously.

As the man untied him, Link's mind reeled. He, Lincoln Thomas, involved in secret service against terrorism. It was the kind of thing he had fantasised about in his youth. And there was nothing to go home to. His friends had abandoned him, and he had come here alone. Clearly this was meant to be. Giddy relief at being spared, fear of what may come, exhilaration at his new 'job', and – predominantly – the effects of sleep deprivation and torture, made Link feel more alive than he had for years.

He had a new purpose. He had a new partner, whom he was thrilled to be teamed *with* rather than against. He felt almost gleeful...

Glee is defined either as jubilant delight, or with the connotation of a smug pleasure that comes as a result of someone else's bad luck. So it may be argued that if pride comes before a fall, glee should come before a *nasty* fall.

How was Link to know that this new partner had been cut loose by his own agency only weeks prior, and was, in fact, listed by them as a 'potential threat to society'? Link felt fairly sure the Yank was on the side of right, though he had some doubts. The man obviously had a penchant for certain antisocial skills, the likes of which Link hoped never to experience again.

Glee gleamed bright on several faces around town that morning. The question was: who would be facing a nasty fall?

KRISSIE BLAINE MOTHERED IN MOTHER CITY!

HOLLYWOOD GOOD-TIME GIRL RIPS UP CAPE TOWN PARTY SCENE!

CAPETONIANS WERE last night treated to yet another celebrity – socialite Krissie Blaine, known for her notoriously wild social life and frequent appearances in the media, usually for bad behaviour. The daughter of internet millionaire, Joseph Blaine, was spotted socialising at various nightspots in Long Street. Witnesses claim she partied into the early hours before leaving in a taxi. It's not clear what the heiress is doing in South Africa, but locals say they expect to see her out and about again.

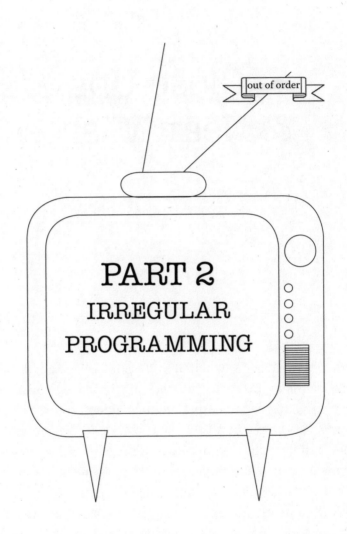

out of order

PART 2
IRREGULAR
PROGRAMMING

4

Close-Ups
& Near Misses

FRIDAY NIGHT WAS when it all went pear-shaped. Although perhaps this is unfair to the pear. It's tempting to wonder how the pear's shape came to denote pandemonium. The pear is shapely. It is curvy in all the right places. Its flavour is mild and sweet, and its colouring unremarkable. All in all, a pear is almost as nondescript as an apple. A more apt alternative may be the durian, a fruit known in Southeast Asia as the 'king of all fruits'. Covered in thorny green spikes, it is a most inhospitable-looking thing and one wonders what ever possessed anyone to sample one in the first place. Also, it has an overpoweringly awful stink, and a flavour that (while praised by its fans) is described as similar to sour cream and onions. The pear seems positively benign in comparison. Perhaps its only crime is that, like other four-letter words, it flows too easily off the tongue.

At any rate, the night it all went durian-shaped was Friday. But that was still days away from when we left a heavily intoxicated Krissie as she made her weaving way back up to her room very early on Monday morning, having just invited a certain young hotel chef by the name of Fahiem to visit after his shift.

Krissie fell onto the expansive comfort of her bed and slept most of the day, oblivious to the fact that the global press was now aware of her whereabouts and scrambling to get some incriminating photographs into their publications.

While Krissie slept high above in her penthouse suite, Fahiem was having a fairly typical day far below, in the bowels of the hotel. Typical as far as what was going on around him, that is... *Inside* of him was a different story. It was not every day that Fahiem was invited up to the hotel room of one of the most famous girls in the world. He was troubled. Beyond troubled. He was in turmoil. As though someone had planted a red-hot coal in the pit of his stomach, a coal that was now growing thorny spikes not unlike those of the durian. Fahiem couldn't imagine what Miss Blaine might want from him – or at least he refused to imagine. He would have to go, of course – one never said no to a guest of the hotel. That didn't mean anything untoward would happen – he could certainly say no in his personal capacity, off duty. Simple. He already had the girl of his dreams – Jackie. Simple. Still, he couldn't stop the burning in his gut.

When break time came, the others in the kitchen gathered around the newspaper, giggling at the unflattering pictures of Krissie Blaine. Fahiem hoped that this development would absorb Krissie Blaine's attention and shift it away from him. He was just considering this when Jackie appeared in the hallway. She raised one stern eyebrow at him then disappeared again. He knew what that meant. He made his way to their special place, the janitorial closet, filled with anxiety. Should he tell Jackie about Miss Blaine's request? What would her reaction be? He shuddered.

The moment the door closed behind him, Jackie pounced, tearing at his pants. She panted. He moaned. Then he made a huge mistake.

'Jackie,' he murmured, escaping her embrace. 'We have to talk.'

'What?' she sneered. 'We don't talk.' As if to verify this, she launched herself at him again, all pushing hands and probing fingers. Again, he jumped away, knocking over a bucket and mop. 'Shit, man!' she hissed, stepping away from the encroaching grey puddle. 'They are not supposed to leave dirty water in here. Heads are gonna roll.'

'Do you love me?' he asked suddenly, taking the gap.

'Now there's water all over the floor!' she said darkly. She turned accusing eyes on him. He cowered.

'Sorry.'

'What did you say?' she said as though all the breath had suddenly gone out of her. Her eyes ballooned.

'Sorry,' he said again.

'Before that.'

'Oh,' said Fahiem. 'I said, do you...'

'I know what you said, fool!' she barked, cutting him off. Despite severe space constraints, Jackie attempted to pace. Her fingers roamed through her hair wildly. Then down to the cross around her neck. Suddenly she stopped and put her hand on the doorknob. 'I have to go,' she said flatly.

'Wait,' said Fahiem, putting his hand against the door. 'Answer me. Please.'

'Don't be so bloody stupid, man.' She tried to turn the knob but Fahiem stopped the door. 'I don't know what's got into you,' she said, 'but you have ruined it. Now get out of my way – I'm warning you.'

'You're scared,' he said.

It occurred to Jackie that she should be speechless, but that was a condition she had never experienced.

'*What?*' she asked dangerously. Fahiem removed his hand and backed away. Unfortunately it seemed that Jackie was no longer leaving – in fact she was now approaching him in a very menacing manner. She was angry.

It just means she loves you, he screamed to himself in his mind. *She's just being passionate.*

'Scared?' she growled, coming closer. 'I don't get *scared*. Scared is not in my vocabulary. So tell me, please,' she said, shoving him against the stock shelves, 'what it is you think I'm scared of –'

'Um,' he whimpered. It had to be now, he decided. Now or never. 'I think,' he whispered, 'that you're scared of loving me.' He flinched involuntarily but Jackie only stared at him. Apparently the fire that had been raging in his belly was now burning in her eyes. It roared there, building in intensity, until finally...

'You little idiot,' she whispered. 'Me? Love you?' Her voice grew louder. 'I will never love *you*. You are *nothing* to me. You're *dirt*.'

'Okay,' he said, keen to bring this nightmare to an end.

'You are an *animal*,' she continued, unabated. 'You're a dirty, disgusting little dog. And a woman like me will never love a dog like you, you –' Jackie broke off, just in time to avoid using the kind of word that would certainly get her fired, opting, instead, to settle for violence. She kneed him in the groin.

A noise somewhere between a sigh and a squeal escaped Fahiem's lips as he crumpled to the floor. The world went white for a moment as a wave of excruciating pain ripped through him, then red as it dulled to garden variety agony and finally black as he lost consciousness.

When he came to, mere minutes later, he noticed two things: one, Jackie was gone, and two, he thought he would never walk again. The pain was so unbearable that it consumed him. He suddenly forgot what a normal, pain-free life was like, and envisioned feeling this way for the rest of his life – which would surely not be for very long since pain like this *had to be fatal*. He cried. He wept. He forced himself to breathe. He prayed. He tried to recall happy times. But mostly he wept. Because once the physical pain started to dull down a little, the emotional pain began to escalate. Not many men get their hearts and their privates broken on the same day.

The things she had said. The way she had said them. It was all too much. Fahiem wept bitterly. Bitterly, he wept. He cursed his own stupidity. He had actually convinced himself that she loved him in her own, strange way. She had called him an idiot, and maybe she was right. It all made sense now. How could he have mistaken Jackie's behaviour as affection when another young woman had shown him just this morning what it *truly* was to be sweet and kind?

The thought of his imminent meeting with Krissie soothed Fahiem. It was a light in the darkness. It was what helped him finally get off the floor and pull himself together. It didn't relieve his physical pain, but it helped get him back downstairs to finish his shift. As he moved gingerly about the business of his day, the thought of Krissie Blaine sparkled around him – on the edges of the cutlery, on the stainless steel of the appliances, on the edges of his newly-broken heart.

It sparkled... with promise.

On the set of *The Rainbow Hotel*, Palesa Moshesh – known to those in the know as MK – also sparkled with promise. It was clear that she had worked on her script and she delivered almost every line perfectly.

She would have delivered them all perfectly, but she didn't want to draw too much attention to herself... yet. Also, it was good for the morale of the others if she, too, occasionally required some guidance from the director. As much as she craved the gold star – and hated faking any lack of astounding brilliance – it served her better to blend in for now. There was no doubt that Saartjie Williams was officially out for her blood and MK needed to keep at least some of the cast and crew on her good side.

Mick had arrived from Johannesburg in the afternoon, and

visited the set. As discussed beforehand, he had gone along
with her act – that of the charming, naïve Palesa. She had been
dying to see her little Wiggy, and was put out to learn that Mick
had left him alone at the Green Point flat. MK didn't push it,
though, noticing a fresh deep scratch on Mick's neck. After a
brief pep talk, Mick had stuck around to watch the rest of the
day's rehearsal. Every now and then, he would laugh out loud at
something (usually MK) and when MK caught his eye, he would
grin happily and give her an encouraging wink.

My number one fan, she thought.

At the end of the day, the director gathered the cast and crew
to thank them for their hard work, his gaze settling on MK as
he spoke. As was so often the case with this young woman, her
outsides displayed something quite different to her insides: while
her face registered the guileless innocence of a simple rural gal,
her mind's smile bore the hallmarks of someone far worldlier
and smarter. MK knew she had impressed – if confirmation was
necessary, she had only to look at the smile Saartjie was doing her
level best to keep plastered across her face. It looked like the card
slot of a particularly hostile and hungry ATM, MK mused.

Once they had all packed up and were on their way out, Saartjie
made a big show of giving MK an über-friendly farewell, kissing
both cheeks and giving her a fervent hug.

'Well done, my dear!' she cooed at MK. 'You tried very hard. I
think you'll be fine. Mickey, my darling,' she said, turning to Mick
warmly, 'so good to have you here. Keep everything on track.
Maybe we can do dinner after work tomorrow?'

'Sure,' said Mick. Saartjie beamed, bade them good evening
and trotted off to her car. MK waved affectionately until she was
gone.

'Good job on winning over the star,' said Mick to MK.

'She hates me,' said MK, dropping the act. 'And it's mutual.'

'No,' said Mick, worry clouding his face. 'No, no, no. Why? She
doesn't hate you. It looked like you two were already fast friends!'

'You have a lot to learn about women,' she sighed. *'Mickey.'* She noticed his look of concern. 'Don't worry, I'll behave like a perfect little angel.'

'You were brilliant in there,' he said, reassured. 'It's going to be a great show.' MK grunted. Mick decided not to pursue the topic and instead count his blessings that MK had agreed to take the role, thus saving him from further trauma, or worse, Talent. When they got into his car, he retrieved the paper from the back seat and handed it to MK. 'This should cheer you up,' he said.

MK's fame-hungry eyes immediately honed in on the pictures of a clearly inebriated Krissie Blaine. Nothing shocking there. It was only when MK had skimmed the caption and accompanying article that her interest piqued.

'This is Cape Town,' she exclaimed.

'Last night,' said Mick.

'She's here...' MK stared at the images intently. Suddenly she found herself prey to a creeping mixture of anxiety, awe, excitement and hatred. Starstruck. By a star she abhorred. It was most perplexing. To MK's mind, Krissie Blaine represented everything that was wrong with the world: she was massively wealthy, and famous the world over for no particular reason. She traded on her stupidity, flaunted the fact that she had never worked a day in her life (nor ever would), and was drop-dead gorgeous to boot. In a nutshell, everything to which MK aspired.

I have to meet her.

'Looks like she's having a grand old time here,' said Mick.

'Hmph,' snorted MK. 'Superstardom Lesson No. 33: There's no such thing as bad publicity. Unless you're too rich, too thin and too stupid to make it work for you.' Mick laughed, but MK remained stony-faced. 'Superstardom Lesson No. 55: Never get drunk in public. It's ugly if you're under thirty, and tragic if you're over thirty. This applies to men and women, but for different reasons: it makes women look cheap, and it makes men louder and thus more likely to pull a Gibson.'

'A Gibson?' laughed Mick.

'As in Mel: a humiliating display of inebriation resulting in verbal assault that angers the world, and invariably requires public apologies.'

'Maybe,' suggested Mick, 'you should rather call that a Mokaba.'

'That wouldn't translate in Hollywood, Mick.'

'Do you really think you're going to make it that far?'

She favoured him with a look of absolute incomprehension, as if to say there could be no other alternative.

'Well,' he muttered, 'of course you should go for it. Anyway, if you're keen to meet Krissie Blaine, I have some good news for you. The party I have planned for everyone on the show this Friday – I managed to book the bar of the Hotel Shmotel.'

'What?' asked MK.

'It's the most exclusive hotel in Cape Town. Although they never reveal who their guests are, it's pretty much a known fact that the world's biggest personalities stay there when they're in town. It's *very* private and *very* discreet, so if Krissie Blaine is in Cape Town, chances are that's where she'll be staying.'

'But,' sputtered MK, hyped up now, 'if it's so exclusive, how the hell did you manage to book it for *our* crappy little sitcom party?'

'Thanks,' replied Mick tetchily. 'Actually I know someone there.'

'Ah,' said MK knowingly. 'One of the Pink Mafia?'

'A friend,' Mick replied archly. 'At any rate, we've got one of their event halls for Friday night. But security is very tight, so you won't be able to go up into the hotel hunting for celebrities.'

'Fine,' said MK, already formulating a way to do just that.

'So what's the deal between you and Saartjie?' asked Mick.

'It's nothing,' said MK, her anger returning. 'She's threatened by me, that's all. Let's just get back to the flat – I can't wait to see my little Wiggy. How is he?'

'Alive and kicking,' said Mick wryly. 'And scratching and biting.'

Around the same time that MK was being chauffeured back home, Fahiem was standing outside the door of Krissie Blaine's suite, trying to work up the courage to knock. He was finding it difficult to stay cool after the day he had had; grief and anger still throbbed through his soul after the confrontation with Jackie, not to mention the pain in his nether regions. Nevertheless, here he was, having decided that a trip to the doctor would have to wait. Finally, he raised his hand and knocked on the door very softly, half hoping Miss Blaine wouldn't hear it.

He heard her coming before the door opened: it seemed she was on the receiving end of a distressing phone call. She waved Fahiem in, but continued barking into the phone.

'Daddy,' she shouted, 'I had, like, two glasses of wine!' Fahiem hesitated, gesturing that perhaps he should go. Krissie yanked him inside and closed the door, fighting on. 'I don't know, Daddy – obviously somebody, like, spiked my drink or something. You know what these vultures will do to get a shot.'

Fahiem deduced that Krissie was indeed aware of the article, but more importantly, so was her father. He lurked near the door, suddenly desperate to flee – straight to a doctor who could tell him his manparts would recover, and then prescribe painkillers to numb both the physical and emotional agony. Krissie Blaine, however, was proving to be a more skilled multi-tasker than he would have imagined: while arguing bitterly with her father, she had somehow managed to open a bottle of wine, pour two glasses and hand one to Fahiem. He took it helplessly but did not drink.

'*I'm* the victim here, Daddy,' she wailed. To Fahiem's astonishment, she proceeded to make the noises of bursting into tears – while simultaneously winking at him and taking a slug of her wine. 'Daddy, I have to go – my dinner's just arrived and I'm, like, starvacious... Fine, I promise not to drink. Bye-ee.' She hung up with a sigh then proceeded to down her entire glass of wine. 'Hi, cutie,' she purred, turning her full attention on the hapless Fahiem.

'Hello, ma'am,' he replied in a tiny voice.

'Call me Krissie,' she said, taking his hand and pulling him towards the couch. 'I love these sofas, by the way,' she said. 'They're really big.' She flung him down onto the couch then sidled up beside him. Fahiem groaned as his pain flared violently. 'Are you okay?'

'Uh, yes,' he said. 'Just a little accident in the kitchen earlier.'

'Oh, that's too bad' she said, looking bored of the subject already. 'Listen, I have a really important question. Did you see the British guy that was with me here?'

Fahiem shook his head, wondering how many men this girl went through in the course of a week. Krissie looked a little disappointed, and wondered to herself what had happened to Link after she had left him to roast by the pool. At least she knew that his phone – with the X-rated pictures of her on it – was still safe and sound in her room safe. He'd probably turn up sooner or later – she may as well enjoy the break for as long as it lasted.

'So tell me about yourself, Frank,' she said.

'Er, it's Fahiem.'

'I prefer Frank.'

'Okay,' he said. 'I work in the kitchen... I'm twenty-one.'

'I'm twenty,' she said brightly.

'Really?' he asked earnestly.

'Yeah,' she laughed, leaning in close. 'How old did you think I was?'

'Well,' he said, keen not to offend, 'you're just so famous.'

'Did you see it?' she asked, suddenly sounding upset. 'The article?'

'Ja.'

'Omigod!' she said, giggling again, then mocking his accent: '*Yaaahhhh...* it's so weird the way you guys say it.' Fahiem laughed too now, feeling slightly more relaxed.

'Well,' he chuckled awkwardly, 'your accent makes me feel like I'm on TV or something. In a movie.'

'Tell me, Frank, a guy as hot as you – you must have a girlfriend?'

'Oh,' he said, unable to keep a moment of sadness from ticking across his face. 'Not really. Sort of. I'm not sure actually.' Krissie gazed into his eyes with a look of compassionate concern. Smoothly, she put one arm around him, and her other hand on his arm.

'Sounds complicated,' she offered.

This was all the encouragement Fahiem needed. He'd been keeping the story to himself for so long, and she seemed so sweet and understanding... He decided to tell her all about his affair with Jackie, minus the racier details, of course. Krissie listened attentively, oohing and aahing in all the right places, squeezing his hand during the particularly unpleasant moments and generally being a comfy shoulder to cry on. By the time Fahiem had finished his woeful tale, his head was on Krissie's chest and her arms were wrapped around him.

'That's awful,' she said. 'Whaddabitch.' The use of this word in conjunction with his true love brought Fahiem swiftly back to reality. He noticed with horror that his tears had run down Krissie's flimsy blouse and wet the area over her small but very shapely breasts. He pulled away abruptly.

'Sorry,' said Krissie. 'But really, it's not cool for her to treat you like that, Frank. There are plenty of girls who would treat you so much better. I'd never hurt you.' He softened, and gave her a grateful smile.

That promise was broken a second later when Krissie grabbed Fahiem's most vulnerable body part. His scream pierced the balmy silence of the evening. Krissie apologised profusely, and when Fahiem had calmed down he came clean about the full extent of Jackie's cruelty. Krissie clucked sympathetically as she created an icepack for him. He took it from her before she could try to apply it herself.

'It's fine,' he said, struggling to his feet. 'You didn't know. I think I'd better be going, Miss Blaine.'

'No, wait,' she said, blocking his way. 'We don't have to... ya know... I mean, we could just, like, hang out... that would be, like, really cool...'

'Okay,' he said. 'Cool.'

Indeed, the evening was cool. But it was clear that certain fires were stirring behind the scenes, and it was only a matter of time before somebody would get burned.

The only other occasion we should delve into before we arrive at the aforementioned durian-shaped night is the weekly W.I.T. meeting, which took place on Thursday evening. This particular meeting was significant in that it was the first for a certain middle-aged newlywed named Martie.

Martie arrived at the home of Jackie de la Rey all-aquiver. She looked forward to meeting decent, God-fearing people like herself, and was anxious to make a good impression. She had wavered over whether or not to bring something. Jackie had told her it wasn't necessary, and they were there for cooking lessons after all, but Martie had been brought up a certain way, and that way dictated that one never visited empty-handed. Martie had decided to make milk tart. She wished she could preface its title with something like: 'Martie's Famous...' but the fact of the matter was that she didn't make a particularly good tart. Indeed, there were those who'd been tempted to preface the 'Famous' in the non-existent title with 'In'. Nevertheless, it was the thought that counted.

And so, balancing her milk tart on one hand, Martie rang the doorbell. Instead of the typical ding-dong, Martie was met by a high-pitched shriek that sounded the tune of 'Jesus Loves Me'. She had just begun to hum along when Jackie opened the door with a big smile.

'Hi, Martie,' she said happily. Then, glancing at the milk tart, 'Ooh, that looks delicious!' Further proof that appearances can indeed be deceiving. Jackie swept Martie inside and into the lounge, a simple but exceedingly neat room.

In an informal circle sat five other ladies: three looked to be in their fifties, one was about Jackie's age, and the last at least eighty. While Jackie made introductions, the flustered Martie tried to keep track of everybody, but the only name that stuck was that of an octogenarian called Wilhelmina. Martie smiled warmly and shook hands with everyone. While accepting a cup of tea, Martie noticed a table laden with sumptuous-looking snacks, including, to her dismay, a milk tart which, while similar in appearance, Martie felt sure was superior to her own.

'Martie made us a milk tart,' said Jackie. The others cooed appreciatively, but Martie waved it off.

'I see you already have one,' she said. 'Let's eat that, and you can keep mine for later. Or give it away.'

'Don't be silly,' said Wilhelmina. 'We'll try yours – in honour of your first meeting. Jackie, cut us each a piece, lovey.' Martie smiled bravely. 'Welcome, Martie,' said the old lady with a smile of such perfect teeth that they had to be false. 'It's so wonderful to meet a new, young member.' Martie laughed, blushing. It had been a good long while since anyone had called her young. 'Now,' said Wilhelmina, 'tell us about yourself.'

'Well, Auntie,' said Martie, using the Afrikaans term of respect for an older woman, 'I've had a very quiet life. Quite boring, really. I'm sure you have much more interesting stories to tell.'

'They've all heard my stories,' chuckled the old duck. 'Please, go on. Jackie tells us you come from good, traditional stock.'

'Oh, yes,' said Martie. 'My father was a priest.'

'Excellent.' Wilhelmina paused to accept the plate Jackie offered her – bearing a slice of Martie's milk tart. 'Lovely...' She took in a generous mouthful. And began to chew: a verb, you may have noted, not usually used in reference to the eating of milk tarts. This tart, however, was less milk and more rubber. But Wilhelmina chewed bravely on, struggling admirably to maintain her composure. Finally, when she had decided it was in chunks small enough to swallow, she forced it down. 'Mmmm,' she addressed Martie, then, turning to Jackie: 'Jackie, lovey, a bit of water please.' Carefully placing her plate on the side table next to her, she suggested chirpily, 'Why don't you show Martie around, Jackie?' As soon as Martie followed Jackie out of the room, Wilhelmina's affable expression crumpled into one of disgust. She passed the plate to one of her companions, who tipped the offending morsel out of the window. 'Shame.'

Martie trotted happily after Jackie on the tour of her small house. It was sparsely decorated with a few, mostly homemade, touches (which Martie could appreciate), and immaculately maintained. Jackie explained that she had only invited the more senior members of the club tonight, and Martie was touched. When they reached the back of the house, and Martie spotted the bathroom, she excused herself to use the facilities. Jackie returned to the lounge.

Martie entered the bathroom and closed the door, gazing at the toilet-roll Barbie perched on the cistern. She moved closer and studied Jackie's handiwork on the flowing dress. Not exactly Martie's cup of tea, but she admired the industriousness of it, and approved of its propriety. Martie did not actually need to use the facilities, but had escaped into the room for a quiet moment alone to gather her wits. She sat down on the closed loo and took a deep breath.

That was when she saw it.

On the back of the door was a very large rendering of the Saviour on the cross. It took Martie's breath away. It was splendid! Martie found herself drawn towards it. She studied the explicit detail in awe. She ran her fingers over it and realised it was a tapestry.

'Oh,' sighed Martie exultantly. She knew she had felt a strong connection to Jackie when she had first met her, but this confirmed it. Martie was overwhelmed with the sense of kinship she felt for the young woman. They would be great friends – she just knew it.

Someday soon, she would introduce her to Gift – *this is my dear friend, Jackie* – and they would get along like a house on fire.

Another bizarre expression, that – a house on fire. Generally, a house on fire is a very bad thing. Things get destroyed and people get hurt, badly. In this tale then, perhaps quite apt description, as you will discover.

For the time being, however, things were still going swimmingly. On returning from the bathroom, Martie noticed in amazement that her entire milk tart had been cleaned out. Two hours later, having thoroughly enjoyed herself, Martie bade her farewells, empty tart dish clutched proudly in hand. It occurred to her momentarily that besides eating their way through a small bakery, they had done no actual cooking. They had received no instruction or wisdom, done nothing, in fact, relating to the idea of Wives in Training. Martie laughed this off cheerfully. They'd had a wonderful time regardless. The other ladies were so friendly! And so interested in her. It was most gratifying. Martie was unaccustomed to being the centre of attention, and discovered she rather enjoyed it. She'd stuck to her resolution of keeping certain skeletons in the closet and skilfully avoided giving away too much about her husband. People always made such a fuss.

The ladies of W.I.T. were equally impressed by Martie. She was definitely conservative, and while they hadn't come right out and asked the difficult questions, they were convinced she was on the same page as them. People are remarkably adept at seeing things as they appear: Martie was an Afrikaans woman of middle age, who had grown up in a small town and had a priest for a father. In their minds, that equated to their kind of politics. They could never have imagined that she was married to a black politician. Nope, to them Martie looked like just the right kind of white, and they were unanimous in their decision to admit her to W.I.T.

Martie was in. She simply had no idea how deep.

Low profiles were the order of the week as the days marched on to Friday: MK kept her head down and did the job on set. She kept her distance from Saartjie as much as possible and focused on doing a good job in front of the cameras.

Krissie Blaine abandoned her wild ways in favour of cocooning in her hotel suite, with her new suiteheart, Fahiem aka Frank. Fahiem did his best to avoid Jackie at the hotel, which wasn't much of a problem since she was doing the same.

Lincoln Thomas remained under the close watch of the man in the island shirt, albeit willingly. The man in the island shirt spent the days 'training' Link, or, put another way, reprogramming him. The Brit was clearly not very powerful in the mental arena, a fact that the man used to his advantage. He had mastered techniques designed to systematically break and then retrain the toughest spies – on Link they worked like a breeze.

The man in the island shirt kept a close watch on Krissie Blaine's hotel room when Link was asleep or indisposed. He had noted with interest the new man spending every evening in her company. He looked like a Muslim. That had to mean something. The man resolved to find out what.

Friday is the day when people feel justified in unseemly behaviour.

After the gruelling workaday drudge of the week, who can blame them?

MK looked forward to the party at the Hotel Shmotel that Friday night. The fact that there was still a day of rehearsals to get through before then bothered her immensely. Four twelve-hour days of this drek had taken their toll. MK tried never to think about the fact that she still had nearly three months of it ahead of her. *The Rainbow Hotel* was proving to be as unoriginal and dull as its sitcom predecessors, and there was only so much she could do to change things without appearing too bolshy. She found herself in a position she feared most people in television reached. Too tired to care.

The other actors were totally over the top in their performances, and consequently entirely unbelievable. Worse, the director seemed to encourage them in this. It was as if they were trying to compensate for a bad script. But in MK's opinion, the script wasn't bad. It wasn't great, mind you, but nor was it Emmy material. Some lines were actually quite funny, but clearly beyond the actors.

Forcing herself to halt this all-too-familiar mental refrain, she tried to get her head back into the rehearsal. The Great Saartjie Williams was once again taking far too much of everybody else's time discussing her scene. For such a legend, she sure needed a lot of work. As it happened, the scene in question was between her character and MK's. MK's character – now named Nono – was asking Saartjie's character for a job. Saartjie's character –Merlene – didn't want to give Nono a job because she considered Nono irresponsible. The scene read as follows:

NONO

```
Come on, Merlene. You know I'm trustworthy.
```

MERLENE

```
I know all about your shady dealings in that
shebeen, Nono. If they were any shadier, you'd
have to hang a moon in there.
```

'Give me the cue, again, please, Palesa?' asked Saartjie.

'Okay,' sighed MK. 'Come on, Merlene. You know I'm trustworthy.'

'I know about all your shady dealings in that shebeen, Nono. If they were any shadier, it would be nighttime in there!'

'That's not the line,' said MK.

'I know, but I think it would be better that way,' replied Saartjie curtly.

MK looked to the director, hoping against hope that he would correct Saartjie. In the time since production started, he'd proved to be pretty spineless in MK's view, and she was getting tired of it.

'Let's try it one more time, Saartjie,' he said. MK cheered mentally.

'No,' said Saartjie flatly.

'Okay,' said the director.

'Wait,' said MK sharply. She made an effort to soften her tone and sweeten it up a little before she went on: 'Why not, Saartjie?'

'It's not funny.'

'Okay...' said MK, nodding. 'But it is funnier than your version.'

'Excuse me,' said Saartjie, swelling with indignation. 'I've been doing comedy for twenty years!'

'But you obviously still need some practice,' said MK before she could stop herself.

'I beg your pardon!' boomed Saartjie.

'Don't beg, sweetie,' grinned MK. 'It's common.'

'*O-kay!*' called the director, finally displaying some assertiveness. 'Good time to break for lunch.' Saartjie stormed off and MK sighed in frustration. It wasn't that the line was all that funny in the first place – it was the principle of the matter. MK was fed up. The director hurried off after Saartjie to calm her down – *kiss her outsized arse* – and the others just stared at MK in shock.

'You didn't have to be so rude,' said Wimpie from the embarrassing purple folds of his dungarees. 'Saartjie is a veterinarian of the small screen.'

It occurred to MK to point out the humour in his mistake, but she thought better of it. The other actors were already looking at her strangely. Time to revert to Palesa.

'You're right – I'm sorry. I'm just very tired today. Please tell her I'm sorry. Thanks, Wimpie,' she finished, pronouncing it 'wimpy'. His brow furrowed into a dark frown but she smiled back innocently. He stalked off.

The rest of the day passed without incident. Saartjie delivered the line as per the script (MK – 2; Saartjie – 1) and everybody did their best to get done as early as possible so they could rush home and prepare for the big party that night.

It's amazing what the promise of free booze can do for teamwork.

At around eight that evening, as the cast and crew of *The Rainbow Hotel* started arriving at the Hotel Shmotel, the sun was still high in the sky. Clouds had begun pouring over the crest of Table Mountain about an hour earlier, and if Krissie Blaine had happened to look out of her window around that time, she would have seen the 'tablecloth' effect she'd heard so much about. (As it turned out, she had not. She was too busy having a grand old time with 'Frank'.) After the clouds had performed their David Copperfield illusion they continued to move down and over the city, slowly turning the blue summer sky into an autumnal grey. This was, after all, the city famous for having four seasons in one day.

MK welcomed this change – she was wearing one of the most expensive dresses she'd ever owned and was not keen on sweating all over it.

Superstardom Lesson No. 41: Sweat is like flip-flops, swearing and sex-tapes – fine in the privacy of your own home, but NEVER in public. Nobody wants to see your bodily fluids when you are famous. You are perfect. Perfect doesn't sweat.

Mick, her escort for the evening, was wearing a gorgeous suit that was obviously very expensive. Alas, not even pricey Italian attire could conceal his growing midsection. MK wondered how he would ever attract a respectable Pink Mafioso with that gut. Still, she was grateful to have a male arm to drape herself over, even if it wasn't a particularly macho one. The upside was that he wouldn't be upset if she met another interesting gentleman, and at the fancy Hotel Shmotel – who knew? For the occasion, MK had purchased a backless dress in white-gold silk organza. It seemed to move with its own grace, falling to her feet in luxurious folds that billowed out behind her in a short train. An avid reader of *Heat*, MK was well aware of the dangers of wearing a train but this was hardly the Oscars. A fact MK became disconcertingly aware of when she realised that, not only was there no red carpet, but there wasn't a single photographer on hand to record for posterity the sublime gown on which she had spent a month's salary.

'No paparazzi,' she sniped at Mick as they made their way up to reception.

'Sorry,' said Mick, thrown. 'You look breathtaking.'

'Not that anyone will know.'

'Unless you meet Mr Hollywood in there,' he said encouragingly.

'Please, we're not allowed to leave the bar. Too common, apparently.' Mick chuckled. 'Besides, Mick, you make me sound like a dumb wide-eyed little girl.' The truth was she *did* hope to meet Mr Hollywood, or Miss Hollywood. She'd even settle for Mr Back-end-of-Arkansas if she thought it would get her closer to the Promised Land. She was dressed the part. This would help should she encounter security when she ventured beyond the bar area. And if her glittering appearance was not enough, there was always the stun gun in her gold-embossed clutch.

That was a last resort, of course. After her frightening experiences with ordinary guns, MK had disavowed violence of any kind, unless it was in the interests of saving her life or facilitating her big break.

Or shutting up sugary Saartjie Williams.

MK stirred from this pleasant daydream as they entered the foyer of the hotel. It was unreal. The only other time she'd been so awestruck was the first time she had visited the legendary Studio 94, the top-secret haunt that had existed in Johannesburg solely for the country's VIPs. Hidden beneath a dilapidated industrial wasteland in town, inside it was a stunningly beautiful haven peopled by the most powerful people in the nation. But that paled in comparison to what MK saw before her now: the foyer seemed large enough to house all the mansions of Sandton. Vast Table Mountain-sandstone pillars stretched to impossibly high ceilings like the arms of gods; the floor, instead of the usual marble, was made of glass, and through it one could see an underground swimming pool – a voyeur's delight from wherever you were standing. MK gasped.

'I'm sure,' whispered Mick in her ear, 'that there must be a Superstardom Lesson about letting your mouth hang open like that.'

MK snapped it shut but kept her gaze on the view beneath her feet. She could happily have stayed there all night. Evidently someone had other ideas, however.

'Good evening, sir,' said a voice behind them, each word perfectly enunciated. 'Ma'am. Welcome to the Hotel Shmotel. This way, if you please.' When MK dragged her eyes away from the floor, she noticed a spectacular young man in a uniform holding his hand out. He turned and started walking, and Mick followed, having to drag the reluctant MK along. She gazed around desperately, trying to take in the rest. Orchids everywhere. Space. So much light. The saffron shades of the early evening visible through a ceiling as transparent as the floor.

Before she knew it, they were inside a bar, and MK's first impression was disappointment – it had ordinary walls. A moment later, as her eyes adjusted and her brain caught up, she was too gobsmacked by the bar to feel cheated about the walls. Again, it was massive – the word 'bar' hardly seemed adequate. The floor was also glass, although now it revealed a garden so achingly beautiful MK could hardly stand it. MK had never been big on plants, but she knew all about aesthetics and this was perfection. Realising she could not spend the entire evening staring at the floor like a moron, she forced her gaze up. Trees from the garden below grew up through openings in the floor and into the bar. It was inconceivable. The bar itself seemed to be some opulent form of treehouse. This was the closest comparison her overwhelmed mind could make, but she knew it did the bar no justice. A treehouse was a wooden box where children could hurt themselves at higher altitudes, but *this...* this was stupendous. It was magnificent. It was sumptuous and all those other adjectives. It was Nirvana... Then suddenly, like a knife tearing through white-gold silk, a Saartjie-shaped figure ripped through MK's vision. She grabbed Mick's arm savagely.

'Ow!'

'Stopstopstopstopstop,' she rambled urgently.

'What is it?' he asked.

'I need a moment to compose myself,' she said. Ignoring Mick's bewildered look, MK shook her hands and lightly slapped her cheeks as though trying to wake up. *Oh my. Oh my. How can I ever set foot back in that dirty, horrible normal world where people just constantly make messes, even of each other?* She took a slow, deep breath, and tried to remind herself that she needed to be focused – now more than ever. She was not MK, the wide-eyed, awestruck rising star; she was Palesa Moshesh, the wide-eyed, awestruck small-town gal. *Hang on... I can work with this.*

'Are you okay?' asked Mick. Silence for a moment.

'Sweetie,' she purred in her best Palesa voice, 'it's like coming home.'

Gleaming from tiara to teeth to toes, MK and Mick joined Saartjie at the bar, where MK noticed that Saartjie was already halfway down a glass of white wine.

'Goodness!' exclaimed Saartjie, all supersweet smiles, 'it's not the Academy Awards, my dear! Although... you actually look a bit like an Academy Award yourself.' She finished with a tinkling laugh that sounded appreciative, but MK knew was actually bigfatbitchery.

'Thank yoo, thank yoo,' sang MK amiably. 'What are you drinking?'

'Dry,' said Saartjie.

'Oh,' said MK. 'How perfect.' MK saw that Saartjie got the jibe.

She also noticed that Mick was grinning like an idiot, clearly oblivious to the blows being exchanged.

Superstardom Lesson No. 99: Face value is worthless.

Saartjie then proceeded to harass Mick about the dinner she kept trying to have with him. The blatant brown-nosedness of it all sickened MK. She took the opportunity to study Saartjie's outfit. A tight-fitting black skirt that did absolutely nothing for her figure, a pair of Sue-Ellen stilettos and a cowboy blouse complete with shoulder pads, rhinestones and tassels across the front. MK fought off rising nausea. She toyed with a possible cautionary Superstardom Lesson based on the ensemble, but then decided there was just too much happening to fit into one lesson. She would have to give it some thought later on. *Yee-haw* was the phrase hammering the tip of MK's tongue but she resisted the urge to let it out.

As big as the bar area felt, it still didn't seem quite big enough for the two adversaries. But nothing was going to dampen MK's spirits. This was going to be an eventful night, no doubt about it.

A different kind of fairytale was happening at higher altitudes, in Krissie's suite. A fairytale of a more adult nature. Fahiem had recovered considerably from Jackie's nasty kick, enough so that he was ready to partake in said adult fairytale. He had spent every evening in the presence of Krissie, and they had connected on what he felt was a very deep level. How could he have known that Krissie Blaine possessed no levels? All in all, she was pretty much a shallow dish. Though it must be said that as far as shallow dishes are capable of feeling, Krissie had grown quite fond of Frank.

Krissie was pretty wild and had a fairly vulgar mouth, but once you got past that, Fahiem found that she was very sincere (read self-obsessed) and actually quite shy (manipulative?). Not unlike most girls of twenty.

From Krissie's perspective, Frank was the antithesis of everything she hated in the guys back home – most notably the married actor she'd been having an affair with just before leaving the States. Frank was gentle, considerate and actually listened when she talked. The other guy (who shall remain nameless) only ever wanted one thing, and the rest of the time had the irritating habit of putting his wife first.

Essentially, Krissie and Frank found in each other a warm, nurturing escape from the pain of their previous partnerings.

It had been wonderful. But it had also been frustrating. At their age, there's only so long you can enjoy the platonic side of a new crush. Finally tonight, it seemed that Frank was sufficiently recovered from his injury to move to baser territory. With great tenderness, they had ventured into the physical wonder of each other. At the present moment, Krissie was using her notorious mouth to treat Frank's battered area to a most soothing and enlivening therapy.

Fahiem lay there staring at the ceiling, dumbstruck by the experience. It was a first for him, and he fervently hoped not a last. When his treatment came to an end, he found himself returning the favour in a wonderland he could never have imagined. With Jackie, there had only been the main course itself, which was always frantic and rushed. She had never been one for entrées... Frank relished each moment with the special kind of reverence made for such firsts. There was no hurry; there was *time*. Somewhere in the distant logic of his mind, muffled cries occasionally objected with condemnation at this improper conduct, but invariably they would again be drowned out in the waves of sensational glory.

Eventually, Krissie forced him away, moaning that she couldn't stand it any longer. From the tone in her voice he gathered that this was a good thing. Ruddy-cheeked, she swung over to the other side of the bed and dug a pack of cigarettes out of the bedside drawer. She lit one and offered it to him.

'No thanks,' he said politely.

'So you really don't drink or smoke?' she asked, dragging heavily on the cigarette. 'Why not?'

'We're not really supposed to,' he shrugged.

'Christ,' she said with a naughty chuckle, 'my father would have a cow if he knew I was messin' around with an A-rab.' Fahiem looked hurt. 'Ya know,' she said more seriously, 'the whole terrorism thing. Has everybody pretty spooked.'

Fahiem nodded.

'I was in New York, you know,' she said quietly. 'The day it happened.'

'Really?' he asked, shocked.

'Yeah,' she said with a smile that had no joy in it. 'It was pretty crazy. One minute you're in New York, having a great time, and it's fun and crazy – I was fourteen – and everything's goin' a mile a minute, because that's New York – it's crazy...' She paused for a moment. 'And then, boom...'

He nodded solemnly.

'Suddenly, it's, like, *so quiet*,' she said. Fahiem felt gooseflesh up his arms and across his back. 'And everyone's in this daze,' she said, 'just silence.'

'Wow,' he said softly.

'So you turn on the TV, you know, just so there's some noise. And, of course, the TV noise is louder than anything else: "*Somebody just flew into the Twin Towers*" blah-blah-blah...' She waved a dismissive hand, but Fahiem could see something else in her eyes. 'It's crazy. How things can just *change* that like, so suddenly...'

Fahiem took her hand.

'Anyway,' she said, 'ruined my vacation.' Her laugh rattled, one thing at the front, something else at the back.

'I don't blow things up,' Fahiem said earnestly. Krissie laughed, this time much closer to actual amusement. She slapped his arm playfully.

'Except me,' she said with a wink that seemed to herald her return. 'I need to party, honey. Let's go out.' Alarm sounded in Fahiem's gut where mere minutes before only fuzzy bliss had hummed. He hadn't thought of this before: he could not go out in public with Krissie Blaine, and risk his parents – or worse, the magazines – finding out about them. The little voice he had so successfully ignored earlier boomed in his head triumphantly.

'Er,' he said, 'why don't we stay here rather? I'd rather be alone with you.' His mind raced for a better excuse.

'But I need to dance, baby.'

'Okay, well,' he stammered, 'let's go to the hotel bar then. There's a party there tonight.' He decided it would be safer to stay at the hotel: losing his job over fraternising with a guest. At least the larger public would be kept out of the loop. Krissie crinkled her nose in a babyish face meant to convey disapproval. 'No, seriously,' he continued hurriedly, 'it's gonna be awesome. And they have a big dance floor. Let's just start there, and then we can see...'

'Okay,' she said brightly, to his immense relief. 'Let's jump in the shower.'

Fahiem hopped to attention and followed after her, offering a silent prayer of gratitude that Jackie was long gone, and that the night shift manager was now on duty.

Jackie cursed the fact that she had been asked to work a double shift. Just so that she could babysit a bunch of local television weirdos. In her experienced opinion, the only thing worse than drunk, snooty rich foreigners was drunk, snooty poor locals in the entertainment industry. How they had even managed to get this venue for their little shindig was beyond her – somebody must've pulled strings. This hotel was far too exclusive (and expensive) for the likes of them.

Stubbing out the cigarette she had only smoked halfway, she began the mental transformation that got her through every shift at the hotel – from man-hating feminist fundamentalist to professional, friendly manager-on-duty.

Game face.

Let the games begin.

Jackie fully expected a bunch of tanked losers, some of whom would attempt a grope. She expected breakages, loud singing, and possibly even the need for security. She did not expect what was coming.

Games, indeed. Tennis, anyone? Only the aim is to hit your opponent with the ball... and not a conventional ball, either, but one covered in green, thorny spikes.

Not unlike the durian.

AD BREAK

The world may be a scary place right now...
But your FACE doesn't have to be!
Introducing the new

❊ GLEAM ❊

Skincare range

This miraculous range of beauty products has a 4-in-1 effect:

❊ Makes you look between <u>ten</u> and <u>twenty</u> years younger!
Remember that sixteen is the new thirty. Gone are the days
of timeless beauty and ageless grace – these days 'tween' is
queen.
❊ A gentle tanning effect brings Los Angeles to your own city!
It's the capital of the world!
❊ Permanently paralyses the area around your lips so that you
have a lifelong pout! Be magazine-ready at all times!

These days you just never know when you'll be caught
on camera –be it YouTube, Facebook, MySpace, or on
your terrorist captors' home video!

Be prepared... to GLEAM ❊

You'll also be helping the environment, as GLEAM is formulated from refuse, turning waste
into wonder! In addition, we only test on animals that are not endangered and were already
sickly anyway – you should see their smiling pouts now!

Bullseye & Black Eyes

MK WATCHED IMPASSIVELY as the vastly intoxicated Saartjie attempted what appeared to be some kind of line-dance with Wimpie. Wimpie had relinquished his trademark dungarees for the night in favour of stone-wash denim jeans, matching denim jacket and neon pencil tie.

A match made in eighties heaven, thought MK.

Mick was at a high table on the other side of the room, talking animatedly to another guy, who looked far too well-dressed to be heterosexual. MK gazed idly from him back to Wimpie and ruminated on the apparent demise of decent, immaculately turned-out straight men – if they had ever existed.

'Ma'am,' said a voice behind her. She turned to see that the bartender had placed a fresh drink in front of her.

'I didn't order this,' she said.

'From the gentleman at the end of the bar, ma'am.'

Keen to remain cool, MK took a moment to adjust her earring, allowing her hand to trail down her neck.

Superstardom Lesson No. 87: Never miss an opportunity to draw attention to your neck. Men love it. You are the impala; he is the lion. If he feels like the hunter, he'll be so much easier to manipulate.

Having delayed turning her head long enough to retain her edge, MK glanced casually in the direction the barman had gestured towards, to get a look at her new Prince Charming...

Hmm. Okay. Not Prince Charming exactly, but maybe his stable hand. The man was in his forties, with dark hair that was just beginning to recede. Tall, with a big build. Very serious looking. MK raised the glass in thanks and took a sip. He didn't smile; only nodded. He certainly had the brooding thing going for him. MK smiled – slightly – and then turned away. He'd have to work a bit harder than that. Prince Brooding took the cue and made his way over. MK raised her glass once again and waited for him to lift his. They clinked glasses and she let slip a low laugh that chimed with sweet, dark promise.

'Hi,' he said, holding out a large hand. 'I'm David.'

'Hello, David,' she said, dropping her rural accent in favour of a more cosmopolitan one. He sounded American. *Excellent.* Instead of shaking his hand, she placed hers in the air, palm down. David again took the cue and kissed it. 'I'm the girl you've been waiting to meet your whole life.'

'Well,' he said, breaking into a grin. 'Lucky me. You gotta name?' MK gave him a coy smile, buying herself a moment to consider this. 'MK' didn't work, and 'Palesa' was not very American. It struck MK that it was high time she came up with a Hollywood name.

'Lisa,' she answered. Close enough.

'So, Lisa,' he said, 'are you staying here at the hotel?'

'Maybe,' she replied. 'You're a long way from home. The States?'

'One of them, yeah,' he grinned.

'One is enough,' she joked, matching his grin with her own.

He glanced around at the people on the dance floor. MK studied his face and decided that he would do very nicely. A real man's man, and, like any American, slightly larger than life. Looked like she wouldn't need to venture into the hotel after all. Unless it was with him, naturally. But she resolved then and there to take it slow. She didn't want to be some local-flavour one-night thing, a notch on a world-travelled bedpost. She needed more. And this guy looked like the ticket. The ticket to America. It wouldn't be all work, of course. He had a rugged kind of appeal that was growing on her by the second. He was pretty delicious, actually.

She could even overlook the garish shirt he was wearing under his jacket. One of those brightly patterned island-style things.

Jackie watched the cast and crew of whatever-the-flippin-show-was-called flailing around the dance floor like a bunch of lunatics during Smarties Hour at the asylum. She recognised the middle-aged coloured lady from TV, and noticed with distaste that she was dancing with a white man. The cheek! And clearly she'd been drinking a lot. *Like they all do*, thought Jackie bitterly. Jackie de la Rey had almost as much contempt for coloured people as she had for blacks. To her mind, their only redeeming quality was whatever white blood they had in them. Their mixed race had several downsides, however: firstly, their black blood (which made them cursed) and their Bushman blood (which meant that they were as primitive as cavemen); and secondly, everybody knew that they were all drug addicts or criminals – or both.

But recently she had begun to hate coloured people more than usual. Ever since that cheeky kitchen boy had told her he loved her. The audacity. It was madness. What had he hoped to achieve, saying something like that? It made her uneasy. It made her angry. Whenever Jackie was caught off-guard, or confronted by something foreign and unknown, she got angry. Anger was pretty much her stock response to life. In this case, however, the anger was shadowed by shame. Since the first day that Jackie had taken Fahiem into the supply closet, the shame that had followed her around since her childhood days of fire-and-brimstone church had intensified manifold. But *love*? Never.

She hated him. She hated him even more since the day he'd made his confession. She hated the fact that she had ever crossed the line with him. She hated the fact that her job was now potentially in jeopardy. She hated the fact that he had said what he said to her. But most of all, she hated the fact that she was no longer seeing him. And, for all of that, she now placed coloured people at the top of her hate-list. She watched the coloured woman howling with mirth as she dragged the white guy around the floor, and felt overcome by a desperate need to take action.

This feeling had been growing for years, like a slow tumour, but in the last few weeks had accelerated exponentially. It seemed harder and harder to maintain the facade of cheery sanity that life – and her job, in particular – demanded of her. Jackie frequently felt fury well up inside her, so potent and explosive it seemed about to erupt at any moment... possibly *this* moment, she thought to herself, watching the self-important TV morons in disgust.

She decided she needed another cigarette. Her smoking had also increased of late. With a strained smile, she exited the bar area and headed for her office and the soothing nicotine that lay within.

Mere moments later, Krissie Blaine and her new beau entered the bar. Fahiem stayed a few steps behind Krissie, partly because he wanted to be inconspicuous, but mainly because when Krissie Blaine entered a room, it was all about her.

Krissie burst into the bar area, whooping. She was dressed in gun-metal grey stilettos and an itty-bitty silver slip, a diamond tiara perched atop her white-blonde mane. The whitish glare of her attire was offset gorgeously by a carefully nurtured tan. Every head in the place turned as one. Krissie grinned at them.

'Hey, guys,' she hollered. 'Let's party!' Grabbing Frank by the hand, Krissie took to the dance floor, whereupon she threw off her heels and began dancing barefoot.

MK forced her face to remain indifferent, although her stomach had apparently been invaded by dozens of elves doing an especially violent Lord-of-the-Dance-type routine. She watched transfixed as Krissie Blaine flung herself around the floor. Clearly she had absolutely no sense of rhythm – not that it seemed to detract from her enjoyment in the slightest. Beside her hovered a young coloured guy who looked mighty uncomfortable. He was quite cute, MK noted. It seemed the celebutante had plucked herself an exotic local fruit to sate her appetite during her stay. He smiled whenever Krissie flopped in his direction, and danced a few tentative steps at her instruction. It pleased MK to note that Krissie was also wearing a tiara – it proved she was on the right track, at least as far as headwear was concerned. As she watched, MK recognised the hyperactive elves in her stomach as nerves. Being in the same room as someone *so* famous had her shaken up, even though she wasn't an avid fan of this particular celebrity. She stared, trying to talk herself back to calm. She had to remain cool at all costs.

Superstardom Lesson No. 28: When meeting another famous person, remain cool – nobody likes a drooler. Remember, if you lose your cool, you risk sweating (see Superstardom Lesson No. 41).

'Excuse me, ma'am,' said the bartender behind her. MK wrenched her gaze away from Krissie and turned towards him. He held out a business card. 'The gentleman left this for you.'

MK suddenly noticed that her new gentleman friend was gone. He'd vanished without saying a word! At least he'd left his card; that was something. She took the card and read it:

David Jones
PRODUCER

Below the words he had written a local cellphone number. The handwriting was small and incredibly neat, so much so that at first MK had thought it was printed on the card. Her sharp mind was quick to wonder why he carried business cards with no contact details printed on them, but as bright as MK was, she was only human, after all. She filled in the kind of answers she *hoped* were true...

He's obviously too important to risk just anyone getting hold of his contact details – so he fills in one card at a time. And he probably travels a lot, so he just puts down the local number he is using at the time.

As gingerly as if she were handling a glass grenade, she placed the card in her clutch, making a mental note to call him the next day (in the afternoon at the earliest). MK turned her full attention back to Krissie. She was shorter in real life than she appeared onscreen, MK noticed smugly. Also, she had somewhat knobbly knees that looked like they'd had one too many stressful encounters with the ground.

MK watched as Wimpie abandoned Saartjie and headed for Krissie with eyes as wide as the flashbulbs of yore and his tongue leaving a wet trail on the floor behind him. Saartjie looked most put out, and thanks to an excess of dry white, didn't bother to hide it.

That's the real Saartjie, thought MK.

Wimpie had obviously asked for Krissie's autograph. She bounded over to the bar counter beside MK, trailed by the awkward Fahiem and a grinning Wimpie. MK realised that this was the first time she'd ever seen Wimpie smile. It was unsettling. Krissie got a pen from the bartender.

'Thanks, gorgeous,' she said, gifting him with an impish smile. Then she turned back to Wimpie. 'Where do you want it?'

'Oh, uh,' he muttered, digging in his pockets for a scrap of paper.

'I have a better idea,' she purred. 'Lift your shirt.'

Wimpie obliged willingly, revealing to those around him the unsightly topography of his chest. Krissie flinched. She placed one hand on his shoulder for support, then with the pen hand began to write. But no ink came out. She stopped and shook the pen before trying again. Still nothing. Wimpie stared into her eyes. Desperately, Krissie began scribbling in an attempt to get the ink flowing. Wimpie yelped in pain, but still the pen did not deliver.

'How 'bout a kiss on the cheek?' she offered.

'Fine!' he sang, temporarily forgetting the reddening welts on his skin. Krissie leaned in slowly. Wimpie's eyes widened in delight. With the speed and agility of a woodpecker, Krissie kissed his cheek. 'Can I buy you a drink?' he asked breathlessly. 'I work in television,' he added.

'Yeah, right,' said Krissie, laughing as though he'd made a joke.

'I do,' he insisted.

'No, thanks,' said Krissie.

'Excuse me, Miss Blaine,' said MK, coming to the rescue, 'I need some advice. Maybe you can help me. Girl talk,' she finished with a subtle wink.

'Great,' said Krissie, catching on. She turned to Wimpie. 'Girl talk.' She put her arm through MK's and turned away from him. Deflated, Wimpie realised his moment had passed and wandered off. 'Is he gone?' whispered Krissie.

'Yes,' replied MK happily.

'Thank you so much, darlin',' gushed Krissie.

'I know how it is, sweetie,' said MK. 'Fans can be a bit much sometimes.'

'No kidding.' Krissie took a moment to study her saviour. 'Hey, you're dressed all in gold, and I'm all in silver. We, like, totally match.'

'Tiara twins,' chirped MK with a grin.

'La-la-love it!' exclaimed Krissie.

MK reflected on how much louder and more marked an American accent seemed in person than it did onscreen. It was remarkable what they did to consonants – the L so heavy and round that one would think they were speaking through a mouthful of slush. Speaking of accents, Krissie had picked up on the change in MK's.

'Hey,' she said to MK, her brow crinkling, 'where are you from? When you were talking to that weirdo, you sounded different. More... African.'

'Oh, sweetie,' said MK, a glint in her amber eyes, 'I have many secrets.' Krissie stared at her with a mixture of confusion and wonder. 'I know,' continued MK, 'that probably sounds strange to someone like you.'

'Well,' muttered Krissie, thinking about her hitherto secret affair with one of Hollywood's biggest stars, 'believe it or not, I have a few of my own.'

'Secrets are a girl's best friend,' said MK.

'I thought that was diamonds.'

'Superstardom Lesson No. 56: Secrets are like diamonds – lovely to have, but if someone else gets their hands on them, it'll cost you.' Krissie laughed heartily at this.

'Superstardom Lesson?' she asked.

'I have a whole bunch,' said MK.

'Tell me some more,' asked Krissie.

'All in good time. I'm Lisa,' said MK.

They clicked like a Louis Vuitton purse.

Fahiem loitered behind the NBFs, feeling distinctly uncomfortable. For one thing, Krissie seemed totally absorbed in lively chat with the young black woman who had just saved her from the drunk guy. Fahiem felt like an outsider. This was mostly due to the fact that he was fraternising at his workplace. The bartender had already recognised Fahiem and given him a sly wink. Fahiem wondered if the night manager would give him grief for being here – or, more importantly, getting involved with a guest. He had a feeling the term 'customer service' had limits.

'Hey!' whispered a voice harshly in his ear. Booze on the breath.

Fahiem spun around, startled, and was relieved to note that it was just another of the partygoers. An older, coloured lady that he recognised from television. Saartjie Someone. She had appeared in several shows that his family had loved over the years. And now here she was, looking far from sober.

'What's a nice boy like you doing with a hussy like that?' she asked him in slurred Afrikaans. Her eyes appeared to be looking in slightly different directions. She leaned on him with her substantial ballast.

'Ag,' he said, taken aback, 'she just needs some help. Getting around.'

'She looks like the type that gets around plenty,' muttered Saartjie bleakly. 'How 'bout you help me?'

'Sure,' said Fahiem uncertainly.

'Dance with me,' she said. Before Fahiem could offer a word of resistance, Saartjie had grabbed him by the wrist with arresting strength and dragged him onto the dance floor. Suddenly she was leading them in a whirling, unsteady boogie. Fahiem smiled helplessly, shooting a brief glance at Krissie – but she was doing shots with her new friend and hadn't even noticed he was gone. Fahiem was forced to abandon his stiff reticence when Saartjie began spinning around with the speed and violence of an unhinged fairground ride. He clung to her for dear life.

Saartjie obviously misread this because she clutched her hefty arms around him in a feverish embrace and began slow-dancing. The frightened Fahiem moaned. Just what he needed: this experience in slow motion. Saartjie interpreted this as a sign of encouragement and squeezed him tighter. She moaned in his ear.

'You're *lovely*,' she moaned.

'Thank you, ma'am,' he replied, maintaining his politeness in the face of this nightmarish turn of events.

A moment later her hands were on his backside, squeezing with such awful intensity he gasped. Once again, she misread his distress for desire, and chuckled. She writhed against him passionately. Fahiem writhed against her, desperately trying to escape. The more he struggled, the tighter she held on. Fahiem just couldn't imagine how this could possibly get any worse.

Until he saw Jackie de la Rey at the entrance, shooting him a look of such malevolent fury that he was almost tempted to jump up into Saartjie's arms and ask her to take him home. He closed his eyes for a second, hoping the awful mirage of his ex-girlfriend/current boss would be gone when he reopened them. It wasn't. When he looked again, Jackie was even closer, making her way over to them. He fought to free himself from Saartjie's grip but to no avail. Saartjie spun around, offering Fahiem a glimpse of the oblivious Krissie, laughing and talking to the other woman at the bar. Another forceful spin brought Jackie back into view; she was standing right before them wearing her widest, most professional grin. Fahiem was terrified.

'Excuse me, ma'am,' she said brightly to Saartjie. 'I need a word with my employee, please.'

'Huh?' said Saartjie. Jackie pointed at Fahiem. 'He's busy,' snorted Saartjie rudely. For the first time since he had met her, Fahiem was beginning to like Saartjie. Jackie's deadly smile didn't falter for a second.

'It'll just be for a moment, ma'am,' she said sweetly. 'Perhaps in the meantime I could organise you a complimentary drink.'

'No,' said Saartjie flatly. 'But I could murder some food. Our snacks are already finished. Five-star *se gat.*'

Jackie called Saartjie all manner of unpleasant names in her mind, but her face registered only the warm, accommodating manner that her job demanded. She could not believe the cheek of this woman.

'Fine,' said Jackie amiably. 'Why don't you take a seat at one of the tables, and I'll have the chef send you something special?' She continued smiling as Saartjie released Fahiem and stumbled off towards a table at the edge of the room. Jackie decided she would be sending the cow a big, fat helping of nothing. The moment she was out of earshot, Jackie took Fahiem's arm and walked him into a corner. 'What the hell are you doing? You are not allowed to fraternise with the guests! But at least you're sticking to your own kind,' she added cattily. 'In fact, she isn't even a guest!'

'Uh,' muttered Fahiem, wondering what her response would be when she discovered that he *was* fraternising with one of the guests – who was nothing like 'his kind' – and in the most intimate manner. 'Sorry, Jackie,' was all he could manage.

'If you're doing it to piss me off,' she growled, 'it's bloody working.'

'I didn't even know you were gonna be here,' he said truthfully.

'Consider this your first warning,' she growled.

Fahiem gulped.

'You little shit,' she spat through teeth clenched so tight he half expected them to crack and crumble into pieces that would bounce down her blouse. 'You little piece of stinking shit. How could you do this to me?' Her words hit him like rapid artillery fire as she advanced menacingly. Fahiem recoiled until he felt the wall behind him.

'I couldn't ignore a guest's request,' he said weakly. 'And do what to you?'

'She's not a guest – she's here for this stupid function,' replied Jackie, deciding to ignore his last question.

'What do you care?' he asked.

Before she could restrain herself, Jackie shoved him roughly.

'Hey!' yelled a voice behind Jackie. 'What the hell are you doing?' Jackie turned to see that the old coloured bag had returned, and had her bleary, cross-eyed gaze fixed in Jackie's general direction.

'It's fine,' said Fahiem hurriedly.

'It's not,' boomed Saartjie. 'I would like to speak to your boss, young lady!'

'No, no,' said Fahiem.

'Ma'am,' said Jackie, struggling for the first time in her life to maintain a businesslike demeanour, 'this does not involve you. Why don't you go back to your party? Fahiem, come to my office.' Jackie grabbed Fahiem's arm and started walking. Saartjie grabbed Jackie's arm and yanked her away from him.

'I said I want to speak to your boss,' warned Saartjie.

'I am the boss,' said Jackie evenly, wrenching free her hand.

Fahiem noticed that Krissie and her friend were approaching, as were several others in the group. This was rapidly turning into a Scene.

'Please ma'am,' he rambled at Saartjie, 'it'sfinereally – I'llcome backjustnowandwecandancesomemore –' A large hand muzzled him into silence – Saartjie's. He saw that she had a dark scowl fixed on Jackie.

'Listen, my girl,' said Jackie in the tones employed by miffed schoolteachers/parents/racists, 'you've obviously had too much to drink. Now calm down and go away or I'll call security, okay?'

'What's going on here?' asked Mick, who had just arrived on the Scene, along with several colleagues, including MK, and Krissie Blaine.

Fahiem was horrified to observe Saartjie's eyes regain sharp focus.

'Ha,' she laughed dangerously. 'Did you just call me "my girl"?'

'Frank?' asked Krissie worriedly. Jackie frowned.

'Send your boss in here *now*,' demanded Saartjie imperiously.

'Ag, shut up, man,' murmured Jackie, her attention now firmly set on the fact that Krissie Blaine was putting her arms around Fahiem in a way that was entirely too familiar. That was the last clear thing Jackie saw before Saartjie Williams slapped her hard across the face. A loud clap rang out. Jackie stumbled backwards.

There was a moment of silence, full of slack jaws and wide eyes. Then two security guards descended, as if from nowhere, and bookended Saartjie between them. She wriggled against them fiercely, shouting.

'She started it! She was pushing him around!' MK couldn't help but smile at the sight of her rival, the Grande Dame of the South African screen, losing face in such grand fashion. 'Let me go!'

'Get her out of here,' barked Jackie.

The guards dragged Saartjie off kicking and screaming. Mick hurried after them, upset by this terrible development with one of his leading ladies.

'My office,' snapped Jackie at Fahiem. 'Now!'

'He's with me,' said Krissie.

Jackie stared, unable to conceal her shock. So *that* was what was going on here. He was with *her*. He was *with* her. *He* was with *her*. She floundered, powerless to surface in the flood of information engulfing her. Suddenly there were fingers snapping in front of her face. A black girl in a gold dress.

'Excuse me, sweetie,' she was saying in a blaccent. 'Jackie,' said the black girl, reading her name badge, 'what exactly is going on here?'

'Who are you?' asked Jackie, staring numbly at the tiara on the black girl's head. It was made of wire and beads, like the lizards and stuff that black guys were always selling on the side of the road, except the beads were gold and looked quite expensive. It matched a very expensive-looking gold dress. Jackie decided she must be from Johannesburg – they were the only blacks that could afford such things. Also, Cape Town blacks still had a little more respect for whites than this one was demonstrating right now.

'You might know me as Miss Kwa Kwa,' said the girl with a radiant beam. Jackie shook her head. 'Anyway, I was asking you what's going on here?'

'Why were you pushing Frank?' asked the American tramp. Jackie blinked, unsure of what to say. '*Frank?*' It dawned on her that there were quite a few people watching, and that she had better make this situation right or put her job in serious jeopardy.

'I...' she struggled, 'I thought he was bothering the other lady.'

'That's no excuse to lose your temper,' said the black girl. 'You are dealing with very important people here.'

'Excuse me,' said Jackie, regaining some of her composure, 'but who did you say you were?'

'All you need to know is that I am a VIP,' answered the cheeky girl. She must've spotted the doubt on Jackie's face, because she elaborated: 'I am an actress and TV personality, and beyond that, I am in the country's top inner circle of celebrities and politicians.' MK had twice in her life been to Studio 94, the now-defunct secret club where there had indeed been many important politicos. The fact that she had not actually met any of them hardly seemed relevant at this point. This was mostly for Krissie Blaine's benefit anyway. MK noticed with joy that Krissie was looking mildly impressed.

'Ag,' said Fahiem softly, 'it was just a silly misunderstanding.'

'It's just that we don't allow staff to harass the guests,' said Jackie with forced gentility. 'I'm sure you understand, Miss Blaine.'

'Well,' said Krissie haughtily, 'Frank is *my* guest. He's here because I asked him to be. Get it?

'I see,' said Jackie, stomach aflame. 'Fine.'

'I think,' said MK, 'that you owe Frank an apology. And Miss Blaine.'

HIS NAME IS NOT FRANK FOR FUCK'S SAKE! screamed Jackie in her mind.

'Yeah,' said the American slut, 'I agree.'

Jackie forced a demure smile, even as her insides burned like the hottest fires in the deepest corners of the pits of hell.

'It's fine,' said Fahiem.

'No,' said Krissie.

'We're waiting,' sang MK to the hotel woman.

'I apologise,' mumbled Jackie dully. 'Truly.'

'What are you prepared to do to make it up to us?' asked MK. She saw something in this woman's eyes she didn't like. MK could think of nothing worse than having to spend one's working life serving other people. She could even sympathise with such a one eventually cracking under the pressure of constantly having to be delightful. But there was something else in this one's eyes. If there was one thing MK was expert at, it was reading people, and she sensed that this one definitely had deep waters. Deeper and darker than most around her would probably ever realise.

'What would you like?' asked Jackie, forcing herself to keep her eyes on the black girl and away from Krissie's hands, which seemed intent on rubbing the shirt right off Fahiem's back.

'I feel like prawns,' said Krissie. 'Ooh, and burgers. You might as well get some pizzas too. And milkshakes.'

Not a vegetable in sight, thought Jackie. *Except you.* She nodded attentively as the American doll rattled off her order.

'Are you sure you'll remember all this, sweetie?' asked the black princess. 'Maybe you should write it down.'

'You can send it up to my suite,' said Krissie. 'We'll go up there. Are you coming, Lisa?' she asked MK. 'We'll have a pyjama party!' Then, turning back to Jackie: 'And some pyjamas for my new friend here.'

MK basked in the glow of true-global-massive celebrity favour. It mattered little that Krissie Blaine would not have been her first choice – or her fiftieth. All that mattered was that in this precious momentous Moment, she was being blessed by the gods of Stardom. She had just been invited *up* – in more ways than one. While she understood that cementing this new friendship (and exploiting it for all it was worth) would not be easy, she had a foot in the door. It was glorious. She could feel the envy radiating from her sitcom cast mates, as well as their silent, desperate pleas to be invited along, and decided it would probably be politic to do so. Her naked ambition wanted to ignore them and keep this moment all for herself, but her mind advised against it. These Hollywood girls were notoriously fickle and capable of swapping NBFs as frequently as their diminutive designer dogs. It would be unwise to throw away the sitcom. For now. And if she were the one who had gotten them into a shindig in Krissie Blaine's hotel room, she'd have them in her pockets. Her power struggle with Saartjie Williams on the set would be settled once and for all... *Superstardom Lesson No. 44: Be kind. It's good to have a bunch of people around who owe you favours.*

'Can these three come with?' asked MK casually. 'Just for a drink.' The group of devotees surrounding MK perked up hopefully, their expressions screaming, Pick me! Pick me! Beside them, Wimpie bobbed his head emphatically.

'Sure,' said Krissie, unfazed. 'As long as they don't steal my stuff. If they want a souvenir, I'll sign a napkin or something. And not the weird one,' she added, pointing at Wimpie. Wimpie hung his head miserably and wandered off.

MK smiled at her trio of actor colleagues magnanimously. They jumped up and down like puppies before biscuits. Before steak. Fillet Mignon. MK gave them a nod and a wink, a subtle reminder that they were forever indebted to her. Krissie took hold of Fahiem's face, and – after a pointed stare at Jackie – stuck her tongue down his throat. MK noticed Jackie flush with colour.

'Later,' said Krissie to Jackie as she passed, leading Fahiem by the hand. The chosen three followed after them deliriously. MK lingered and spoke to Jackie in a low voice.

'Careful. You look like the kind of girl who could get in a lot of trouble.' Jackie stared at her in disbelief. Just then Mick rejoined them, out of breath.

'Saartjie's okay,' he groaned. 'I put her in a taxi.'

'Good,' replied MK.

'I'm so sorry about that,' he gushed to Jackie. 'She had a bit too much to drink. I'm so sorry.'

'No problem, sir,' said Jackie. 'Excuse me.' She walked off.

'I have to go, Mick,' said MK. 'Party in Krissie's room. Wanna come?'

'No,' he said. 'I should get back to...' He gestured vaguely in the direction of the man he'd spent most of the evening talking to. He was still sitting at their table, apparently waiting for Mick.

'Oh,' said MK devilishly. 'Is Mickey going to get lucky?'

'MK,' he said earnestly, taking her arm. 'Promise me something.'

'You know how I feel about promises.'

'Promise me,' he said insistently, 'that before you run off to Hollywood, you'll at least finish the sitcom first. I'll be screwed if you don't.'

'Well,' she said, casting her gaze at his companion, 'you may be getting screwed before then anyway.'

'MK –' he said worriedly.

'Don't worry,' she said as she walked off after her NBF, 'you'll have another heart attack if you're not careful. Besides, I signed a contract, remember?' She waved one last time before disappearing from sight. Mick worried. As if something as trivial as a contract would ever restrict MK from doing just as she damn well pleased. He decided that there was nothing that could be done about it now. Let Monday bring whatever it would. It was Friday night, and Mick Emmott decided that he would focus – as his good-but-sometimes-exasperating friend MK constantly urged him to do – on getting a social life. With that, he marched back to his table.

From the darkest corner of the room, a man watched the end of the Scene thoughtfully. As it happened, he was the same man that had bought MK a drink and left her a card inscribed with the name 'David Jones'. He was the man in the island shirt. The same man who had tortured and 'reprogrammed' Lincoln Thomas. The same man who was keeping surveillance over Krissie Blaine, believing her to be part of a massive terrorist conspiracy aimed at deadening American – and by extension, western – minds. The man who now – thanks to a tiny device he had planted on one of Blaine's heels while everyone was distracted by the fracas – could hear what was going on in her room. MK, or as he knew her, 'Lisa', thought he had left some time ago, but the man in the island shirt was masterful at becoming invisible.

The African beauty he had met was not part of his investigation. He had slipped into the bar under the guise of belonging to the television party show happening there. It was merely an in. Meeting Lisa had been a pleasant distraction while he marked some time. She was breathtaking. As a native of the US of A, he had seen his fair share of skinny girls (in the ever-present media) and horribly obese ones (in daily life). But Lisa was neither of these: she was not skinny; indeed, she was voluptuous –in all the right places. Her skin was the colour of chocolate milk and looked too soft to be believed. Her eyes were the gorgeous hue of coffee, just the strength he liked it, too. And she was smart. He knew this from the look in her eyes. (Like MK, the man had developed a keen sense for reading people, although even he was powerless to fully appreciate the extent of MK's superior mind.)

I'm the girl you've been waiting to meet your whole life.

He shuddered just thinking about it. How soft her skin had been when he had kissed her hand...

It unnerved him.

The man in the island shirt had been in love only twice in his life, and both incidences had been of the unrequited sort. Dolly Parton had been the first. He had loved her from the first moment his folks had played a record of hers, when he was just five years old. Initially it had been about the music. Dolly always sounded like she was havin' such a good ol' time, and he was a man (kid) who liked havin' fun. Later, it was her face and... other generous endowments. To the young ███████, Dolly had epitomised what it was to be American: she had started out dirt-poor, worked hard and made a success of herself, and was wholesome and polite and blonde. And dang, she knew how to raise the roof with her foot-stompin' tunes. Throughout his youth, and right up to his early adulthood – including the first few years of his service – he had ached with love for Dolly. He had even (secretly) hoped that his work would one day bring him into contact with her, should she ever require protection, for example. Like that Whitney Houston movie, except maybe called something like *The Dollyguard*.

Alas, he had never had the pleasure of meeting her Dollyship, and after some years in his chosen line of work, had fallen for a new target. So to speak. The First Lady. Like millions of other Americans, he had spotted her on television. His love had grown slowly over time, and it was not until he had gotten the coveted job of providing security for the President's family that it had really blossomed. Agents were forbidden from making conversation with their wards, of course, so day after day he would stare at his prize from behind his sunglasses, dreaming of the moment she would summon him into a White House bedroom and let him – among other things – run his fingers through her perm.

The other guys would joke about how unattractive she was, but he did not agree. She was a little overweight, granted, but the man appreciated this far more than the drug-addled coat racks that the media fixated on. Also, the First Lady was classy. She wore only Nude Beige lipstick (a smidgeon), never wore skirts above the knee, and never used bad language. Most importantly, she and the man shared the same favourite song – 'The Star-Spangled Banner'. He had come to care for her deeply and felt very protective of her. Which was why things had turned out the way they had...

Fifty thousand Americans had witnessed the man tackle the First Lady. And millions more had seen it on live television. In the media frenzy that had ensued, it hadn't seemed to matter at all that he'd been trying to save her life. The event had been a massive concert staged in honour of the troops serving their country in Iraq. The man had already been on high alert since learning of it – he was convinced that terrorists would seize the opportunity to do some damage. During the fireworks show that had taken place at the start of the festivities, the man had grown agitated, and increasingly worried about his secret love, Mrs President. When one especially loud firecracker had boomed overhead, the man hadn't thought – he'd simply reacted, diving on top of the First Lady, and taking her to the ground. In the tumble, her modest skirt had been yanked high enough to eliminate any trace of modesty. In a devastating twist of fate, the First Lady had that morning decided to wear a pair of underwear her husband had recently given her as a joke. Over the crotch area was the Presidential Seal. And across the expansive section that covered her posterior were the words: FIRST LADYBOY. In case anyone had missed it live, there'd been countless reproductions in the press. Even when the President had issued a 'request' for the media to stop showing the image (with subtly threatening overtones), the internet had continued to spread the visuals around the US, and around the world.

The damage had already been done, however, with headlines like 'OH, BOY! HAVE WE SEEN TOO MUCH OF THE FIRST LADY?' in the more reputable press, and 'STAR-SPANGLED TRANNIE?' in the tabloids. Much was made of the disturbing moniker on the over-exposed underwear: what exactly did 'Ladyboy' mean? Surely, not what it sounded like? As it happened, 'Ladyboy' was simply an affectionate nickname President Chris T. Tain had come up with for his wife years ago when she had gotten a disastrous short haircut. Regrettably it had stuck and now the whole world was drawing bizarre conclusions.

The President's advisors (having already proven a significant lack of skill in this field) had instructed him to tell the press it had been a 'wardrobe malfunction' and was actually supposed to have read: FIRST LADYTOY. Needless to say, this had unleashed a whole new wave of parody. Either the president was a pervert or a dimwit – he just couldn't win.

Somebody had to pay. The man in the island shirt had been singled out. Not only had he tackled and humiliated the First Lady but, to make matters worse, he had hesitated after exposing her. In the epileptic flashing of camera bulbs it had taken him a moment to get his bearings and realise what was now on show. He had then proceeded to try to fix things – by grabbing and yanking at the First Skirt as its owner lay screaming. Then he had pulled out his weapon to locate the terrorists. Thousands of people in the crowd had begun to scream. Just then, three other agents had pounced, disarmed him and taken him into custody. His seniors at the agency had been most unforgiving. Aside from all the transgressions mentioned before, it was pointed out that he had not leapt to rescue the *President* when he'd suspected danger. This was the nail in his coffin. His superiors had been wary of him for some time now anyway – they found him to be altogether too quiet, obsessively neat and frankly more than a little creepy. He carried a picture of Dolly Parton in his wallet. He never slept.

Thus he had been relieved of his duties, and further listed as someone to keep an eye on. In their opinion he was the type who might one day pick up a rifle, find the nearest rooftop and play a little game of shoot-the-civilian.

This heartbreaking turn of events proved too much for the man. All of the neurosis and paranoia he had for years been keeping barely contained and channelled into his life's work now broke loose. His obsession became manifest. He vowed to continue his work, alone. He had been trained well enough to do so. He just had to keep one step ahead of his ex-bosses.

When he intercepted the intel that a dangerous person had been planted in South Africa by Muslim terrorists, he hopped on a plane and said goodbye to his fatherland, the land of the free and the home of the brave, and headed for the tip of Africa to fight for freedom. He discovered a land also free, but ostensibly braver than he had expected. Despite the unimaginable crime levels, people carried on – happily. He came from a place both wealthy and peaceful, yet gripped by fear. He found this nonchalance in the face of death intriguing, but wrote it off to third-world ignorance.

When Krissie Blaine arrived in a veil of secrecy, his theory was affirmed. She was an agent of terror, a threat to the free world, and he was going to be the one to expose her. But not yet. First he would uncover the whole network, from the top down. And when he bust it open, he would return home a hero.

It bothered him that his new interest, the darkly gorgeous Lisa, had gone off with the Blaine girl. He hoped she would not be sucked into anything untoward. Still, it could prove useful, having an insider on his side. The Blaine girl was darn good at her act, but it had to be an act. Nobody could be that stupid. No, clearly she was an excellent actress, one who had chosen to use her talents in pursuit of Terror rather than an Oscar. (In the man's mind, the Oscars were, of course, also linked with terrorist plots, but that was another story.)

She was fraternising with a Muslim youth – that was undoubtedly significant. In fact, his first major breakthrough. Soon he would need to have a talk with the kid. In his special way. The way that made folks very talkative.

Violent thought also raced through Jackie de la Rey's mind as she sat in her office, nursing her tender cheek and bleeding knuckles. The cheek was thanks to Saartjie Williams; the fist was Jackie's own doing. The second she had made it to the privacy of this little haven, she had punched the wall with such ferocity that she'd scraped off some skin and possibly done some internal damage. She cleaned up her hand and dressed it, but felt no pain. She felt only rage.

Tonight was one for the record books. Not only had she had to endure a snotty American bimbo (something she was fairly accustomed to), but she'd then been slapped by a drunk coloured and humiliated by a darkie princess who obviously thought she was something special. That had hurt the most.

The way she had lorded it over her like that. Boasting about the fact that she knew celebrities and politicians! Big deal – they were probably all as black as her. Jackie was an ancestor of De la Rey, one of the greatest, most visionary politicians who had ever lived. He had fought the British when they'd flippin' owned the world, and if he were alive today, he would fight its current owners if they got in the way of his people. Well, he was dead. But his dream lived on in people like Jackie. She could see the future and it was bright. And white.

It took her ages to calm down. She had to fight with everything she had against the urge to go home, fetch her gun and do some serious damage. She forced herself to focus on her larger objectives. They could not be ruined by a thoughtless, reckless act of violence.

The face of Miss Kaka – or whatever she had called herself – burned in the front of her mind. People like her were the problem. Her and her VIP flippin' friends. As the minutes wore on, these thoughts began to crystallise into an idea. A plan. A sword of terrible power, tempered in the flames of her fury. The girl had said she was in with all the top players... That could be useful. Jackie could certainly use that. For information. Perhaps even as a weapon. Images of sending the hapless Miss Whatever into a meeting of the top political figures in the country, loaded from head to toe in high-grade explosives, danced in Jackie's mind like fireflies.

All her years of intense but aimless hatred and anger seemed to culminate in this moment. Jackie saw an opportunity to take action. At last she had some kind of plan. The specific game plan could be refined later, but its kick-off was obvious...

She would kidnap Miss Kaka. And make her the first prisoner in a war that was about to begin.

6

Weekend Viewing

SOME PEOPLE SPEND Saturday mornings sleeping in. Others get up and about early, keen to maximise their break from the bleak streak of the working week. Some catch up on their hobbies – gardening, scrap-booking, internet porn. Swimming pools, movie theatres and malls fill up, as do beaches and tourist attractions.

Krissie Blaine was of the sleep-the-day-away variety. Unlike most people, she did not have a week of hard work to recover from, although in her mind, life was not easy. Constantly being seen at the right parties, premieres et al, and always in the right clothes, was very draining.

This particular Saturday morning proved an exception: Krissie actually managed to rise before noon, and, bored without Frank (who had returned to his day-job, deep in the pits of the scullery), called her NBF, Lisa.

MK was thrilled to get the call. When the party had moved to Krissie's room the previous night, Frank had crashed fairly soon, anxious about being downstairs on time for work. MK had worked her magic like never before: using all of her wiles, every ounce of charm and her considerable smarts, she'd sung a song so melodious and catchy that Krissie was now a fan for life. Today Krissie wanted to hear some more.

MK arrived at her suite promptly. After much girl talk and general bonhomie, they played dress-up (taking about two hours to settle on just the right outfits) and finally left the hotel in search of adventure.

MK was as much of a tourist in Cape Town as Krissie, and the two delighted in sightseeing, posing for countless pictures together and generally being the loudest people wherever they went. MK enjoyed the fact that she would soon be appearing in all the local papers and magazines – and would probably also be fielding interviews about being a superstar's NBF – but this did not satisfy her as much as she expected. The fact of the matter was that her nuclear mind was already ticking over, trying to find ways to spin the hype into a successful and sustainable career overseas.

Superstardom Lesson No. 26: Contrary to popular belief, fame and fortune is hard work. You are working every second of the day. If you can't handle that, perhaps you should aim a little lower: like continuity presenter.

To her surprise, MK found that she actually quite liked Krissie. Behind her sex goddess exterior there was actually a warm young girl who wasn't as stupid as she looked. Granted, she'd probably never be a crossword champion, but she wasn't stupid. In fact, at times, she seemed very typical of her age: slightly naïve and occasionally awkward. Almost endearing.

Krissie had enjoyed meeting the local people. Even the photographers – they were far more polite and respectful than the paparazzi back home. To her dismay, however, she had spotted one or two familiar faces – obviously some of the bigger publications from abroad had sent their people to shoot her. She resolved to adopt the approach she employed back home: pretend they weren't there and carry on with life. She found an ally in Lisa in this regard, who stepped in whenever someone got a little too pushy.

In-between the scenery, the cocktails and the endless posing for cameras – including cellphone cameras – Krissie wondered idly what had become of the British jerk who had tried to blackmail her.

The Brit in question was lost – and not in any metaphysical sense. He had no idea where he was or how he had gotten there. Lincoln Thomas came to under a piece of cardboard on the side of a quiet little street. The sun was nearly gone; the world around him was turning the darker shade of twilight. Further down the street he could see lights and hear people. He groaned as he sat up, still smarting in several places from his recent torture/training at the hands of the Yank.

After a moment spent piecing together the recent days in his mind, Link was overcome... but not by fear, or a desperate urge to run – to the nearest sane person, the nearest telephone or police station. No. He was overcome by a sense of *purpose*. Until this very moment, purpose was not something Link had ever concerned himself with. Never one to shine in any particular area, Link had lived a life most ordinary: born to decent but somewhat severe parents, Link had moved through the stages of his life as though on autopilot. After an unremarkable school career, the young Lincoln had embarked on the most prosaic of paths: get paid, get drunk and if you were lucky, get laid. Lincoln rarely got lucky, given his dependable tendency to disrobe when intoxicated. Over the years, he had done various jobs (mostly in construction, and, more colourfully, dressing up as a Viking for local tourist stops. Visitors found him suitably gruff and unsightly). Yes, purpose was merely something he occasionally heard mentioned on telly.

This had all changed, however. Lincoln Thomas was on a MISSION. Earlier in the week he had been cursing fate for putting him in the path of the savage American man in the fruity shirts – now he saw that it had indeed been fate, but the good kind. He saw that his whole non-life – the sad daily grind, his loser friends, being dumped by his loser friends, and his subsequent trip here alone – had led him to this point. All so that he might be chosen to help save the free world.

Link was now a believer in the Yank's theory. Well, not theory – fact. It made sense. Of course the terrorists were behind the tabloid obsession that currently had the first world in its grip. What other explanation could there be? During Link's 'training', the Yank had described their tactics as mass distraction, designed not only to keep minds away from more significant world events, but also to numb them. People just weren't aware of the dumbification (the Yank's word) sweeping over them. Link had not realised his own stupidity until he had been woken from it. But that was behind him now. He saw the truth and would do whatever he could to help others do the same. He was now an agent. Although Link was not sure exactly what organisation the Yank represented, he felt honoured to be its newest recruit.

Now if he only could figure out what his mission *was*. He had been dumped on the streets with nothing but the clothes on his back. Glancing down at said clothes, he realised that he was wearing a pair of beach shorts and a lively island shirt – obviously courtesy of his new partner. Link searched the pockets of the trousers and found a note. He unfolded it and found a photograph inside. It was the Muslim youth that Krissie Blaine had apparently shacked up with. The note read: FOLLOW HIM. It then listed directions to the Hotel Shmotel, with the staff entrance marked. Link slumped. How the hell would he get near the hotel in the first place? He decided that if he could just get close enough to see the staff entrance, he could follow the boy anywhere he went from there.

With a grunt of discomfort, Link got to his feet and dusted himself off. It felt good to be able to stretch his legs.

'Excuse me,' said a miffed voice from above. Link looked up to see that he was being watched by an old lady from the balcony of a flat. She looked like a sour old duck. 'What are you doing down there?'

'Just having a nap, luv,' he replied cheerily. 'Don't worry, I'm leaving now.' He gave her a wave and strolled off down the street, towards the busy main road below.

Twenty minutes later, as he was walking down the busy main road, a car slowed down and pulled up alongside him. Inside was a man Link didn't recognise. The man was in his fifties and looked furtive. He gestured for Link to approach. Link assumed that the man had to be one of their own – a colleague of the Yank's – with some important message. Nonchalantly, Link sauntered over to the car and got into the passenger seat.

'Evening,' said Link with a knowing smile. 'You got something for me?'

'I think so,' said the man, also smiling now.

'Right,' said Link, 'give it to me.'

'Not here,' said the man anxiously.

'All right.'

'You're a big boy,' said the strange man. 'I'll bet you're rough.'

'Well,' said Link reflectively, 'As rough as I need to be. To get the job done.'

'Good,' said the man excitedly. 'Are you active or passive?'

'Definitely active, mate,' said Link, keen to give his new employers the right impression. 'I'll do whatever it takes. You've got the right man.'

'How much?' asked the stranger excitedly.

'Hmm,' said Link. He hadn't even considered the question of payment; until now the thought of saving the free world had been reward enough. 'Dunno.'

'I see,' said the man, taken aback. 'What can I get for two

hundred?' There followed a long moment of silence during which Link slowly began to piece together the bigger picture. Latent instinct came to the fore, warning him there was something dodgy on the go. Then Link noticed the man's gaze settling with sweaty glee on Link's crotch.

'*BLOODYHELL!*' bellowed Link as he fled the vehicle and slammed the door. 'I'm no bender, you bloody fool!'

'That's not what it says on your forehead,' shrieked the man as he sped off, panicked. As the shocked Link watched the car race off, he realised that the word 'GAY' was obviously still tanned onto his forehead. Cursing, he continued his trek down the road. Thankfully, he was not propositioned again.

After what seemed a very long distance, Link approached a busy cluster of bars and restaurants alive with nightlife. Suddenly he was struck by a desperate desire for a beer. It had been some time since he'd had a beer. Too long. An almost inhumane period of time for someone so intimate with the beverage. Surely a ten-minute break from his mission wouldn't do any harm? Just long enough to wet his lips and refresh him for the journey and work ahead...

Link lumbered into the first bar he saw and, with the tunnel vision of the very thirsty, honed in on the bar counter. He ordered a beer from the muscled bartender (who must've removed his shirt because of the heat), and took a moment to revel in the joy of being in a pub. The moment his drink arrived, he took a long, greedy gulp.

'R10,' shouted the bartender over the thumping dance music.

'Oh,' said Link. He stuck his hands in his shorts pockets, desperately hoping that the Yank had left him with some dosh. Nothing. 'Er...' he sighed dejectedly.

'Here,' said a voice beside him, as the hand of the speaker placed a R10 note before the bartender. Link turned to thank his benefactor. With dismay, Link observed that his Good Samaritan was plainly a case of mutton dressed as ram. Although middle-aged and balding, the bloke had styled what remained of his hair into a spiky quiff that Link presumed was meant to be trendy. Also, he was wearing a sleeveless vest and obscenely tight jeans that highlighted rather more of his physique than Link would have liked to see. Clearly, he was an uphill gardener, a shirt-lifter, a *poof.* Just as Link began to bemoan the fact that he was being forced to endure a second fruitcake in one night, his surroundings finally began to come into focus: multi-coloured lights, glitter ball, artsy photos of half-naked men and a clientele consisting of well-groomed males and a small number of women of questionable orientation. It was a bender bar.

'Shit,' murmured Link.

'It's a pleasure,' snipped the bugger who had just bought him his beer. 'First time?' he asked, looking Link up and down.

'Thanks for the beer,' muttered Link grudgingly before taking another swig.

'You're not from around here,' observed Link's sponsor. Of this much he was certain, but he could not fathom exactly where such a creature *had* come from. He sounded British, although he was wearing an outfit that belonged in Hawaii. But the pom's origins were not what had sparked his interest. He had paid for the beer based on seeing the pom from behind, and from behind he'd looked like a big, rugger-bugger type. From the front... he had a deep pink complexion that appeared to be the after-effects of either chronic sunburn or exposure to some evil chemical; the word 'gay' was tanned onto his forehead, and, most disturbingly, he had no eyebrows. It was most unsettling. From the back, he'd looked like just the straight-acting kind of giant he loved – he'd looked like potential. From the front, he elicited a different response – morbid curiosity. 'I'm Owen.'

'All right,' said the browless wonder gruffly.

'What happened to your eyebrows?' asked Owen, choosing not to mention the incriminating graffiti on Link's forehead. Link drained off the rest of his beer, deciding this was a better idea than punching the fairy's lights out. He replaced the glass on the counter and belched.

'Wow,' murmured Owen. 'Want another one?'

'Aye,' said Link immediately. In his forty years on the earth, he had never refused a free drink. 'But you should know I'm no bender,' he declared, 'despite what my forehead may say.'

'Fine,' said Owen before ordering another beer for what was turning out to be tonight's piece of reality entertainment. 'So,' said Owen once Link had his next beer, 'the brows: was it some kind of prank? Like a bachelor party or something?'

'Something like that,' nodded Link. 'What's your excuse then?'

Owen laughed, genuinely tickled. After a moment, Link relaxed a touch and laughed as well.

'I'm not staying,' said Link flatly. 'And keep your hands to yourself.'

'Believe me,' said Owen, 'that won't be a problem.'

'So what do you do when you're not flapping about in places like this?'

'I flap about in an office,' said Owen. 'Yourself?'

'I'm not at liberty to discuss that,' said Link gravely, borrowing from the countless spy movies he had watched over the years. Owen laughed again. Link scowled at him and the laughter stopped. Link gulped down the second beer with the speed and ease of a practised professional. God, it was good to have beer again. Beer was the one thing that convinced Link that God existed. He burped.

'Bless you,' said Owen.

'I'll have another,' said Link. 'Then I must be off.'

'Sure,' said Owen. Far from being offended at having a mile expected of him after offering an inch, Owen was very curious to see what would happen when this bizarre guy got drunk. Maybe he'd talk some more. Owen was a firm believer that truth was stranger than fiction, and loved nothing more than meeting the people who demonstrated this fact. He was a devout fan of reality television: meeting this guy was like watching a live episode of *Big Brother*. Well, maybe something like *Queer Eye on the Straight Barfly*.

'I'm Lincoln, but you can call me Link. Long as you don't try anything funny. And tell your fruity mates too.'

'Fair enough, Link. Let's get you another beer.'

Sunday mornings find some people sleeping off the excesses of Saturday night, and others attending church (some to atone for the excesses of Saturday night). Some read the paper in bed, while others prepare picnics for the countryside or visit flea markets. Some wake up alone, others with the love of their lives. Some wake up beside people that featured prominently in the excesses of the previous night, and try – as politely as possible – to get rid of them, or escape. And every morning somewhere in the world, someone wakes up with a crazed kitten pawing at his face. Sometimes there are claws.

This was how Mick Emmott was jolted into consciousness on this Sunday morning. MK's demented kitten, Wiggy, was standing on his chest, swiping violently at his face, apparently trying to create a patchwork pattern in blood. Mick yelped, bolting out of bed and away from the demented furball. He stood against the cupboard, catching his breath and getting his bearings. He stared wide-eyed at the kitten, which was now sitting placidly on the bed with all the cutesy innocence of a laminated poster captioned with something inane like, 'I is too cute – can you furgive me?'

'Mow,' he meowed sweetly. Mick marvelled at the cat's acting ability. Anyone would swear Wiggy was just the loveliest darn little thing on four booties, but Mick knew better. He knew the evil that lurked behind that creamy fur coat.

'I suppose you're hungry,' Mick mumbled. 'As usual.' He made his way to the kitchen, pausing to note that his bedroom door was ajar. He knew he'd closed it before he went to sleep last night, to protect himself from a midnight cat attack, but the cat was wily. Clearly his rapidly expanding weight served him well in forcing open doors. 'MK!' called Mick, knowing she wasn't there.

Obviously off living large with her NBF, Krissie Blaine. And here I am – the spinster with the cat.

As Mick poured the pellets into the dish, Wiggy flopped onto his back at Mick's ankles, batting them with his paws. Then he sank his teeth into them. Mick shrieked, hurrying to set the food down before the beast to curb its murderous attention. Wiggy settled in front of his meal, happily ignoring Mick. For the time being, anyway. Just as Mick began to consider the contents of his medicine cabinet, and whether any of it could be used to tone Wiggy down a touch, his thoughts were interrupted by a soft but insistent knocking at the door.

'Yes?' he barked.

'It's Mrs Siegl from next door,' called a saccharine voice from the other side.

Mick sighed. That painful woman. MK had filled him in on the miraculous coincidence. Hastily, he pulled on his robe and opened the door. She stood there, all sensible fabrics, pastel hues and the pungent lavender perfume apparently favoured by pensioners the world over.

'Good morning,' chirped Mick as brightly as possible.

'Is it a bad time?' she asked, eyeing his robe with patent disapproval.

'Nope,' he sang. 'Just feeding the cat. What can I do for you, Mrs Siegl?'

'I heard screaming,' she said with the slightest hint of scolding.

'Ah,' laughed Mick. 'The cat was trying to eat me,' he explained, only half-jokingly. Her eyes widened. 'My lateness with his lordship's breakfast obviously didn't go down well.'

'Oh!' she chuckled humourlessly. 'Of course the building doesn't actually allow pets, not that *I* mind, of course.'

Liar, thought Mick.

'My nerves are just a bit rattled at the moment,' she said. 'Last night I saw a very suspicious-looking man sleeping on the pavement. He looked like a thug. I said: "Excuse me, what are you doing down there? This is a respectable building, not a nap area. Now please move on at once!" He left quite quickly after that.'

'Well,' said Mick, 'we're fortunate to have in you the vigilant watchdog that we do.' Her smile wavered at this analogy.

'Quite,' she said. 'This area just isn't what it used to be. All sorts of undesirable elements making their way in. There are constantly people walking up and down the street. And vehicles just *cruising around*.'

Mick snorted.

'I'm not one to judge, of course,' she continued. 'But I just don't see why they have to *loiter* around here. Loitering is still against the law, you know. Not that it's enforced in this country. I'm not one of those people who like to complain constantly about things, mind you. People like that are just negative nellies, I always say.'

Mick nodded, battling to contain his mirth.

'I think it's wonderful that we live in such a free country and all, I just don't think people should be free to wonder aimlessly up and down our streets, that's all.'

Mick bit his tongue so hard he tasted blood.

'In my experience, people are never wandering *aimlessly* – unless they're on a sightseeing trip or a nature hike. In which case, aimless wandering can be rather pleasant. But when people are doing it in the city, there's usually some other agenda.'

'Right.'

'Sometimes in the supermarket you get people who seem to be wandering aimlessly. Dawdlers. It's so frustrating when you're just trying to get your shopping done. But the youth today just don't seem to know where they're going. I blame television.' She stopped suddenly, thrown. Mick saw in her eyes that she had just remembered that he worked in television. 'I don't mean quality programmes like yours, of course,' she gushed. 'Listen to me gabbing on. I admit: I'm still such a fan of the wireless.'

'Yes, of course,' said Mick, 'Well, it is a wonderful thing.' He hoped that the lull in the conversation would be a cue to Mrs

Siegl that their little visit was over.

'As a child,' she launched forth fondly, reminding Mick of her thick skin, 'it was quite the event to listen to the wireless. After dinner, we'd all sit together and listen for a short while before our bedtime.' Mick struggled to imagine a time when Mrs Siegl had actually listened to anything except her own voice. She went on: 'I always wanted to stay longer, of course. There was something about the voices on the air in those days that was so comforting. Unaffected. Today it's so different. Not that I'm one of those old fuddy-duddies to bemoan the march of progress, of course.'

'Of course,' sighed Mick, feeling his freedom slip slowly away like the golden age of the bloody wireless.

'There's very little I can listen to on the wireless these days,' she carped. 'It's so noisy, and yet nobody is really saying anything. And the music! Goodness, that's changed since my day!'

'I'm sure a lot has changed since your day,' said a voice coming down the corridor. It was MK, arriving home in the kind of couture one would expect to see on the runways of Milan – obviously courtesy of Miss Blaine. 'Good morning!' she breezed, ignoring Mrs Siegl's beady-eyed appraisal.

'Hi,' answered Mick flatly.

'Are you just coming in?' asked Mrs Siegl innocently. 'That's quite an outfit for a Sunday morning, my dear. So... adventurous.'

'Well, it is the first day of the rest of my life,' replied MK with appropriate pizzazz. She smiled as Wiggy came padding into the corridor. He curled around her legs, purring happily. 'Hi, baby.'

'Better not let anyone see him,' advised Mrs Siegl in a helpful tone. 'The building doesn't allow pets. Not that I'm complaining. All God's creatures and so forth.' She put a conspiratorial finger to her lips.

'Have a good day, Mrs Siegl,' said Mick, stepping aside to let MK in.

'You too, dears.'

She was still waving when Mick closed the door.

'I can hear her flat-bottomed old-lady shoes shuffling away,' said MK. 'Who'd have thought one of the devil's servants could wear such harmless shoes?'

'Don't be unkind,' said Mick.

'Don't be fooled by the act, Mick – she's evil.'

'She's lonely,' said Mick dismissively. He was keen to change the subject. 'Like your cat. Since you've hardly been here, his reign of terror has gotten worse.' He pointed to a fresh scratch on his nose to emphasise his point. 'He broke into my room this morning and attacked my face.'

'It's his way of showing how much he loves you,' she said, cuddling the fluffy little charmer.

'I'd hate to see him angry then,' retorted Mick. 'Have a good weekend with your new gal pal?'

'She's actually very nice.'

'Then maybe next time you should take Wiggy to meet her.'

'Thank you for babysitting,' MK said sincerely. Mick softened. 'Did you stay in last night?'

'I went out for a little while,' said Mick.

'To a gay bar?' asked MK eagerly.

'You make it sound like such an event. It's hardly Disneyland. Although there were people in costumes trying to get a ride.' Mick laughed at his own joke. 'Did you get lucky?' asked MK. 'Did you see your friend from the hotel? Was he wearing a costume? Did you try any rides?' she teased.

'Funny,' said Mick.

'Well, I have a date tonight,' purred MK triumphantly. 'Maybe if it goes well, we can go on a double date some time.'

'With whom?' asked Mick, alarmed. He had never known MK to go on a date without some ulterior motive. Sometimes he thought she'd stay single forever – she just didn't seem the type to fall in love. Mick then took a moment to hope that *he* would find someone. Otherwise he and MK could wind up living together into their golden years, and as much as he adored her, this frightened him.

'A tall, handsome stranger,' she said mysteriously. 'I won't say any more for now.' Mick sighed, exasperated. She turned the talk back to him: 'So how was your date last night? I want to know. I want to know that he has the right intentions.'

'It was fine,' he replied. 'Quite eventful, actually,' he added, beginning to smile. 'There was this English guy there who was a total weirdo. He had no eyebrows. I don't know if you've ever seen someone without eyebrows, but it's quite disturbing. He looked like an alien. And not the best-looking guy in the first place. He got so tanked that eventually he started dancing on the tables.'

'I'm sure the gays loved that,' grinned MK.

'That's not unusual,' conceded Mick. 'But then he took all his clothes off.'

'Even better.'

'No. Believe me, no. It was hideous. But of course, all the other drunks in the place went wild. And this guy was lapping it up, which was weird, because he was obviously straight.' MK raised a sceptical eyebrow. 'No, really,' said Mick. 'He was a real yob. But he was going crazy up there, like he was living out some rock star fantasy. Anyway, it only lasted about five minutes and then he was kicked out. He got quite nasty after that, but they got rid of him.'

'The world's full of crazy people,' said MK with no hint of irony.

'So why aren't you with Krissie? You bored of her already?'

'Nah,' said MK. 'She's spending some quality time with Frank. Besides, I need to get ready for my date tonight.'

'Now?' asked Mick.

'Oh, Mick, my dear friend,' said MK mock-woefully, 'you really know nothing about women, do you?'

Not far away, Lincoln Thomas was waking up to an especially vicious hangover: his head felt like it had been used as target practice for rock-throwing Bedouins, and his mouth was as dry as the desert these Bedouins roamed. Fecking Bedouins. Although each miniscule movement intensified the agony, he lifted his head and opened his eyes. He discovered with horror that he belonged to the Sunday morning camp that wakes up beside an awful stranger – in this case, male.

Although it hurt to do so, he retraced the events of the previous night as best he could. From this blurry set of images, he plucked the face of his current bedmate. It was the bender who'd bought him beer all night. Owen. Link noticed that he was naked: not necessarily a cause for concern, given his predilection for getting naked when he was drunk. He lifted the covers gently and was even more relieved to note that Owen was wearing boxer shorts.

In trying to get out of the bed as innocuously as possible, Link knocked over a lamp, which shattered very bloody *nocuously* (his own word). Link cursed to himself. When he heard Owen stir behind him he leapt out of the bed.

'Link?' said Owen, squinting into the light. Link grabbed the nearest object to hide his shame. As it turned out, this was a large inflatable penis. Owen observed the bizarre image before him: an awkward, nude pink man clutching a large plastic member. 'What are you doing?'

'What are *you* doing, mate?' spat Link dangerously. 'I think *that's* the question. What the hell am I doing in bed with you?'

'Nothing, nothing,' rambled Owen, waking up quickly. 'We were just talking – and drinking – and we must've passed out. Nothing happened!'

Link paused, then decided he believed Owen. There was no amount of booze in the world that would ever compel him to... urgh, it didn't bear thinking about. As casually as possible, he sidestepped across the room, keeping the ridiculous inflatable in place as he moved. Owen was reminded of the hippo ballerinas in that cartoon movie. Link tried to bend over to extract his clothes from the piles of discarded laundry all over the floor. Nice place.

He struggled to bend and pick up and keep covered, so Owen kindly averted his gaze.

'Thanks,' mumbled Link. He got dressed faster than ever before.

'I'll make some coffee,' said Owen.

'No!' shouted Link, advancing on him menacingly. Link wanted to grab him by the scruff of his shirt but he wasn't wearing one, and Link was not about to clap hands on his bare flesh. Tone would have to suffice. 'Listen, if you tell anyone about this – any of this – I'll hunt you down and put you out of your misery like a sick dog, understand?' Owen nodded furiously. Link took a breath, and in slightly less ominous tones, added: 'And cheers for all the drinks, mate.' With that, he was gone.

Owen shook his head. Nobody would believe him anyway.

The moment Link reached the street, the sunlight hit him like a panga to the brain. He staggered, groaning in pain. But there was one thing that was worse than all of this, and more dangerous: the Yank. Link realised he had abandoned his duties by getting blotto in benderland. He hoped against hope that the Yank's own surveillance had kept him from discovering Link's mistake. Panicked, he stuck his hands in his pockets to make sure he hadn't lost the map, photo and instructions. There they were. His relief was so great, it momentarily eclipsed his discomfort.

Owen was making himself coffee when the doorbell rang. He was stunned to find Link standing on his doorstep wearing a sheepish grin.

'Mate,' said Link amiably. 'I need a bottle of water... and taxi fare. And maybe a headache tablet or three.'

'No problem,' said Owen. Anything to get rid of this psycho. Owen needn't have worried – he'd never see Lincoln Thomas again.

The Sunday sun was still high in the sky when MK embarked upon her date with destiny (aka David Jones, Producer) early in the evening. They met in Camps Bay, at a gorgeous restaurant across the road from the beach. The sun was setting over the ocean and a row of palm trees lined the street. Behind them were the mountains. Every detail was bathed in the golden evening sunlight. David Jones was wearing another island shirt, although in this context it made more sense. It occurred to MK how beautiful everything looked in this light, including her date. He smiled broadly as she walked up the steps to meet him.

Don't trip, don't trip.

When she reached the top, he kissed her cheek. He smelled divine. Of course she knew he was thinking similar things about her. She had taken a moment to appreciate the rich tone her skin radiated in the surreal light. It was helped, of course, by a light dusting of faintly glittering powder on her shoulders. And she, too, smelled irresistible. In the words of Coco Chanel: 'A woman without a fragrance is a woman without a future.'

'Hi, handsome,' she beamed.

'You're a vision,' he said. Not very original, but his sincerity made up for it. 'I thought we could start with a walk on the beach before the sun goes. Maybe get some ice cream.'

'As long as it doesn't spoil your appetite, young man,' she said with a lilting laugh. He laughed too. Before MK could offer her hand, he had already taken it. He led her down the stairs. They walked slowly, taking in the spectacular view. A few minutes later, armed with ice cream (strawberry for her, coffee for him), they crossed the street and made their way onto the beach. He removed his sandals and offered to carry her shoes. MK handed them over, so swept away in the moment that she broke one of her own rules...

Superstardom Lesson No. 63: A lady never removes her shoes in the presence of a man. Feet are so terribly pedestrian, and superstars don't do pedestrian. Besides, those shoes no doubt cost a fortune – make them pay for themselves.

The sand was impossibly white and fine and felt more glorious than any pair of shoes that MK could imagine. She was overcome by it all. Although MK had been born in the mountains, mountains rising from the sea were something else. To MK, being in the place where the water met the land felt almost spiritual. The sound of the sea was so powerful, yet soothing. The ocean stretched out forever. Somewhere on the other side of it lay her dreams. MK could understand why so many people flocked to the sea every year. It was special. It was hard not to sense that there was indeed a bigger picture. Suddenly she felt very small in a very big world.

'Hey,' said David softly. 'You look a million miles away.'

'Oh,' she said with a forced laugh. 'I wish.'

'Why?' he asked. 'What's wrong with here?'

'Um,' she said. 'Nothing.' And, looking at him at that moment, she meant it.

He smiled at her and took her hand. They kept walking, in silence. There seemed to be a tacit agreement between them that conversation wasn't necessary. It was nice. In MK's opinion, people rarely said anything significant, for all the talking they did.

A breeze had picked up and MK folded her arms. David offered his jacket, but she refused. He suggested that they go back up to the restaurant for dinner, and she agreed. There was only so much beauty and perspective she could handle at one time. For a moment they looked at each other, not moving, and MK wondered if he would kiss her. He did not – instead he held out his arm and grinned chivalrously. She locked her arm in his and they headed back.

'You know,' he said as they ambled, looking at the mountains, 'I grew up in the mountains. In Montana.'

'Me too,' she said. 'Although they're probably smaller than the ones in the US. Everything is bigger there, I believe.'

'Yeah,' he laughed.

'Montana,' she mused. 'Like in *Brokeback Mountain*?'

'That's right,' he said, laughing again. 'Although I never kissed no cowboys.'

'It looks so beautiful.'

'It was,' he said.

'You don't live there anymore, obviously,' she said.

'No, uh,' he said hesitantly, 'California.'

'Where the hills have big, white letters on them.' She saw bewilderment on his face. 'Hollywood.'

'Oh, yeah, Crazytown.'

'Do you ever miss the mountains?' asked MK suddenly. It had been on her mind to press him for details about Hollywood and his life there, but this other question had popped out from nowhere.

'Sure do,' he said, his smile returning.

'Me too,' she said. And she meant it.

They walked the rest of the way in silence, finishing their ice cream with their free hands.

When they reached the restaurant, MK excused herself to the powder room while David got them a table. In the privacy of the bathroom, MK leaned against the sink, suddenly overcome by a strange sensation. Her pulse was racing a little faster than usual, and she simply felt... dizzy wasn't quite the right word. Woozy... also not quite right. Just *strange*. It had started on the beach. The rhythm of the waves as they broke on the shore. And she'd had a moment of *doubt*... that was so unlike her it almost felt like the emotion belonged to someone else. For a split second the beauty of the sea had been replaced in her mind by a darker vision: the sea as a perilous obstacle between her and her dreams, black and deep and full of dangerous things waiting to pull her down into its depths. MK had never doubted herself before, never. As for the fact that she'd suddenly started talking about home – Kwa Kwa, in the mountains – and *missing* home... Until now, MK had been totally content never to see it again. What the hell was going on?

Displaced. That was the word. She felt somehow displaced. She felt as though things in her mind had been displaced. The thought that MK had been doing her considerable best to suppress suddenly surfaced like a kraken and overwhelmed her: someone had *done something to her* back home in Johannesburg. She had lost a week of her life. Someone had been there, doing something... That was the reason she had run; run away, here, to Cape Town. Ever the model of resilience, MK had forced this incident into the past, left it behind her, put it on a shelf in her mind and closed the cupboard door. Suddenly, however, it had burst forth to the front of her mind. What had happened to her? What if it wasn't over? What if they came after her again?

The flush of a toilet behind her pulled her back into the moment. A stall door opened and a cleaning lady emerged. She greeted MK and MK greeted her back with a deferential smile. The lady paused and touched MK's arm.

'Are you all right, my dear?' she asked.

'Yes, Ma,' replied MK. 'Just need to touch up my lipstick.' The woman didn't look convinced, but nodded and left anyway. *Lipstick. That's a good idea.*

MK turned to face the mirror and took out her lipstick. It never failed to cheer her. Forcing herself to ignore the slight tremor in her hand, MK pulled herself together. There was no sense worrying about answers she simply didn't have; she needed to stay focused on the task at hand – charming Mr Hollywood out there. There were worse ways to spend a Sunday evening. He *was* rather delectable. Best she stuck to what she knew. The rest would unfold as it must.

She was feeling better already. Consoling herself that her moment of weakness had simply been brought on by the headiness of the beach, MK joined David at the table and went to work with a renewed sense of purpose.

MK had been right about the cause of her episode; in fact, it *had* been brought on by the steady pounding of the surf. Whatever strange seeds had been planted in her mind during her lost week were only waiting for the right trigger – a trigger that relied partly on sound. A sound not unlike the one she'd heard on the beach, but not exactly like it... which was the only the reason the trigger had not been activated.

If it had been, the evening would certainly have turned out very differently.

As it happened, the date was great. MK found David to be a warm, genuine man, despite his noticeable fixation with keeping things on the table perfectly aligned. He ordered a good bottle of wine, but had only one glass. The rest of the evening he drank coffee, rather a lot of it. MK had two glasses of wine, but paced herself so as to remain clearheaded. The conversation seemed focused on her, and MK worked hard to keep her story – the story of 'Lisa' – straight. David Jones seemed very interested in her, which was flattering, but it kept her from learning more about him.

'That,' she said, daubing her mouth with her serviette, 'was delicious.'

'I can't believe you had chicken when we're at such a good seafood place,' he said with a chuckle. 'The prawns were outstanding.'

'I don't do crustaceans,' she answered gravely.

'This is interesting. Why not?'

'They're scavengers, bottom-feeders. They eat the garbage of the sea.'

'Mmm,' he said, casting a disgusted look at the prawn remains on his plate. 'Thanks for sharing that with me.'

'Sorry,' she laughed. He waved good-naturedly. 'You must deal with a lot of bottom-feeders in your job,' she said casually. He looked surprised at this. 'As a producer,' she added.

'Oh,' he said. 'Oh, yeah. All the time.'

'What's the funniest thing that's ever happened to you at work? I'd love to hear what it's like in Hollywood. It must be fascinating.'

'Well,' he said coolly, 'not to be rude, but, uh, I don't really want to talk shop while I'm on vacation. I'm trying to get away from all that.' She nodded apologetically. 'Besides, I don't know what the world finds so interesting about it. They're just a bunch of people doing jobs like everyone else – except they get paid ridiculous amounts of money to do it.'

'That's the dream for a lot of people,' she said, careful not to include herself in this statement.

'I guess...' He trailed off, looking very bleak all of a sudden. He folded an empty sugar packet neatly in half, making sure the corners were perfectly aligned. Then folded it smaller. His eyes focused on the project with intensity. The mood had changed. MK needed to change it back.

'I have some tweezers, if you'd like,' she offered with a smile. David looked up, wide-eyed, as though stirred from a troubling daydream, and then broke into a smile. He laughed and put down the packet. It looked like it had required some effort to do so; his eyes glanced back down at it briefly. MK reached over and took his hand. 'You're kind of high-strung, aren't you?' she asked gently. He made an indistinct noise. She grinned. 'It's the disease of the modern age.'

'We're living in scary times,' he stated solemnly.

'I'm sure they've said that throughout history,' she said reassuringly.

'Maybe,' he said, putting on a relaxed smile. He told himself to get it together. He had been undercover before – the act was permanent, you never let it drop (little did he know that MK had a similar philosophy). It felt strange, however, acting in his private life. He really liked this young woman. And he was lying to her about almost everything. Except Montana. He decided that as long as he kept honest about the stuff that really mattered, that would have to do, for the time being. 'You're a smart little lady, aren't you?'

'I hope that wasn't a joke about my height,' she said.

'It was a compliment. It's nice to meet someone who doesn't play stupid, because that seems to be the fashion these days. People don't realise how dangerous that can be.'

If you only knew, she thought.

'Anyway,' he said brusquely. The waiter approached just then to clear the plates. 'Will the lady have dessert?' asked David, trailing his fingers over her hand lightly. 'Or a coffee, or something?'

'We already had ice cream,' said MK. 'No, thanks, I'm fine.'

'Just the bill, then,' said David to the waiter.

'Quick question,' said MK, once David had settled the bill (and left a decent tip, she noticed). 'Your business card. Why are there no details printed on it? You wrote your phone number on it by hand.'

'I could tell you,' he whispered playfully, 'but then I'd have to erase your memory.'

'Ooh,' she whispered equally playfully, 'a man with secrets.'

'If you only knew.'

'I have secrets too,' she said under the guise of playfulness.

'You have secrets?' he asked, in mock-horror, '*and* you don't eat seafood. I don't think we should see each other again, Lisa.' MK laughed heartily at this. He stood up and pulled out for her chair for her. 'Walk you to your car?'

David walked MK back to her (Mick's rental) car. The moon had risen. The sea was darker than the sky. MK noticed the sound of the surf and decided not to hang around for too long.

'I have an early call in the morning...' she said.

'Gosh,' he joked, 'buy a girl dinner, walk on the beach, and she doesn't even put out!' She slapped his arm lightheartedly, laughing.

'I'm not that kind of girl,' she declared dramatically.

'What kind of girl are you?' he asked, a touch more seriously.

'Hmm,' she said, drawing in close. 'I'm just a peaches 'n' cream kinda girl, looking for a meat 'n' potatoes kinda guy...' He smiled, impressed.

'Well,' he said, getting closer, 'since we won't be seeing each other again, how about we don't see each other tomorrow night at, say, seven-forty-two?'

'Make it eight,' she chuckled.

They drew closer. David put his arms around her. She shivered, delighting in the anticipation. Their lips were mere millimetres apart...

'Thank you, medem!' called a voice behind them. David spun around instantly, and MK grabbed his arm.

'It's okay,' she said quickly. 'It's the car guard.' They broke into awkward laughter. David trailed his shoe over the ground aimlessly while MK dug out R5 and put it into the happy clapper of the guard. The guard grinned a toothless grin of thanks and hopped off to another couple who were approaching their car. MK turned back to David, looking apologetic, but before she could say a word he took hold of her and kissed her full on the mouth. It was brief but memorable.

'To be continued,' he said, before walking off, a noticeable skip in his step.

MK caught her breath. She reeled. Her heart skipped the proverbial beat. Her knees did not go weak, but she felt adrenaline rushing through her legs. She'd never been kissed like that before. It was... a thousand adjectives flooded through her racing mind, but none seemed adequate. There are moments language can never quite capture. It was certainly pleasant. It was very pleasant. So pleasant she still felt it physically charging through her body like a tide.

Uh oh. I'm in trouble.

Trouble was certainly headed MK's way, although from the last place she would have expected. Some distance away from the seaside majesty of Camps Bay, Jackie de la Rey was busy with her own special kind of Sunday-night service. She sat on the edge of her bath, smoking a cigarette and chatting to Jesus – the tapestry on the back of her bathroom door.

Ever since the crushing events of Friday night – the cursed TV party that had ended with the horrifying revelation that Fahiem was screwing the American tramp, and Jackie's humiliation at the hands of the black princess – Jackie had hit rock-bottom. She called in sick over the weekend, and spent the time at home, crying, screaming, praying, breaking things, weeping, crawling around, flailing, beseeching, bellowing, smashing things, sobbing, raging, bemoaning and thrashing around on the floor. Even her toilet-roll Barbie had paid a price: Jackie had ripped clumps of blonde nylon hair out of the little head, burned the face and body with cigarettes and ripped up the knitted dress. Bizarrely, Jackie had still replaced it after her outburst. It now stood atop the cistern, like a ghoulish guardian of the loo paper.

'I have suffered,' she said to the tapestry, 'like you. You rose three days later, and tomorrow I shall rise.' Such delusions of grandeur are of course commonplace among lunatics. 'The time to wait is over.' Jackie smoked the last of her cigarette and tossed into the bath where the corpses of other cigarettes lay discarded. 'And when the war has begun, and my people – Your people – start being heard once more... I'll quit smoking for good.'

Jackie headed for the door and gave the wall-hanging one last look. She stopped dead at what she saw. It was wet. Immediately her eyes went up to the Messiah's face. It was wet. She ran her fingers over the fabric. It was moist. Where she had stitched droplets of blood, it was moist, and where she had stitched tears, it was moist. She dropped to her knees.

'Oh, Lord,' she moaned, enrapt. Her humble tapestry – her own personal display of devotion – was weeping *real tears*! It was a miracle and a sign. A sign and a miracle. While one may have argued that the Lord's tears were a sign of sorrow at Jackie's planned actions, Jackie read them as approval. Encouragement. A blessing from Above, right here in her own humble little home. He had seen her tears of suffering and answered them with tears of solace. Jackie cried again.

When one is in a state of immense agitation and emotion, perception is typically skewed. This was the case here. Had Jackie been in control of her faculties, she might have first investigated the cause of the damp, perhaps even grown irked by the fact that something was wetting her prized work. Had she investigated, she would've spotted the dripping coming from the ceiling above the door. In the course of her violent weekend, Jackie had done immeasurable damage to her house, including her plumbing. This morning's paper had been plastered with images of Krissie Blaine and her NBBF (New Best Black Friend), Miss Kaka, seen around town. So incensed was Jackie that she had proceeded to stuff the entire newspaper down the toilet, in the irrational conviction that that was where the offensive pair belonged. After repeated flushing, this blockage had resulted in a build-up in the pipes, which had then resulted in a leak in the pipe above the door. The only sign a sane person would have allotted to what was clearly a plumbing issue, was 'out of order'.

Jackie de la Rey, however, had strayed somewhat off the path of sanity, and was now frolicking in the perilous back alleys of madness. She had been toying with the idea of kidnapping both Miss Kaka and Krissie Blaine, but she now saw that Krissie was not necessary. The desire to punish her was born out of petty personal issues ('jealousy' was not a word Jackie allowed herself to use with regards to Fahiem's new flame), but ultimately had nothing to do with her purpose. The black girl did.

Jackie tried to regain her composure. She needed to be back at work at the Hotel the next day with her best game face on... because the next time the black bitch showed up at the hotel to visit her NBF, Jackie would be ready. She would take her, by any means necessary.

Sunday evenings are generally a quiet affair. Many people either begin thinking about the week ahead, or do their best not to. Some continue partying in defiance of the fact that the weekend is coming to an end.

Martie and Gift Yeni were always in bed early, reading.

Krissie Blaine and Fahiem Abdul took advantage of the fact that his delicate region had recovered sufficiently for them to consummate their relationship. They did so with gusto, repeatedly...

MK sat in her bedroom, trying to revise her lines for work the next day, but kept catching herself daydreaming about the man she knew as David Jones, and the way he had kissed her. There was also the troubling episode she'd suffered after the beach...

The man in the island shirt abandoned his surveillance of the Blaine girl and her terrorist companion after it became clear that they would not be doing much for the rest of the night, apart from engaging in an intimate version of East-meets-West. Also, he was continually being distracted by thoughts of his evening with the intriguing Lisa, and the kiss that had topped it off...

Nearby, Lincoln Thomas sat on the pavement in a spot where he could see the staff entrance of the Hotel Shmotel. He'd witnessed the Muslim kid arrive hours ago. He guessed he wouldn't be emerging any time soon. His hangover had subsided a little and he was starving. Was he expected to just sit here the whole night? Eventually he nodded off, and dreamed of greasy bacon butties...

Jackie de la Rey set her alarm clock and got into bed, much calmer than before. Tomorrow was a big day...

Indeed.

WHAT'S ON TONIGHT?

- **5:00pm HEART SONGS** Mirabella reveals to Becky the truth about Roark's dark past. Faith and Caesar celebrate their anniversary, while Marco plans to redecorate the town square. More heartwarming moments in this US soapie.
- **6:00pm JOZI DAYS** Thembi warns Estelle about Jabu's shady past. Meanwhile, Thandi celebrates her record deal and Jimmy decides to redecorate the shebeen. Switch off after a hard day's work with this scintillating local daily drama.
- **6:30pm SHE TALK** Is ironing really dull? We explore this with a panel of experts.
- **7:00pm NEWS** Catch up on the day's events from one point of view!
- **7:30pm TWO MUCH** More marital mayhem and hilarity, as Karen decides to redecorate the lounge. International comedy at its best.
- **8:00pm INSIGHTS** More and more communities are opting to begin, instead of a Neighbourhood Watch, a Neighbourhood Blindspot: this is where people simply ignore what's happening with their neighbours. They say it is inspired by the President's attitude to neighbour trouble.

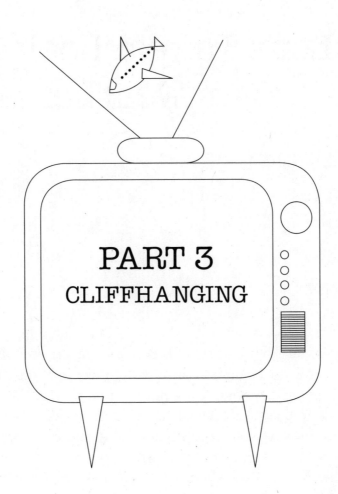

PART 3
CLIFFHANGING

'Let's Take a Look at Your Weather'

THE TENSION ON set was palpable. A humming, metaphorical cloud of blue hung in the air. For most of the crew, this was simply the usual blue associated with Mondays. If the cloud had been visible, they would have noticed that it intensified around Saartjie Williams, darkening to a deep indigo, almost violet. She was uncharacteristically quiet and unsocial, and the others responded by keeping their distance.

When MK (or Palesa in this circle) arrived, she was aglow with a far brighter shade; let us say cerise. The other actors flocked to her, still thrilled by their party in Krissie Blaine's suite on Friday night – thanks to MK. As they flapped around her, cooing and giggling and talking about seeing her pictures in the paper, like a bunch of sugared-up schoolgirls, their bluish shade mingled with her pinkish shade, resulting in a soft lavender colour that was cheerful and soothing.

Saartjie *hated* lavender. She hated the fact that Palesa-flipping-Whatsername had gotten their cast mates into the Hollywood bimbo's hotel room, and now had them all eating out of her hand. More than anything else, Saartjie hated the fact that she was now the One Who Got Drunk, Punched Someone and Got Kicked Out. The humiliation stung worse than a wasp attack. By wasps who had stopped to dip their stings in chilli juice and pepper. Saartjie could feel that her power base had shifted – right out from under her. The greetings of her colleagues had said it all: the mumbled hello minus eye contact.

'Saartjie, my dear,' said MK, who appeared beside her as if by black magic. Unlike the others, she had no trouble maintaining eye contact with Saartjie, and was, in fact, giving her a look that hovered between sympathy and concern. Her voice had a matching tone. 'How *are* you?'

'Fine,' said Saartjie as breezily as possible. 'And you?'

'I had such a wonderful weekend!' gushed MK. 'But I'm sure you saw the pictures in the paper.'

'No,' lied Saartjie.

'Oh. Well, you should read the paper, sweetie – it's how we keep in touch with the world we're living in.'

Saartjie nodded slowly. That had backfired.

'And I met a lovely gentleman on Friday night,' enthused MK, aiming the salt right at Saartjie's wound. The sympathetic concern returned to her face. 'Of course that was your terrible night... I'm so sorry.' She squeezed Saartjie's hand, and gazed meaningfully into her eyes. Saartjie wrenched her hand away and answered in a low voice.

'You're loving this, aren't you?'

'I don't know what you mean,' replied MK guilelessly.

'Be careful, little girl,' warned Saartjie venomously.

'Pity you didn't take that advice on Friday,' beamed MK. 'And I'm not even talking about when you got booted out of the hotel in front of the whole team – I'm talking about the outfit you were wearing.' Saartjie tensed visibly, and MK could feel that she wanted to attack – physically.

'You're a great actress, lovey,' said Saartjie evenly. 'But I'm better.' She turned and walked away. MK was impressed, but felt sure that it would come out sideways later. The whole thing seemed so petty now, compared to the Hollywood prospects she was presently courting with Krissie and David, but MK just couldn't help herself. Saartjie Williams got under her skin. She epitomised everything MK resented in show business: minor talent with major celebrity and a core of obnoxious bitterness.

Please don't ever let that be me.

A trace of Saartjie's violet had inked MK's cerise. It was going to be a long day. They'd all be lucky if *The Rainbow Hotel* wasn't pounded by a freak storm.

The newest member of Wives in Training – who had no idea of the storm her membership would soon be placing her smack-bang in the middle of – worked in her kitchen amidst her own metaphorical cloud, a cirrus of lemon yellow. Yellow had always been one of Martie's favourite colours and she was in a wonderful mood. Martie was baking. Well, 'baking' would imply practised ease and hint at success, so let it rather be said that Martie was *experimenting*. There were only four days until the next W.I.T. meeting and Martie needed to perfect something that she could take along with pride.

Initially, she had insisted on trying to improve her milk tart, but after numerous unsuccessful attempts, Gift had begged her to stop. He'd had the lucky job of being the official taster. Eventually, however, he could take no more. Aside from the taste (which he could have endured for the sake of love), the tarts had caused some alarming developments in his evacuation process. He neglected to inform Martie of these, so we shall leave it at that; suffice it to say, milk tart was summarily banned from the connubial home.

Having survived the weekend, Gift was off on important meetings, the details of which Martie barely understood. Happy to be left alone with her recipe books, Martie decided to branch out.

Like many other things, the internet was something Martie had never encountered before meeting Gift. At first she had resisted it, writing it off as too complicated. Her early attempts at 'surfing the web' had felt as difficult as she'd imagined actual surfing would be. It was like trying to paint a Rembrandt with a lump of coal, or trying to play the piano with boxing gloves on, or trying to get out of jail if you were Schabir Shaik, or trying to fix the economy if you were Robert Mugabe... unlikely to succeed and, frankly, embarrassing.

With a little patience and perseverance, however, Martie got the hang of it, and while she was unable to achieve any of the feats listed above, at least she could read all about them online. The internet lived up to the hype – it really was as if the world were at her fingertips. She tended to avoid the news, however, deciding that it was harmful to her happiness, and so she had not seen the photos of Krissie Blaine and her new cohort. No, today Martie wanted to dive for recipes – the more exotic, the better. She wanted to offer the other ladies something they'd never had before.

In the search box, Martie typed 'exotic', then paused for a moment and added 'Asian'. Finally she opted to add 'pie', and clicked search. One of the first listings that caught her eye read: 'Asian cream pie'. Sounded like just the ticket. She opened the page, and gasped at what filled the screen. The Asian lady on the screen was most certainly not baking! Evidently a 'cream pie' was something *very* different to what it sounded like. She slammed her fingers on the keyboard to try get rid of the offensive image, but only succeeded in bringing up another – equally explicit – picture. Martie shrieked and put up a hand to cover it. With the other, she grabbed the mouse. Her shaking hand made lining up the cursor with the little X that closes the window tricky, but finally she managed to close it.

One hand over her mouth, and the other over her heart, Martie told herself to breathe. How disgustingly awful! Why anyone would... It was best not to think about it. There was room enough in hell for the creators, participants and viewers of such filth. Just when her heart rate had returned to normal, a box appeared onscreen advertising another sin of the flesh. And then another. The panicked Martie closed them but no sooner than she had closed one, two more would materialise in its place. Words and acts that Martie had condemned her entire life – and a few she'd been blissfully unaware of – invaded her monitor. Eventually she pulled the plug and ran away, fleeing the perverted purple of the study.

Well. So much for exotic. Martie decided that her old recipe books would have to do. They might contain the sort of classic, old-fashioned cuisine some people snubbed these days, but perhaps in some senses, the old ways were preferable. Anyway, that could wait – Martie had lost her appetite.

The dishes needed doing. Yes, it would do her good to clean something.

The man in the island shirt had already cleaned his entire hotel room (the staff never cleaned to his standards, so after the first day he had requested that they rather bring a cart of cleaning supplies to his room and let him do the rest). The Blaine girl was still asleep so there wasn't much surveillance to be done. He turned his attention to writing a poem for Lisa. After last night, he was feeling particularly inspired. He was not the world's greatest poet, not by a long shot, but he derived some therapeutic release from writing. It was about the only useful thing he'd gotten out of the mandatory counselling stint his superiors had forced him into after the First Ladyboy debacle, and before he had vanished.

He had no intention of giving Lisa the poem, or even showing it to her – it was just for him. Who knew? One day, at the end of a long, full life and illustrious career (having regained his credibility by busting open this terror plot, of course), he might include some of the poetry in his memoir.

> **As dark and bewitching as the night**
> **But as arresting as full moon**
> **You gave to me your sweet delight**

He paused for a long moment, then added:

> **I hope it comes back soon**

He frowned.

> **~~I hope it comes back soon~~**
> **I'm lost in the monsoon**

He nodded, happy with the change, and then began copying it onto a new piece of paper. He couldn't stand looking at the crossed-out line. He whistled as he worked, 'The Star-Spangled Banner', and froze midway through his inspired word, 'monsoon'. Inspiration just kept on coming: he was suddenly struck by an idea of absolute genius. He would write words about Lisa to the tune of 'The Star-Spangled Banner'! And make it so good that he *would* show it to her! Perhaps even sing it to her. He had a decent voice, when he concentrated.

What would he call it? 'Star-Spangled' worked pretty well... Star-Spangled Something... He put aside the other poem and took out a fresh leaf.

> **Star-Spangled Lady**

> **Oh us at the beach by the dusk's golden light**

Pleased with this opening, he continued on for the next hour or so, crafting one verse of clumsy imagery that he was immensely proud of. It ended with his reworking of the final two famous lines, as such:

And the star-spangled lady sweet kisses shall give
In the land where we are free and the home where we'll live.

Hey, not everyone has the gift of verse. What it lacked in imagination, it made up for in sincerity. It still needed some work, but the man was satisfied with this start. He began daydreaming about the moment he would sing it to her. The fancies ran wild – atop the Statue of Liberty, maybe even here on Table Mountain. Never in his wildest imaginings, however, could he have guessed he'd be singing it at 30 000 feet, while losing altitude rapidly.

Fahiem helped the others clean the kitchen after another hectic lunch run at the Hotel Shmotel. He treasured moments like this, when it was a little quieter and he could take the opportunity to get some thinking done. The last week or so of his life had been eventful, to say the least. Most men Fahiem's age would have been dancing with delirious joy at being in the enviable position of being Krissie Blaine's lover. Not that Fahiem wasn't enjoying it... but after the initial flush he'd realised his desire was strictly of the physical variety. And Fahiem was a romantic at heart. Making love with Krissie would be wonderful if there were any actual love involved, but Fahiem had come to see that this would never happen for the two of them.

Just as he was considering exactly what this meant, a surprise visitor appeared in the doorway – Jackie. She smiled serenely as she entered and issued the head chef with a special dietary request for one of the guests. Fahiem's stomach lurched – he had not seen her since Friday night, when Jackie had been slapped by that actress and then put in her place by the others. He was terrified. But, just as swiftly as Jackie had entered, she exited again. Strange. Why was she not dragging him off to the closet to punish him?

Fahiem ran after her. He caught her in the hallway, and touched her arm. Immediately he retracted his hand as though for fear she may bite it, but she only smiled on in that bizarre, tranquil way. He'd never seen anything like this expression on Jackie's face and found it fairly unnerving.

'Yes?' she chimed sweetly.

'Are you okay?' he asked.

'I'm just fine, thanks,' she replied, 'and you?'

'I feel bad... about Friday night. And Krissie. I think I've made a mistake.'

'I see,' said Jackie in managerial tones, although her face registered a slight shift in mood. A hint of discomfort. 'In the kitchen? Because you know you really should discuss that with the chef – he's your direct superior.'

'I'm talking about *us*,' said Fahiem urgently, wincing in anticipation of the backlash that was sure to follow. But Jackie only stood there, motionless, for a long moment.

'The time has come,' she said slowly. 'None of that matters now, because war is about to begin, and you and I are on different sides. The fires are coming – for me, flames of glory, but for you... the fires of hell.'

Fahiem stared.

'You shouldn't have touched her,' she added viciously before turning and leaving. Fahiem watched her go and then let his eyes settle on the carpet. His mind spun, repeating what she had just said to him. He thought her smile had been unnerving, but that was nothing compared to the words that had escaped it.

Clearly she was not happy, but where was the anger? Her roaring temper, her rage – the thing that made Jackie, Jackie. Something else had taken its place, and although it came packaged in a thin smile, it was far darker than anger. Ignoring the icy prickling running up his spine, Fahiem hurried back to the kitchen, to the simplicity of cleaning utensils.

Jackie returned to her office and closed the door. Then she opened her drawer and took out a utensil of her own.

A big, shiny gun.

Across town, our very own traditional weapon, MK, was about ready to blast. A new director had come onboard this week, and MK found three things about him absolutely intolerable: he changed the script at will and encouraged the actors to do the same (which would be fine, if he had the faintest idea of what was funny); he didn't have the faintest idea of what was funny; and he adored and blatantly favoured Saartjie Williams. As if all of this wasn't frustrating enough, he took every available opportunity to expound his creative vision and methodology. An impressive ego for someone whose biggest claim to fame was a soup commercial.

The bragging MK could deal with – the favouritism was another matter. So far, a whole scene of hers had been cut to make way for a 'comedic sequence' for Saartjie, and the majority of MK's laugh-lines in the rest of the episode had also been given to Saartjie. This was proving difficult to bear, as the episode they were rehearsing had MK's character in the major storyline. Needless to say, Saartjie was loving every second of it and had given MK many a victorious look throughout the day.

In the last few minutes a discussion had begun between Mr Director and Miss Doyenne which, for MK, was proving to be the fateful straw that would surely cause spinal damage to the proverbial camel. A not-so-subtle suggestion had been made (by Saartjie) that the storyline be switched around to put *her* character at the centre of the plot, and this suggestion was currently being seriously considered (by HRH The Director).

'Sorry,' said MK in the light voice of Palesa, 'but surely we can't just rewrite the whole episode – we're shooting it tomorrow. And we've all learned the lines.'

'Oh, Palesa,' hummed Saartjie with the air of a veteran addressing a novice, 'the most important thing we can do here is serve the work...' MK nodded, reluctant to agree as she had the impression this was going somewhere objectionable. 'And of course we honour the words,' continued Saartjie with thin humility, 'but our larger goal must be to serve the show as a whole. If the director suggests an idea that is funnier...'

'You suggested it,' put in MK. Saartjie ignored this and continued loudly.

'If a funnier idea is put on the table, we're obliged to consider it.'

'Yes, yes,' said the director. 'Quite so.'

'Of course,' added Saartjie, a malevolent gleam in her eye, 'if you don't think you'll be able to make the necessary adjustments by tomorrow, just say so. I can work with last-minute changes – comes from my years on the stage.' The director, who had never been anywhere near the stage in his life, nodded approvingly.

'You are an inspiration, Saartjie,' said MK. Then refusing the bait: 'But I don't think I'd be able to make the changes by tomorrow.' Saartjie's eyes flashed. Backfire. 'I'm very slow with learning lines,' MK finished.

'No, you're not,' Saartjie snapped, unable to keep anger out of her voice. MK, playing the wide-eyed novice Palesa to perfection, looked away, embarrassed. Saartjie turned to the director. 'I think she can manage it.' MK turned up her act, looking very uncomfortable, as though she were letting down the team.

'I'm sorry,' she said in a tiny voice, 'I don't want to let you guys down.'

'It's fine, sweetie,' said another actress, coming to her defence. This young lady had been one of the lucky guests in Krissie Blaine's suite courtesy of MK – naturally. 'Besides, I actually think it's funnier the way it is.'

'What do you know?' barked Saartjie viciously.

'I'm sorry,' cried MK, upset. Cue waterworks. An inspired performance, thought MK coldly as she put a quiver in her lip and wiped away the tears. 'I don't want it to turn into a big deal. I'm doing my best.' The director moved closer and put his hand on her shoulder. Saartjie jumped off her chair.

'She's faking it!' she screamed. 'The whole thing is an act!'

MK began weeping bitterly.

'Stop that, you little drama queen!' yelled Saartjie savagely, pointing her finger violently in MK's direction. '*Stop it!*' The next moment was classic MK: her mind did something totally at odds with her body. As the cool, businesslike mind counted off new points for herself, the person known as Palesa flung herself into the arms of the director, in uncontainable distress. It was masterful. The director put his arms around the wretched creature protectively. Saartjie fairly jumped in rage. She flew over to the pair and screamed herself hoarse, inches from MK: '*StopitstopitstopitSTOPIT!*'

'*Aaaaaahahahahahaaa!*' wailed Palesa

'Saartjie!' called the actress, shocked at her colleague's cruelty.

'Enough!' shouted the director, also aiming his ire at Saartjie.

'I don't believe this!' shrieked Saartjie. She looked around, desperate to find someone else who was seeing through this horrible little upstart's act. But around the silent room were only stony faces. Shock. Distaste. Hostility. No one made a sound. 'I don't believe this,' she repeated breathlessly. She felt sick.

'What is your problem?' muttered the other actress at Saartjie, putting her arm around MK comfortingly. The other actors gathered around MK, throwing dark looks at Saartjie, Public Enemy Number 1. While everyone scowled at her, Saartjie looked over at MK, and what she saw broke her. MK winked.

Saartjie ran, ran as fast as her tracksuited legs would carry her, out of the studio and out of sight. MK snivelled miserably, accepting a tissue from one of her comrades, and thanking them for their supportive words. The crew stood motionless – a garden of denim sunflowers, waiting to see which way the sun would go. Not even Wimpie went after Saartjie.

'I think that's a wrap for today,' said the director, pointlessly. With a final squeeze of MK's shoulder, he headed off, a touch reluctantly, to find Saartjie. You just never knew what these actresses were capable of after such a scene. He half expected to find a Saartjie-shaped hole in the wall, only to pass through it and find her wandering in the traffic, tearing at her hair. *Hmm*, he thought as he wandered off, *that could work as a commercial. "Is your shampoo not living up to its promises?"*

The silence was broken by a muffled, vaguely electronic voice chanting: 'I'm ringing! I'm ringing! Better shut me up before I start irritating people!' MK dug in her purse and took out her cellphone. She walked away from the others.

'Sorry, guys,' she said with a sniffle, 'excuse me...' Her co-workers gave her compassionate looks as she headed for the privacy of the green room. 'Hello,' she said in a perfectly normal voice.

'Hey, bitch,' sang Krissie on the other end, in her typically loud American register. 'I'm bored. You wanna hang?'

'Hi,' said MK, effortlessly shifting gear. 'Actually I have a hot date tonight. But we've finished early today, so I guess I could come visit for a while.'

'Cool, I can help you get dressed and do your makeup!'

'Okay,' chuckled MK. 'See you soon.'

When MK entered the dressing room to grab her things, it was empty. No doubt Saartjie was having a meltdown elsewhere. After a quick, shaken farewell to her co-workers, MK packed Palesa away and headed for the door. As she was leaving the building, Mick caught her. He looked shaken too, although his mood was genuine.

'What the hell just happened?' he demanded, out of breath.

'Ask your leading lady,' said MK simply, before stepping around him.

'Hey,' he said, taking her arm. 'I somehow doubt I'll get the full story from anyone else. *Palesa...*' he added significantly. MK rolled her eyes.

'There is no story,' she said. 'Miss Thing in there was playing writer, director and star. She wanted to change the whole bloody episode, Mick. The director wrapped us. Ask anyone.'

'I love you,' he said angrily, 'but don't forget that I am your boss.'

'She left,' said MK. 'Not me.'

'Why?'

'If you're looking for the prima donna, find Saartjie Williams. Apparently she doesn't need anyone else in her show.' Mick stared at her, trying to do the impossible and read her. 'Stay calm. You have to look after your heart.' She pecked him on the cheek and was gone.

A storm had definitely hit. Mick wondered if the show would survive. It never occurred to him that MK might not.

Martie's cloud had darkened too. The cheesecake she had attempted just refused to set, remaining a big bowl of biscuit-bottomed mush, and her carrot cake had done the opposite and hardened to the consistency of a nutty brick. How could baking be so flipping difficult? All Martie wanted was to be the deft, radiant homemaker she so often saw on television – swooping in to treat her husband with scrumptious little snacks after his long day at the office. Like a super-heroine, but in a colourful apron instead of a cape. Why was that so hard?

Martie wished she were the kind of person who could break things when she was this upset – another thing she often saw on TV. She envied those people who could just fling things across the room dramatically. It always looked somehow thrilling...

After a moment's hesitation, she picked up the carrot cake/rock. She couldn't. Could she? Well, maybe, just the cake – no sense in breaking the plate. Having replaced the plate on the counter,

Martie held the loaf-shaped cake in her hand. It was heavy. A shiver of excitement ran through her. Martie raised the cake then paused, hand in mid-air, and wondered where she should throw it. Was she over-thinking this?

'Hi,' said a voice behind her.

Martie spun round, startled, and without another thought, flung the cake at the intruder. Gift yelped as the cake bonked off his forehead, and crumpled to his knees.

'What are you doing?' he moaned.

'Oh my goodness,' she cried, hurrying to his side. Not a super-heroine, after all, but a villain. 'I'm so sorry, Baas – I thought you were a robber!'

'Fine,' muttered Gift, touching his forehead gingerly. 'But where did you get the brick? Why is there a brick in the house?'

'It's a cake,' she moaned miserably.

'You do realise you're supposed to put *flour* in those,' he barked. 'Not cement mix!'

'I'm sorry!' Big, bright tears glistened in her eyes. Gift sighed.

'It's okay, Fat-cakes,' he said softly.

'No,' she wailed, 'it's not. I'm a terrible wife! First the pornography, and now this!' Before Gift could argue the terrible-wife point – and question the pornography remark – Martie had scurried from the room, crying.

Gift had only seen her this upset once before: the day he had acquired food poisoning from a particularly ambitious Sunday roast she had attempted. Well, not day... more like forty-eight hours. He knew that at these moments Martie was best left alone. In an hour or so, once she had prayed sufficiently to calm herself down, he would take over the job of consoling her from higher Hands. In the meantime, Gift decided to make an ice pack for his head and offer a small prayer of his own.

Please don't let me be concussed. A trip to the hospital at this point would not go down very well.

MK entered the lobby of the Hotel Shmotel like she owned the place. It could happen. Especially considering the way things had been going lately. Between her new celebutante friend and her Hollywood producer love interest, the possibilities seemed endless. She felt on the brink of something spectacular, and she liked the view.

The problem with walking around with one's head in the clouds, however, is that a small obstacle on the ground might easily be missed. MK did not notice Jackie de la Rey watching her from behind the reception desk.

Jackie's weather had suddenly brightened immeasurably at the sight of her mark, and now matched the glorious, sunshiny, blue-skied, beachy-keen day busy winding down outside. With her usual friendly professionalism, she marched up to MK and put on a big, deferential smile.

'Hello ma'am,' she said.

'Hi,' replied MK. 'It's you.'

'Miss Blaine asked me to come and fetch you,' said Jackie. 'She's in the retail area.'

'The retail area?'

'The hotel hosts branches of some of the higher-profile stores,' said Jackie, 'in case our guests don't feel like leaving the hotel. At the moment she's in Prada.'

'I see,' said MK, wondering if Krissie was shopping for her date tonight. Prada. Butterflies danced in her stomach. 'Which way?'

'Follow me,' said Jackie, heading towards the lifts.

'I hope,' said MK as they waited, 'that you haven't been pushing anyone around since last time.'

'Oh no,' answered Jackie. 'I must apologise again for that. I had worked a double shift that day. Not that that's any excuse.'

'No,' agreed MK.

A melodious *ding* signalled the arrival of a lift. When the doors opened, Jackie waited for MK to get in first and then followed. Jackie pressed the button marked 'Basement'. MK frowned.

'Basement?' she asked. All of a sudden the hotel woman's other hand was holding a gun, aimed right at her. MK noted randomly that the gun was very large indeed, but before she could utter a word of protest, it exploded. Pain seared through her leg and she collapsed to the floor. Rather than focusing on the fact that she had just been shot, MK's single thought was, *I've been outplayed*. 'What?' was all she managed before the world turned upside-down. Somewhere in the middle of it was the hotel girl. Grinning...

Jackie replaced the gun in the back of her skirt and bent to lift the unconscious princess. Grunting, she grabbed MK's lifeless body beneath the arms and dragged her out as the lift doors opened. Nobody was around. Excellent. She had prepared a story, of course – *too much to drink at the bar, helping her back to her car* – in case she encountered a nosy passerby. Not that it mattered. Once Jackie was gone, it wouldn't matter who found out what.

She wasn't planning on coming back.

Above ground level, Fahiem was just leaving via the staff entrance. He had put Krissie off for the night, deciding that he needed to spend an evening at home with his family. Not that Krissie had seemed especially disappointed. She was going to be dressing that Lisa girl for some big date. Part of him hoped that Krissie would then go out herself and find a new boy-toy to occupy her time – Fahiem no longer wanted the position. Any of them. Not without love.

Jackie popped into his mind just then. His unease at the way she had seemed earlier returned. It was quite worrisome. In the privacy of his own head, he admitted that he still loved her and wanted nothing more than to be with her. Well, he wouldn't complain if her temper improved and she occasionally demonstrated her affections in a manner more suited to human beings. Heck, it was his fantasy – that Jackie would become the loving, devoted wife of his dreams.

As he ambled down the street towards the taxi stop, he did not notice the scruffy Englishman following some distance behind. Lincoln Thomas didn't know whether to rejoice or cry when he finally saw the terrorist boy emerging from the hotel! He'd started to wonder whether the young Muslim had moved in there permanently. The downside was that he now had to follow him – and Link was in desperate need of a bath, a beer and a bed.

Living on the streets was tough. Link had often fancied the idea of travelling the world like this – with nothing but the shirt on his back. He'd been cured of such romanticism in the last two days, however. He had tried to use his time at the mercy of the elements to tan over the word 'gay' on his forehead, but the difference in shades had remained, only redder. His face was now obscenely sunburned. Despite his accent (clear proof that he was a tourist), passersby had been strangely reluctant to give him change. Eventually, a kindly fellow Brit had handed over a donation and Link had at least managed to eat a little and buy some water.

Still, despite all this hardship – and the lack of communication from his partner – Link felt inspiration returning at the sight of the Muslim kid. *The mission must go on.* Link was a link (if you will) in the chain that was ultimately going to nab and imprison a whole bunch of crazy, antisocial Arabs. He felt sure. He was, after all, in the service of a top-secret US governmental agency. If this kid led him to others in the network – terrorist bosses – Link would be first in line for some of the shining glory he had been denied his whole life.

He felt better already.

When Fahiem stepped into a minibus, Link hesitated for only a moment, and then followed. The kid had no idea who he was, anyway, and he couldn't lose sight of him – the Yank would have a fit. Grudgingly, he handed over most of his remaining change and squeezed in beside three other people. Goodness, they really packed them into these local taxis. The driver's eyes drifted to Link's forehead.

'All right,' he groaned. 'Move on. Just a prank by my stupid ex-girlfriend.'

The bus lurched forward and Link clung to his seat.

Let the adventure begin.

The (original) man in the island shirt was not enjoying his surveillance as much as was Lincoln Thomas. In fact he was growing more perturbed with each passing moment. He knew that Lisa was supposed to have come to Krissie Blaine's suite – she had told him she'd be stopping there before their date, and he'd overheard Krissie's side of the phone call with his listening device.

That was hours ago, and Lisa had not arrived. He'd watched anxiously as Krissie had called her repeatedly and left message after message asking where she was. The Blaine girl had evidently given up, however, and was now lying slack-jawed in front of the television. So much for the weight of NBF status.

It seemed unlikely that Lisa would stand up Krissie Blaine... well, actually that was a definite possibility. He felt quite certain that anyone with half a brain would only be able to tolerate the painful girl in small doses. And Lisa was certainly very intelligent. When Lisa had befriended Krissie, he had questioned this briefly before deciding that even very smart people got overwhelmed by celebrity. Maybe the novelty was wearing off for Lisa. But that still didn't explain why Lisa's cellphone was off.

He decided to put this – and other niggling thoughts (like this country's notorious crime rates) – out of his mind. She had not yet stood him up – their date was only in half an hour. *She must have turned her phone off to have a long bath, and to take extra care getting ready for our date.* Stepping into the shower, he daydreamed about taking Lisa home to Montana one day, to the mountains. He pictured introducing her to his parents and laughed out loud. Their faces at seeing their strapping American (white) son with an African (not white) woman. This would be worth revealing his true identity.

It struck the man that the first woman to reciprocate his interest was so different from his earlier loves. Dolly Parton and the First Lady were so... American. That was fine – if anyone adored America it was him. But it was refreshing to realise that there was a world outside the United States, one where not *everyone* wanted to kill you...

Some distance away, the woman of the American's daydreams was slowing regaining consciousness, and wondering if she had survived an attempt on her life. MK's head felt as if it were full of molasses – thick, syrupy and bitter. Her chin was touching her chest, due to the inordinate weight of her head. She was obviously sitting up. Further physical stocktaking revealed that she was in a chair – the small, plastic sort one might find in a school. Her hands were bound behind it, and when she moved – sluggishly – there was a pain in her upper thigh. On her skirt was only a small bloodstain. Evidently not a mortal wound then.

Where am I?

With considerably more effort than it should have required, she lifted her head. *Have I been drugged?* MK tried to retrace her steps as best as she could: she remembered the scene that had ended her day on the set, then arriving at the Hotel Shmotel and imagining being its owner one day... That woman. Short red hair, little up-turned nose, the slightest hint of an Afrikaans accent. The hotel person. Jackie. She'd followed her into the lift, and then she'd pulled a gun. *And fired it... I think.*

MK gazed back down at her thigh and the pathetic bloodstain. Not very dramatic. She found she was able to wiggle her leg slightly, and although there was pain, it was wholly bearable. MK would've imagined a gunshot wound to be far more painful. Maybe it was just a flesh wound.

But WHY? Granted, MK had given Jackie a hard time about Friday night's debacle, but surely that didn't warrant vengeance on this scale. MK could understand a girl's need for payback, but let the punishment fit the crime! She groaned, longing desperately for a clear head – the kind of thing you took for granted until it was gone, like good health or free parking. It was quite clear to MK that, however this situation turned out, she was once again at the heart of criminal activity, albeit as a victim. Dammit, did she just attract this drama? Why did this kind of nasty stuff always have to happen to her when all she wanted to do was con her way into international stardom?

She lifted her head again to take a look around. Bathroom (low-end). Bath full of cigarette butts (disgusting). A Barbie-doll toilet-roll dispenser with knitted dress... MK did a double-take. The doll had been disfigured. With half a head of clumpy hair, melted face and torn dress, the thing looked like something out of a horror movie. Either one where malevolent toys came to life and embarked on a grisly rampage, or one where a demented sicko defaced dolls while he planned his murders (always deliciously elaborate, stomach-churningly gruesome and loaded with clues and taunts aimed at the frustrated police). Either way, MK was suitably chilled. She never imagined her fame would come as result of being the victim of some nefarious serial killer.

With a shiver she turned away from Bloodbath Barbie. Which was when she got the *real* fright of her life. At first she thought it was a bloodied man in the doorway, which was why she screamed. A second glance revealed it to be a picture, a sizeable tapestry hanging askew. Of Jesus, apparently. It was a hideous rendering. One might have argued that this was apt, given the heinousness of the moment depicted, but MK would not have agreed. Aside from its graphic attention to detail, the handiwork was not very skilled, which transformed the piece from nerve-racking to nerve-shredding.

MK broke into a cold sweat, so scared was she that she completely failed to realise this was breaking a Superstardom law. Just then the tapestry moved. MK shrieked as the door swung open. Jackie entered and closed it behind her. MK was grateful to note that in her hands were only a cigarette and a lighter. No scalpel, saw or other device of torture.

'Look who's awake,' said Jackie without emotion. 'Her majesty.' Sarcasm dripping. She slouched past MK and sat on the edge of the bath, lighting her smoke. MK watched numbly as she sucked on that cigarette with everything she had.

'What do you want?' asked MK, determined not to show her fear. Jackie laughed wearily as though the answer was too big for MK to grasp. 'Is this because of Friday night?' Jackie smoked on silently. 'Not a great conversationalist, huh?'

'I've spent the last six years of my life talking to people,' said Jackie reflectively. 'People who want things, people complaining about things. Mostly complaining. Celebrities, politicians, people like *you*,' she spat.

'Hmm,' mumbled MK, 'I'm guessing you don't mean actresses.'

'Funny,' said Jackie, not amused. 'People don't listen anyway. They only pretend to if they think it's gonna help them get what they want. I'm sick of getting people what they want. Now, I'm gonna talk, and people are gonna start listening!'

'But you just said...' MK began, before stopping herself. Pointing out her captor's inconsistencies was probably not the best idea, she decided. 'So why am I here? And why did you shoot me?'

'Ag, man,' said Jackie impatiently, 'it was just a tranquiliser gun. Relax.'

'You shot me with a tranquiliser gun?'

'How else do you take down an animal?'

Anger flushed through MK's emotional cloud, a shot of scarlet through the murky fear. She knew she had to keep her wits about her, stay cool, if she had any hope of getting out of this alive.

'I see,' said MK evenly. 'So what happens now?'

'Ha,' said Jackie, with a snort. 'War, my girlie. War.'

Okay, thought MK, *she's prone to hyperbole. I can relate.*

'And lucky you,' continued Jackie, 'you're the spark. And if you're not careful and don't do exactly what I say when I say it, you'll also be the first casualty.'

'You've been following me,' said MK. 'Since Joburg.' The confusion on Jackie's faced seemed genuine. MK went on: 'You drugged me and did God knows what to me for a week.'

'Watch your mouth,' snapped Jackie, throwing an apologetic glance at her tapestry. She took a final drag of her cigarette and tossed it in the bathtub, running the cold water for a moment to extinguish the butt. The other butts floated around in the stream before settling on the bottom again.

'I love what you've done with the place,' said MK. She had only a second to regret this before Jackie slapped her hard across the face. Lightning flared in MK's cloud. Ooh, this bitch was going to pay. All this time she'd been battling Saartjie Williams – all for that stupid show – when what she should have been doing was trying to figure out who'd been after her. Instead of sticking her head in the Cape Town sand, fine and soft as it was. Now, here she was, at the mercy of this pleb with a bad haircut, and evidently about to become a pawn in what appeared to be some kind of political statement.

I blame sitcom, thought MK ruefully.

'Don't be cheeky,' scolded Jackie. 'You've forgotten your place, all of you. Too busy stealing ours from us.'

'Are you serious?' asked MK as gently as possible.

'Dead.'

'Wow,' said MK. What else could she say? It crossed her mind to ask Jackie if she'd ever heard of a place called Orania. She kept quiet.

'You ever heard of De la Rey?' asked Jackie pompously.

'Uh,' muttered MK, 'I've heard *about* the song but I haven't actually heard it.'

Jackie glowered.

'You mean the guy,' said MK, correcting herself. 'History was not my favourite subject. But I know a little, yes.'

'It's not history,' snarled Jackie. 'It's the future.'

'Fine,' said MK. 'How do I fit into this exactly?'

The doorbell chimed a protracted, discordant tune. It sounded like a warped version of 'Jesus Loves Me'. MK must've looked surprised because Jackie explained it to her.

'It's broken,' she mumbled. 'I might've chewed the wire or something.' Jackie stood up, suddenly anxious, and started scanning around the bathroom. MK tensed: she was not keen to experience an anxious Jackie. She watched as Jackie pulled a roll of cotton wool out of the cabinet. 'Open wide,' she whispered as she approached. The bound MK didn't have much choice, and sat helpless while Jackie forced a big chunk of it into her mouth. She gagged. 'Now,' said Jackie, 'don't make a sound. I'm going to get rid of whoever that is.' Then, just before she exited: 'I have a real gun, too.' The door closed behind her.

MK slumped. This was very, very bad. She felt tears welling, but refused to let them fall. For a woman obsessed with control, it was most upsetting to lose it. A snippet from an Oprah show flashed through her mind: the show had been about handling life-threatening situations. The expert had said – and Oprah had repeated – that if someone tried to abduct you, you should never let the perpetrator take you to the second location. And here she was, at the second location...

Bloody Oprah.

The Montana man's heart sank in tandem with the sun. Lisa was more than fifty-one minutes late. In his experience that was never a good sign. Forty to forty-five minutes could still be conceivably explained by a delay, such as traffic. Fifty minutes late without a call was rare, but it happened. Fifty-one minutes was a very, very bad sign.

His gut was sounding the alarm, and not just hunger growls. His switch into business mode was instantaneous. The agent in him berated himself for not getting more information on Lisa. He did not have an address. He knew none of her associates, except Krissie Blaine – and she had no idea where Lisa was. In fact, he didn't even know her last name. Sloppy. Stupid, careless and sloppy.

Fifty-five minutes.

Action.

Martie wore a smile that looked part apologetic, part fraught.

'I nearly killed my husband,' she moaned.

When Jackie first saw Martie on her doorstep, her first instinct was to get rid of her. But when Martie opened her mouth and said *that*, Jackie grabbed her by the arm and pulled her inside. She remembered that, at their first meeting, she'd gotten the distinct impression that Martie was a battered woman. Hell, the husband had obviously pushed her too far tonight. Jackie could not turn her away. An Afrikaans woman was, according to her fervent beliefs, at the top of the hierarchy. Besides, Jackie realised she was going to need some help now that the war had begun.

'Don't worry,' rambled Jackie, 'my mother nearly killed my father once.'

'I was just trying to make the perfect cake for our next meeting,' said Martie.

'Right,' said Jackie, not really listening.

'I feel like such a failure,' continued Martie. 'That's why I came. I'm sorry to just arrive unannounced. It's rude. But I need your help.'

'Yes,' said Jackie, tuning back in. 'That's what I'm here for. And you'll help me. That's the whole point, Annetjie.'

'Martie,' corrected Martie.

'A-hah,' nodded Jackie, stealing a concerned glance down the hallway. 'Listen to me. I know you're very new, and I wish we'd had more time to educate you, but I have a good feeling about you. I know you'll be loyal.'

'Of course.'

'It's begun,' said Jackie gravely. Martie saw an intensity in

Jackie's eyes she'd never detected before. Jackie grabbed her by the shoulders and leaned in close. 'I've taken action. It's time for you to prove yourself.'

'Oh,' said Martie, thrown. 'Well, I've been practising a lot,' she stammered, referring, of course, to baking, 'but I don't think I'm ready.'

'I have a prisoner in the bathroom,' said Jackie.

'You know how some people just have bad luck with plants,' said Martie, 'well, I think I'm like that with...' She stopped. Jackie's words sank in. *I have a prisoner in the bathroom.* 'Prisoner in the Bathroom?' asked Martie uncertainly. 'Is that some kind of dessert?' She blushed at the memory of the Asian cream pie. You never knew these days.

'The war has begun, Martie. I took a darkie prisoner, someone with friends in high places. They'll have to listen to us. Our journey out of the black darkness and into the white dawn has begun.'

Martie's face remained frozen in the curious smile she had adopted for the dessert question. Her mind ran overtime, trying to process everything Jackie had just said to her. She tried to put her finger on exactly when she had stepped out of reality and into this nightmare. Suddenly little things that her eyes had caught sight of when she'd arrived, but which hadn't computed at the time, began coming together: the tears in the couch and the eviscerated cushions (not from an excitable pet), the broken window (not from a neighbourhood child's stray cricket ball), the smell of spilled liquor... Martie allowed her eyes to dart around the room once more. New sights assailed her: the slanted coffee table with the battered, splintery surface that last time had been smooth, polished and topped by a neat doily and a vase of fresh flowers; a hammer on the floor nearby and shards of the shattered vase around it. *The war has begun*, she'd said...

'Jackie... what happened?'

'I know, it's scary,' said Jackie comfortingly. 'Nobody likes war.

But our grandchildren will thank us. And look on the bright side...'

Martie shuddered. War? Madness? The 'black darkness' and the 'white dawn'? A picture was forming for Martie, one that seemed very unlikely to have a bright side. She looked at Jackie, waiting to hear it.

'You'll never see your husband again,' smiled Jackie.

It was a clear, balmy evening in Cape Town that night.

Not that it mattered. Personal weather has little to do with the climate, and around town jet-black clouds were exploding with crashing thunder and blinding lightning.

the AD BREAK

anti-anthem

Are you tired of... great-looking hair

Are you spending a fortune on... freshness that lasts for days

Do you ever wish you could... stop bad odour

Introducing a revelation in... getting ripped off

Are you sick of... cut prices

Once-in-a-lifetime opportunity to... feel bloated and without energy

Will leave your breath smelling like... lavender

Long-lasting... trouble satisfying your partner

Feel like a new person... that kills insects on contact

Great-tasting and nutritious... stains in your toilet

Have hair that... fights greasy, built-up stains

Because you're worth... low prices, guaranteed

The future begins... with a bowl of cornflakes

Guaranteed... to be sold to people under the age of 18

Happiness is an investment... (batteries not included)

Our friendly consultants will treat you like... dirt and grime

8

Night-Owls &
Other Birds of Prey

TO SOME, THE appeal of television is as simple as having background noise. Silence can be a scary thing: an empty darkness that quickly becomes inhabited by terrifying things like thoughts. And nowadays thoughts are scarier than ever. Television is the consummate antidote to thought. All you have to do is sit back and switch off. Fill the room with the comforting glow and chatter, the dependable friend that is always there and will never do you any harm.

Mick Emmott was not television's biggest fan, having been in the business for so many years, but there were times when, like most other folks, he enjoyed nothing better than to put up his feet in front of the tube and shut down active thought. Tonight was not one of those occasions. Faced with the very real possibility that the entire production of *The Rainbow Hotel* could be shut down indefinitely, the last thing Mick wanted to do was look at a bloody TV.

After a draining three-hour negotiation with Saartjie Williams that afternoon, Mick had returned to his flat, fed the cat and wept into his pillow. He had then prepared himself a healthy but delicious dinner. Mick had been over forty when he'd taken up his first hobby – knitting. The only thing he'd managed to achieve was one exceedingly long, pink scarf, which had proved useful in two ways: it had saved MK's life the year before, and then, after a wash, had been handed over to a children's home and subdivided into smaller scarves for the coming winter (by a more skilled seamstress). They'd managed to get fifteen scarves out of it. Mick had felt unburdened, both physically and emotionally. It was a fitting end to a taxing period in his life. Since then, he had started attending cooking classes. Cooking relaxed him, and provided him with the wholesome diet his heart needed.

Now that dinner was over, Mick felt better, but still far from calm. The talk with Saartjie had gone round and round in circles and ended with an unpleasant ultimatum: Saartjie had declared that either Palesa should leave the show or she would. Either way, the whole shebang would be delayed and hence very costly. Not to mention the pressure from the broadcaster.

Mick forced himself to put it out of his mind. He was off the clock now. He picked up the book he was currently reading – the latest New Age spirit-lit that everyone was talking about – and paged to his place halfheartedly. It was not especially gripping and rarely revelatory. Essentially it was the same old stuff he'd heard a million times before, but under a catchier title. Create your own reality, etc....

In a few short hours he'd be wishing he could create his own reality – or at least undo the one he was finding himself in – but we're not there yet. Mick's eyes glazed over. Half of the damn book was made up of quotes by other people. Over the years Mick had read books about secret codes, prophecies, inner power, outer abundance, and wandered down the road less travelled with Da Vinci and others. He had explored nine insights, four agreements and seven habits to be successful. Evidently neatly numbered answers were a profitable enterprise.

A knock at the door. Either MK had lost her key or Mrs Siegl from next door was going to ask him to turn down the TV, mistaking another neighbour's for his. The man he observed through the peephole didn't look familiar.

'Yes?' called Mick through the door, simultaneously scrolling through his cellphone for the number of the police, with the practised skill of a Johannesburger.

'Hi there!' called the man in the bright singsong way only an American could. 'You don't know me, but I'm a friend of Lisa's. I need your help.'

'Lisa?' asked Mick. 'No Lisa here.'

'Yeah, I know she's not here, but I need to find her. We kinda had plans tonight and she didn't show...'

Mick clicked. He was talking about MK. *Lisa? Soon she's going to have so many personas, she'll need a phone book all of her own.* Another knock, slightly more urgent this time. Mick opened the door and smiled. The man pushed past him, inside the flat, and closed the door. Mick stumbled backwards, afraid.

'Don't worry,' said the man. 'Well, I'm worried,' he added then paused, sombre, to think for a moment. He went back to the friendly smile: 'Do you know where Lisa is?'

'Um,' said Mick. 'No. I'm Mick, by the way...'

'Yeah, Mick Emmott,' interrupted the man. 'I know. You can call me David. Do you have any idea where she could be?'

'She does her own thing,' said Mick, still trying to get on the same page. 'Sorry, but you say she stood you up. And you came here? Did she give you this address?'

'No,' said David. 'And she didn't stand me up.'

'Then how did you get this address?' asked Mick.

'I don't really have time to explain everything, Mr Emmott,

let's just say you'll discover tomorrow that your production office has been broken into.' Mick gaped. David flashed an impossibly white smile: 'But don't worry, I'm not the bad guy. We need to find Lisa.'

'Okay,' said Mick, fingering his phone. 'Why do I get the sickening feeling something is going on?' Mick stopped when David suddenly cocked his head to the side as though listening to a distant sound. Or a voice... that only he could hear.

'You should come with me, sir,' said David suddenly.

'I'd really rather not.'

'Oh come on.' Too friendly.

'No,' said Mick.

'Come on,' repeated David in a far less amiable tone, taking Mick's arm.

'She'll probably come back here,' cried Mick helplessly.

'I don't think so, sir,' said the man darkly, 'and trust me – I'm usually right about this kind of thing.'

Lincoln Thomas stuck out like a sore thumb in the middle of the Cape Flats. A very red, sore thumb. He'd first become suspicious when he'd gotten out of the taxi earlier that evening. The driver had given him a frown that seemed to suggest that Link was crazy. Fine, so it looked like a bit of a poor neighbourhood, but Link wasn't fazed. He had mates in London who lived in council blocks not unlike some of the ones he could see around here.

'Are you sure you're getting out here?' the driver asked.

'Aye,' Link muttered, hurrying to extract himself from the tin-can death-trap before Fahiem got out of sight. The driver snorted and wished him luck, although not in the sincerest of tones.

It took Link a good few minutes of walking before he realised that he appeared to be the only white (red) face around. Didn't bother him. He'd also observed that the residents all seemed to be what he'd heard South Africans call 'coloured'. They were apparently not included under 'African', speaking a different language and with a different culture entirely. It was a funny distinction to Link – back home there was no such thing as 'coloured'. Funny country, this.

None of these observations caused Link any alarm. He felt at ease among poorer people. He was one of 'em. Only reason he'd gotten this holiday was because he'd won some money on the horses, money that equated to quite a sum here. He'd gotten a few curious glances along the way, but he was starting to get used to that. Besides, he had to focus on the task at hand.

The Muslim kid had noticed Link get off at his stop, and along the way had looked back several times. Link was doing his best nonchalant not-following-you-mate impression. How convincing it was, who could say? When the kid disappeared into a small house, Link ducked around a corner and waited to make sure nobody emerged to check him out. After a few minutes, he continued on to the house. It had a low wall, which Link jumped easily. He then made his way around to the side of the house and squatted under a window, which he guessed belonged to the lounge. He heard voices.

The smell of dinner was intoxicating to the malnourished Link. Well, such important work obviously had a cost. Link settled down beneath the window and tried to be strong. Over the next hour or so, the smell of dinner, the warm evening air and the easy family chatter had lulled him into a very sleepy state. The grass underneath him was a veritable luxury compared to the concrete he'd been stuck on for the last while.

Sleep crept up on Link slowly, deliciously, secretly. By the time it showed itself, it was too late to do anything about it. Link succumbed.

Sleep wouldn't be the only thing that crept up on him that night.

'Give me your phone.'

'What for?' asked Martie, not keen to hand over her only

remaining link to the sane world outside of Jackie's Little Broken House of Horrors.

'I need to make a few calls,' said Jackie, holding out her hand.

'Where's yours, dear?' Martie tried to sound casual.

'Broken,' said Jackie. 'I used it to fix the toilet,' she added bafflingly.

'I'd love a cup of tea,' said Martie.

'*Phone.*'

Martie handed over her phone with a shrill cackle that was intended to be more of a chortle. She hoped it would either satisfy or distract Jackie enough so that Martie could edge towards the door.

'Okay,' said Jackie happily, 'let's have tea.' As though dealing with a guest at the hotel, Jackie gestured courteously towards the hallway and waited for Martie to go first. Martie nodded gratefully and headed for the corridor, praying harder than she'd ever prayed in her life. And Martie Yeni prayed a lot. A *heck* of a lot.

'The, er...' said Martie, gesturing towards the closed bathroom door.

'Prisoner,' said Jackie.

'Yes... should we make some tea for him?'

'It's a female,' said Jackie.

Dear Lord, thought Martie, *she's imprisoned her maid.*

'We should gather the other ladies,' said Jackie thoughtfully.

'No,' said Martie suddenly. The last thing they needed around here was more Crazy. Jackie frowned at her, so she softened her tone: 'Not yet. I'm here. Let's first discuss how I can help.'

'Okay,' said Jackie, switching on the kettle.

Martie noticed with mounting dread that the kitchen had not escaped whatever fury Jackie had unleashed upon the rest of the house. The remains of much crockery were scattered over the floor. The microwave lay on its side, its door agape like the mouth of a death mask. Jackie looked through the cupboard for teabags, tossing things out as she went.

'I've only got rooibos,' she said.

'Fine,' said Martie. She looked on in horror as Jackie took two used cups from the sink, gave them a cursory wipe with a filthy dishcloth, then plonked them on the table and placed a teabag in each. 'Jackie,' she began earnestly. 'You and I... we're both strong in our faith.' Jackie smiled at this, nodding. Martie was heartened as she went on: 'I think I've been sent here to help you... by...' Martie pointed skyward.

'I agree,' said Jackie.

'Good. I just think maybe the help you need is not what you think it is.' She noticed a trace of suspicion in Jackie's countenance and hurried on, 'I mean, what do you think He makes of all this?'

'It's His plan,' answered Jackie bluntly.

'You see,' said Martie, unable to ignore this blasphemy. It was simply not acceptable to assign a divine purpose to such insanity. It was flat-out wrong. 'I don't think so, my dear. A prisoner?'

'A prisoner of *war*,' emphasised Jackie.

'She probably has a family,' said Martie. 'She's probably a very nice person. Things are different these days.'

'She's a monkey, man.'

'Heavens,' gasped Martie, paling. 'She is a human being. Look, Jackie, I understand, okay, I was raised just like you, my first husband was like that too, but times have changed and we have to catch up. I'm reading a wonderful book right now by Steve Biko...'

Martie was silenced as Jackie's fist swept across the tabletop, sending the teacups flying into the wall.

'*What?*'

'Jackie...'

'Who the hell do you think you are? What the hell are you talking about? And why are you reading a book by that terrorist? Are you telling me you're some kind of darkie-loving *liberal*?' She spat out the last word as if it were a *Fear Factor* snack.

'Excuse me,' said Martie, standing. 'That's quite enough. You need to learn some respect, missy. I am married to a black man, and I won't listen to any more of this!' Martie trailed off as Jackie scampered out of the room. Just as Martie took a step towards the corridor, she reappeared with a large gun.

'You're an enemy,' said Jackie.

There was a gun on the table.

Noticing Mick's worry, David picked it up and put it in the holster he was wearing under his jacket. By the window was what looked like surveillance equipment. Mick wondered what the hell MK had gotten herself into this time.

'Please,' said David affably, 'have a seat.'

Mick sat down on the edge of the bed. David switched on a small monitor and on the screen appeared Krissie Blaine, stuffing her face with room service. Mick stared. David smiled.

'I'm not a stalker.'

'If you have to say that, I wonder...' said Mick. David laughed at this, but Mick could hear the stress in his voice. This guy obviously had it bad for MK. 'So what do we do now, secret agent man?' asked Mick.

'Who told you that?' asked the man, suddenly grim.

'I was joking,' said Mick.

'Oh,' said David before forcing a laugh. 'We wait.'

'Is that it?'

'For now, yes,' said the man, with an air of authority that was a complete sham. He wanted to do more, but without the resources he'd had at his disposal when he was officially on the job, he didn't know what else he could do. At least now he had the two most tangible links to Lisa under his watch. He began to hum.

'I know that tune,' said Mick. 'The Star-Spangled Banner?'

'Something like that,' muttered the man.

Where are you, star-spangled lady?

The lady in question had a new cellmate in the makeshift P.O.W. camp that was Jackie's bathroom. MK could not believe her eyes. It was Martie Dippenaar. Well, Martie Yeni now, she supposed. She had read the stories in the press about the marriage. How the hell she had wound up here? It was a sick cosmic joke.

MK was relieved that Jackie hadn't stuck around after tying up the unconscious Martie. She could hear her murmuring on the phone in the other room. MK tried to brace herself for the moment Martie awoke and saw her sitting there. No doubt she would find a way to blame her for this. For all MK knew, it was her fault that Martie was here. If the psychotic Jackie was waging some kind of personal vendetta against MK, maybe she was targeting people from her past. But why Martie?

Martie stirred, grimacing in discomfort.

'Hewwo,' said a nearby voice that sounded like it was talking through a mouthful of something. Martie opened her eyes. When she saw the speaker, she froze. 'Supwize,' said a young black woman Martie recognised.

'You...' gasped Martie, stunned. It was Miss Kwa Kwa: the girl who had ruined Martie's old life, and in so doing, facilitated her new one. The devious, conniving girl who'd pretended to be stupid but was really dangerously clever. The reason that several lives had been put in peril last year. Despite the fact that these events had resulted in Martie meeting Gift – and the fact that Martie was a believer that everything happened for a reason – she found she could not muster any goodwill for the troublemaker. It was a face Martie had hoped never to see again in her life, had prayed she'd never see, in fact. Now here it was, stuffed with an excess of cotton wool. 'Dear, God,' said Martie aloud. 'Give me faith.'

MK coughed; a piece of cotton had lodged in the back of her throat. Desperately, she tried to breathe through her nose. But the coughing had sucked it further back. MK panicked and started writhing in her seat.

'Wait!' cried Martie. With some effort, she stood awkwardly, the chair keeping her bent. Groaning she staggered closer to MK and stopped. Tears were streaming down the girl's cheeks. Martie looked into her eyes, considering how to respond with no free hands. 'It has to be done.' She leaned in, as though for a kiss, clenched some of the cotton wool protruding from MK's mouth between her teeth and pulled. A large clump of soggy cotton was wrenched free. Martie spat it out. With greater control of her mouth now, MK balled up and spat out the remainder. Martie clunked her chair back onto the floor and breathed heavily, apparently overcome with the trauma of having come so close to MK. MK took a few minutes to catch her breath and regain her composure.

'Thanks,' she muttered.

'Pleasure,' said Martie.

'What are you doing here?' they asked simultaneously.

'I said, what are you doing here?'

Link felt an unfriendly foot nudge his belly. He rolled over and *smell of grass* opened his eyes. Above him stood three young men that Link guessed were not members of the local scout troupe. The big giveaway was their abundance of tattoos, many of which looked like they'd been done at home. Or worse, somewhere with lots of bars, regulated activity and an excess of free time.

'Evening, lads,' said Link amiably.

'He sounds like a lekker ou larney, né?' said one of the boys. Link had no idea what this meant, but, coming from Yorkshire, he could appreciate a regional dialect.

'I think you very lost, ou pel,' said another.

'Do you boys live here?' he asked.

They shook their heads, grinning wickedly. Link stood and threw a worried glance at the window. Nobody inside appeared to have heard what was happening – yet. Link hopped the wall, over to the pavement side, keen to remove this scene from the premises of the group he was supposed to be watching. The other three followed and surrounded him.

'Now,' said Link, 'I'm here on very important business. So I think you should just keep moving.'

'Is it?' said the one with the antisocial foot – apparently the leader. He was short a few teeth, notably those in front. 'What kind of business? Nobody does business around here without our permission...'

'Ah,' said Link. Sounded like a gang thing. He wondered if they had any ties to the terrorists.

'I know what kind of business you're looking for,' spat one of the henchmen unpleasantly. 'We see lots like you, coming from overseas, looking for some fun with our girls. Or boys,' he said, poking Link's forehead.

'Oh, no,' said Link. They advanced on him menacingly. Link began to retreat. He was always up for a good rumble, but he was horribly outnumbered here.

'*Dzay!*' screeched a voice behind him. A woman was leaning out of the window Link had been napping beneath until a short while before. She waved a phone in the air. 'You get out of here now, you little bliksems! I'll call your mothers!' This apparently struck a chord with the three, who wavered only for a heartbeat before beating a hasty retreat. Link stared. The woman turned to him and spoke in a kindlier tone: 'You'd better come inside.' She pointed to the front of the house and disappeared from view.

Link found himself wandering around to the front entrance. He hadn't anticipated direct contact with these people. He was neither trained for it nor sure that the Yank would approve – his instructions had been simply to observe. But there didn't seem much choice now.

Without so much as a peep of objection, Link allowed himself to be shuffled into the house by the woman. *Into the lion's den...*

'We have to get out of here.'

'How?' asked Martie weakly.

'I don't know,' said MK, 'but there are two of us now.'

After filling each other in, MK and Martie agreed that Jackie was plainly mad and obviously dangerous. As they whispered, they heard the sounds of other women arriving and gathering in the lounge. Thus far, no one had come in to see them. No doubt too busy being subjected to the frantic rhetoric of Jackie de la Rey, which was audible from the bathroom. Martie gazed at the tapestry of Christ and shook her head sorrowfully.

'It's scary, that thing,' muttered MK.

'It reminds us that we're in greater Hands,' snipped Martie. 'Let's ask ourselves: What Would Jesus Do?'

'Or,' said MK, 'What Would MacGyver Do?' Martie clucked disapprovingly. 'Maybe we should just keep quiet until one of us has a bright idea.' MK sighed with the burden of being the only genius in the room. Not only did she have herself to worry about, but now she'd have to try to get this dim woman out. What was it about MK that seemed to attract taxing women? Martie, Jackie, Saartjie... MK recalled Friday night. Saartjie had slapped Jackie. Because Jackie had been pushing Fahiem around... why would a manager react so strongly to catching an employee with a guest?

MK's speciality in life was People. If there were a doctorate, or a Nobel Prize, or any other such recognition for this skill, few would be able to compete with MK's credentials. This was her greatest gift. But so much had happened that night. MK recalled her first, gob-smacked impression of the hotel, the dynamics between the sitcom folk, and meeting David Jones and Krissie Blaine – she may have missed some important details. With everything that had been going on, the hotel manager had not seemed a priority in MK's mind. She'd been totally forgettable. Until today, of course. MK cast her mind back to the Scene that night, and re-examined it, putting Jackie into sharp focus.

When Krissie had been gabbling eagerly to her at the bar, MK had noticed that Saartjie was leading a deer-in-headlights Fahiem in a passionate dance. *Poor kid.* Jackie had approached them and taken Fahiem to one side. After an intense exchange, Jackie had shoved him, which was when Saartjie had re-entered the fray. That's when The Moment struck MK... Just after she and Krissie had joined the others, but just before Jackie had made the remark that had gotten her slapped by Saartjie, Jackie had shot a look at Krissie. At that moment, Krissie had been pawing Fahiem like a lovesick teenager, and the look in Jackie's eyes had been... *jealousy.* And in the aftermath of the trauma, MK had not only chastised Jackie – and in so doing, allied herself with Krissie – but had made statements fluffing up her own importance. MK realised that in trying to impress Krissie she had made an impression on Jackie; an unstable element just waiting for a catalyst, who had watched her beau trot off with one of the biggest sex-objects on earth. Throw some radical political views in there, with MK claiming to be connected to the top politicos of the other side, and you had a cataclysm.

'Oh, wow,' said MK, taken aback by the revelation, and her expert unearthing of it, 'I may have an idea.'

'Usually,' said Martie, 'I'd worry, hearing that from you.' She sighed with resignation. 'But in this case, I have to hope that God is working through you, and not the devil.'

'Shut up, Martie,' said MK irritably. As loud as she could, she called out: 'Jackie! Jackie, sweetie! Can you come in here for a second, my lovey?'

The silence was only slightly less awkward than it had been when Mick had first arrived at David's hotel room several hours back. Mick was starting to get cabin fever in the tiny space. The decidedly strange David had done nothing but stare at the monitor. So far, they had observed Krissie watching television, Krissie sitting on the phone talking to her mother in the States (a longer, more banal conversation Mick had never heard in his entire life – even the odd bit of insider celeb gossip hadn't been that juicy), Krissie drinking a bottle of wine in front of the TV, Krissie picking skin from her heels in front of the TV. Still, David stared, as though willing Lisa to arrive or call.

'It's late,' said Mick pointedly.

'Yes,' replied David.

'Maybe she's gone back to the flat.'

'She would've called. Your note said it was urgent.'

Mick sighed. Initially, he hadn't been the slightest bit worried about MK, knowing her as he did. She could be *anywhere*, with *anyone*. Of course he could only argue this so far with David without revealing certain details that Mick was sure MK would rather he didn't. Then Mick remembered MK's story in Joburg about someone 'stealing' a week of her life. At the time, he had not really believed it. MK was prone to exaggeration. And outright deception if she thought you had something to offer. He wondered if the whole story hadn't simply been an excuse to come to Cape Town and have a place to stay. When shooting had begun – without incident – he'd forgotten all about it. But now he was beginning to wonder...

'We can't just sit here anymore,' declared David.

'Um, hang on a minute,' said Mick. 'I think maybe there's something I should tell you...'

Wilhelmina was the oldest member of W.I.T. An octogenarian on the verge of becoming a nonagenarian, Wilhelmina had been born in 1918, the same year as Nelson Mandela (this naturally marking the only commonality the two would ever have). Those early years of her life had been the defining era for the Afrikaner nation, and in the decades that followed, bitter dissent and wrangling had forced people to take a position. Wilhelmina's family had planted themselves on the far Right. Her formative years had been spent growing up in a toxic garden where Jan Smuts was a Brit-loving traitor to his own people. Wilhelmina had been just twenty-one when her father had joined an organisation that opposed South

Africa fighting on the side of the British in World War II, and which fervently believed that the Nazis were the way of the future.

It was some years before several of its members found greater success in the National Party, and many more unfortunate years before their ultimate downfall. Wilhelmina had been around for most of what had to be the country's darkest century; certainly its most infamous. To her mind, however, the apartheid years had been the highlight, when everything had been as it should. A sentiment Wilhelmina, and others, had passed on to subsequent generations. In this way, even as the toxic garden was torn down, bitter seeds continued to bear bitter fruit.

Jackie de la Rey had met Wilhelmina some years back, as a casual acquaintance of Wilhelmina's grandson. While her grandson had left to attend a mixed university in Johannesburg, with the kind of acceptance Wilhelmina abhorred, she had seen in Jackie potential. Wilhelmina, unlike most of these youngsters today, had seen first-hand what a bit of determined action could achieve, and had taken the lost Jackie under her wing. Over the years she had moulded the kind of young, powerful leader she was too old to become herself. Her mastery had been such that Jackie had never fully realised the extent of Wilhelmina's role in W.I.T.

As far as Jackie de la Rey knew, the whole thing was her baby. Wilhelmina differed with Jackie on certain points – Jackie's insistence that men were to be placed subservient to women, for example. That was just silly. A war needed men. But Wilhelmina knew this merely stemmed from Jackie's experience with an abusive father, and hoped that when it came to the crunch, Jackie would re-evaluate this misguided notion.

Clearly, the crunch had come. Wilhelmina had been most put out to receive a phone call from Jackie demanding her presence at her house – at such a late hour. Nevertheless, she'd come, and been updated on Jackie's latest activities. Wilhelmina disapproved of the rashness of Jackie's actions, although there was little she could do about it now. Jackie was boasting about the high profile nature of her prisoner, and ranting that her demands to the government would soon be heard by their brethren around the nation as the call it was: rise up.

Truth be told, Wilhelmina secretly hoped that the actual day of reckoning would occur only after her departure from the planet. As much as she wanted the Change to happen, she'd grown quite comfortable in her cushy retirement village. It now appeared, however, that she'd be around to watch it unfold.

As these thoughts stewed in Wilhelmina's aged but keen mind, the ladies around her chatted excitedly. Only four others had been invited – the most senior and trusted members of W.I.T. While the remaining members shared their ideology, it wasn't clear if they'd be able to take action if it came right down to it. This left the four sitting in Jackie's lounge with Wilhelmina. Studying them quietly, Wilhelmina doubted their military prowess.

At least they were heavily armed.

Down the hall, in the bathroom, Jackie sat on the edge of her tub, smoking. She blew a thick plume in Martie's face, causing her to cough.

'So what?' she barked at the black princess.

'I'm just saying,' said MK, 'that I'm very in with Krissie Blaine.'

'There's nothing she can do for you now,' snorted Jackie.

'She has a lot of money...'

'Is that what you were after?' sneered Jackie. 'Typical African.'

'No,' said MK calmly, filling her vivid imagination with pictures of bloody revenge. 'I mean, money that you can use – for your cause. Money can buy you a lot of things...'

'We have enough weapons here to blow us all the way to Table Mountain,' Jackie announced. MK ignored the bloom of fear in her gut and went on.

'Yes,' she said. 'But what are you going to do? Just go down in flames in this house? What if nothing happens after that? What if your statement doesn't wind up being big enough to spur people into action?' MK noted with satisfaction that Jackie was listening. 'Besides, wouldn't you love to stick it to Krissie Blaine?'

'What do you mean?' asked Jackie sharply.

'We've all fantasised about taking down someone like her,' said MK conspiratorially.

'Not me.' Martie, prim and self-righteous.

'Shut up,' snapped Jackie and MK in unison.

'She has everything,' continued MK, adding a touch of venom. 'She's a spoiled brat who feels entitled to take *anything she wants*.' MK saw a sparkle of agreement in Jackie's eyes, and she knew that Jackie was thinking about Fahiem. 'Even when it doesn't belong to her.'

'Ja,' said Jackie.

'So take something from her,' said MK. 'Use me.'

'What's in it for you?' asked Jackie suspiciously.

'Just let me live,' said MK. 'And her,' she added, glancing at Martie. Jackie considered this for a moment. MK hoped against hope this would work.

'It would be nice to teach her a lesson,' snarled Jackie. Confusion then swept over her face. 'But that's not part of the plan. She may be a dumb, blonde, self-obsessed bitch, but that has nothing to do with my goals...'

'I'm talking about your plan,' put in MK helpfully. 'She probably owns a private jet. And if she doesn't, she can afford one...' Jackie blinked, lost. 'Here, you're just another crank caller with a bunch of old women and some guns. But in the air, on a plane... People would have no choice but to listen.'

Jackie's jaw dropped, as did Martie's.

'What? Are you talking about some kind of nine-one-one thing?' asked Jackie, confusing the US emergency line made famous by television with the other, much-televised event. Jackie sputtered: 'You think I'm going to do something like those crazy Arabs did? Fly into something?'

'No,' said MK patiently, 'of course not. I'm just saying, you can escape and go wherever you want. And if it comes to it, you could just... you know, *threaten* to fly into something. That could be pretty persuasive.'

Martie began reciting the Lord's Prayer under her breath.

'Think about it,' said MK. 'Those terrorists got the whole world's attention. And Islam is the fastest growing religion in the world.' Jackie's eyes widened. 'Yep. Now, you could just get the attention... without actually doing any harm.' Of course MK had no intention of allowing it to go that far – she just needed to let someone know about her predicament.

'I love it,' Jackie declared with a grin. Suddenly she was up and out the door again, back into the house. MK sighed loudly. She noticed Martie staring at her with dreadful condemnation.

'Please,' said MK. 'I'm just trying to get us out of here.'

'And straight into hell,' stated Martie.

Lincoln Thomas waved farewell as he left the house of the Abdul family, accompanied by Fahiem. Having been rescued from the three thugs earlier that evening by Fahiem's mother, he'd been welcomed into their home like an old friend. Mr and Mrs Abdul had insisted he join them for dinner.

Naturally, questions arose: how had he come to be in their area? Was he lost? What was he doing here? Link thought faster in that particular half-hour than he had in the ten years before it. The tale he concocted involved a group of mates that had decided they no longer wanted anything to do with Link (this part was inspired by real-life events), but before they'd left him out in the cold, they'd played a number of mean-spirited pranks on him – the tanning thing, the eyebrows, locking him out of his hotel suite and lastly, sending him out here. The family ostensibly bought it, as the conversation moved easily on to general things.

Although the family was indeed Muslim, they were nothing like Link had imagined they would be. For starters, they dressed just like normal people. In fact, aside from the lack of alcohol at dinner, they seemed normal in every respect. They were warm, engaging and convivial. Mrs Abdul displayed a sense of humour that was at times quite earthy. The whole picture was not at all one of religious fundamentalists. Link reminded himself to be cautious, however – the man had warned him that these days, terrorists blended in and could appear quite ordinary. Frankly, Link was relieved that no booze was on offer – he needed to keep his wits about him. After some time, Link realised that out of all the social occasions he'd endured sober – and there weren't many – so far this had been the most enjoyable.

The topic of Islam came up. Link asked to know more, partly out of investigative probing and partly out of interest. Before all the madness of 9/11, Link had known little about Islam; since then, he hadn't dared ask. The Abduls answered all his questions with quiet sincerity. There seemed to be no hint of fanaticism about their faith. Link was surprised to learn that essentially their values were not too different from his own. Well, his parents', perhaps. He was absolutely shocked to learn that Islam and Christianity had shared roots – they even shared a few prophets. Link could have listened to Fahiem's parents all night. But unfortunately the lesson was interrupted by Fahiem's cellphone ringing. After a few minutes out of the room, Fahiem re-entered and announced that there was some kind of emergency situation at the Hotel, and that he would have to leave at once. To Link's relief, the Abduls insisted that Fahiem accompany him back to town.

Fahiem hated lying to his parents, which was why he told them there was an emergency at the Hotel. What he omitted to say was that a hysterical Krissie Blaine had phoned and demanded his presence in her Hotel *room*. She refused to go into details over the phone, but whatever it was... it sounded serious.

A short time before Krissie had called Fahiem, she had received a disturbing phone call of her own. About thirty seconds before that,

Mick Emmott had finished telling the American known as David about MK's 'lost week' in Johannesburg, and her suspicions that some mysterious person(s) was after her. David had listened with his characteristic frown, albeit a darker, more pronounced version.

'So,' said Mick quietly, 'do you think that could have anything to do with her disappearance?' David narrowed burning eyes at him. 'I suppose I should've mentioned it sooner, but I just thought she was overreacting. And frankly, I don't even know who you are – why would I tell you anything?'

'Fine,' said David hollowly.

'What now?' asked Mick.

They were interrupted by the tinny ring of a cellphone. Both men turned to the monitor that showed Krissie Blaine's suite.

Krissie was drifting off when her phone rang. She moaned and tried to ignore it, oblivious to the two men watching her on a monitor from a hotel only blocks away.

'Answer it!' cried Mick and David in unison. When the ringing stopped, they gasped in horror as Krissie smiled in sleepy contentment.

Britney Spears sang, grunted and groaned again as Krissie's phone started up a second time. Krissie cursed the day she'd ever chosen this damn song as her ringtone. With practised irritation, she snatched up the offending instrument as two men watched from afar with bated breath.

'Yeah?' she demanded snottily. 'Oh, hey, bitch,' she said, brightening. 'Where were you earlier? How was your date?'

'It's her,' said David under his breath.

'Can't we hear what MK's saying?' asked Mick.

'I don't have a bug on her cellphone,' snapped David before shushing him.

They watched as Krissie listened for a long moment. Over the next few minutes her sunny expression collapsed, first into disbelief, then shock, then fear.

'So I need you to arrange a jet for us,' said MK slowly into Jackie's phone. 'And meet us at the airport. You need to use your status to get into a private entrance and onto a private airstrip. And make sure you get a qualified pilot,' added MK emphatically. 'Someone who knows what he's doing. Do you understand?'

Jackie frowned suspiciously and grabbed the phone away from MK.

'And if there's any cops, somebody will get hurt,' she screamed into the phone. 'Now get a pen and write down these directions.'

MK prayed that Krissie had gotten the unsubtle hint to notify someone important, someone with the skills to take down a terrorist without any civilians getting hurt.

David and Mick watched helplessly as the frightened Krissie scrawled something down on a piece of paper, tears streaming down her cheeks.

'Fine,' she whined. 'One hour.' She ended the call, looked at her phone like it was some foreign, hostile thing, then put it down, and scanned the room with the panicked confusion of a pensioner at an arcade.

'Let's go,' ordered David, standing suddenly.

'Where?' asked Mick.

'Time to blow my cover,' said the man resignedly. 'Quickly.'

Gift paced around his lounge, frantic. Martie had left the house – badly upset – hours before, and had still not returned. Her cellphone kept going straight to voicemail. It was very unlike her, and he feared the worst: car accident, hijacking, and a plethora of uniquely urban possibilities.

Desperate to go off in his car and search for her, but compelled to remain at home in case she (*or someone official with bad news*) turned up, Gift was beside himself. Eventually he settled on writing a note explaining that he would be back shortly, with the intention of sticking it on the front door before heading out. After scrawling the message and gathering his cellphone and keys, he rushed to the front door and flung it open. He nearly fainted dead away at the sight of the man standing there on his doorstep.

'Dammit!' he yelled. 'Jeremiah!' he howled, walloping his old friend on the arm. 'What the hell are you doing here? What are you doing in Cape Town? Do you know what the time is?'

'Gift,' said the man, 'do you remember Miss Kwa Kwa?'

'*What?*' Gift reeled. Here he was, on the verge of a serious nervous attack due to his missing wife, at some ungodly hour of a Monday night, and now his ex-friend, Jeremiah, the left-wing nutjob – who had not so long ago insulted said wife by breaking one of her hand-painted plates – was on his doorstep, out of the blue, asking about a name that Gift had not heard for roughly a year (and had fervently hoped never to hear again). 'What the hell are you talking about?'

'We don't have time for all the details...'

'We don't have time for *any* of the details, Jerry!' Gift barked, pushing past him and closing the front door. 'I'm in the middle of an emergency here.'

'Well,' said Jeremiah harshly, stopping Gift's hand mid-lock, 'we're in the middle of a *crisis*. Potentially a national crisis.'

'I'm no longer in the government,' snapped Gift. 'And neither are you, in fact. So if there is a national crisis, let the authorities deal with it. I have to go and find my wife.'

'Is your wife a member of an organisation called W.I.T.?' asked Jeremiah.

Gift stopped dead at this.

'Yes,' he muttered, 'but I'd hardly call them an organisation. They bake cakes and stuff. How do you know this? Have you and *your* organisation been spying on us?'

'The police received a call earlier tonight from someone calling herself the leader of W.I.T., Jackie de la Rey...' Jeremiah raised an eyebrow here, but Gift only stared at him as if he were insane. 'Our sources informed us of it. Apparently she wanted the message given to someone in government, but of course it's after hours.' Gift shook his head, as though he were not keeping up. 'She is claiming to have a political prisoner – Miss Kwa Kwa...'

'Why,' snarled Gift, 'would some tea-and-cookies housewife club have a political prisoner? And Miss Kwa Kwa? Is this some kind of practical joke? Because it's not funny!'

'It's no joke,' said Jeremiah. 'We suspect your wife is with them.'

Gift's mouth opened but nothing came out. He stood, frozen, as all of this information rocketed around his brain. It was certainly conceivable that Martie, feeling a failure as a wife, could've turned to her fellow members for support. It was a good lead. As for all this other malarkey, it sounded like typical Jeremiah – left-wing paranoia. How he had come to be here, and how he knew anything at all about Martie's club, were considerations better left alone for the time being, disturbing as they were. Resolving to get more answers later, Gift headed for his car.

'Where are you going?' asked Jeremiah, following him.

'To find my wife,' barked Gift.

'You're not going to the W.I.T. house, are you? It's not safe.'

'If your little story is true,' said Gift, 'there should be police crawling all over the place. I'll be perfectly safe.' Shaking his head incredulously, Gift unlocked his car. With one deft move, Jeremiah grabbed the car keys.

'I'll drive,' he said threateningly.

Gift threw his hands up and went round to the passenger side.

'No one is there yet,' said Jeremiah solemnly, once they were inside the vehicle. 'The police are treating it as a crank call. They won't contact anyone from government, and haven't sent anyone to investigate.'

Gift shook his head, too irate to speak. Jeremiah started the car, and Gift hoped that they were indeed headed to Jackie's house, where he was sure he would find Martie trying to perfect a milk tart under the patient eye of her club's chairlady. There'd be no drama, no hostage situation, and everything would be just fine.

Hope does spring eternal.

While Krissie waited for Fahiem to arrive, she calmed herself with one of her mother's 'calm pills', which she washed down with the last of the wine in the bottle she'd opened earlier in the evening.

The knock at the door was a relief. Krissie hurried to answer it and end the awful solitude she'd been weathering since Lisa's terrifying call. Sweet, eager-to-please Fahiem would go to the airport for her, and sort all of this out. And as soon as he was gone, Krissie would take another pill and sleep the sleep of the oblivious. She was too rich for this kind of trauma.

She wrenched the door open without checking who was there, and was badly startled when a tall, muscular man in a freaky shirt barged in, followed by a nervous-looking pudgy guy.

'Miss Blaine,' said the tall one sternly, as he closed the door, 'please don't panic. I'm with the government.' He frowned slightly, then added, 'The US government.'

'Oh my God,' she exclaimed, 'an American!' She flung her arms around him, sobbing. As gently as possible he forced her away and spoke into her eyes.

'We're aware of the situation,' he said. He and Mick had lingered at the surveillance monitor after the call from MK and listened in on Krissie's call to Fahiem, thus filling in the blanks for themsleves. 'And we're coming with you to the airport. Everything is under control now.'

'No, no,' she murmured, 'I can't go to the airport. What if something happens to me? I'm very rich and very famous and my folks have been warning me my whole life about becoming another Patty Hearse.'

'Hearst,' corrected Mick.

'Miss Blaine,' said David, 'I'll be with you the whole time. Meet your new pilot.'

'Him?' asked Krissie doubtfully, glancing at Mick, 'he doesn't look like a pilot. He looks like... what do you call those people who make sausages?' Mick huffed, indignant.

'No, ma'am,' David interjected, 'I'll be your pilot.'

'Can you fly?'

'Yes,' he said, 'but hopefully it won't get that far. Let's go.'

'Wait,' she said, 'my boyfriend's coming.'

The man reflected for a second: although his first impulse had been to ignore the boy, it occurred to him that the boy's presumed terrorism skills could come in handy. Also, he would hopefully be followed by the Brit. The man wasn't sure how he felt about this, but supposed every extra body could prove helpful.

'You can call him on the way,' he said. 'Tell him to meet us at the airport.'

'Get up,' said Jackie, training a handgun on MK. 'We have a flight to catch.'

MK stood, grimacing at the pain in her body from having been in a seated position for so long.

'You too,' said Jackie, pointing her weapon at Martie.

'Me?'

'Yes.'

The door opened and Wilhelmina peered inside.

'Jackie,' she said, 'can I talk to you for a moment, please?'

'No,' replied Jackie flatly. 'No time.'

'Are you sure this is wise?' asked the old woman. 'It sounds very risky. At least here, nobody knows where you are, dear.'

'We can't just sit here forever! Is everybody ready to go?'

'We're not going with,' said Wilhelmina firmly.

'Yes, you are!'

The old woman just shook her head, as though informing a

petulant child that there would be no more sweets.

'We've been talking,' she said, 'and we've agreed that this is not the best course of action. It's been suggested that we reassess...' Jackie stared at her with a blend of incredulity and rage. Wilhelmina smiled serenely.

'I agree,' Martie chipped in hopefully.

'You don't make those decisions!' shouted Jackie at Wilhelmina. 'I am the leader and we will do what I bloody say! You'd love to be running the show, wouldn't you, you old bag? But you're not. Now get out there and tell those cows to get hoofing – we have new pastures to secure!'

Wilhelmina said nothing for a moment, then nodded slowly.

'As you wish,' she said, and disappeared.

'Maybe you should just hear them out,' said Martie.

'Shut up,' grunted Jackie as she loaded up her tranquiliser gun.

'What's that for?' asked MK, alarmed. 'You can't tranquilise me. I'll be a dead weight, and then what? You'll have to carry me.'

'Just in case.'

Jackie bent before her tapestry and muttered a few unintelligible words to it. Martie shook her head sadly. MK considered kicking Jackie but quickly thought better of it. Then what? They waited as Jackie finished her prayer and removed the tapestry from the hook. She began rolling it up.

'He's coming with us,' she said reverently. 'Move.'

Jackie backtracked carefully out of the bathroom and down the corridor towards the front of the house, keeping her two followers at gunpoint the whole way. When they reached the lounge, she barked an order.

'Okay, the prisoners come with me. I'll need a driver.' Jackie noticed the surprised faces of her prisoners, staring into the lounge behind her.

Jackie spun around and saw that the room was empty. The front door stood open. They had left. Fled like cowards. Fury welled up in her like searing lava. Her gun went crashing into the glass of her (once prized) cabinet. She swore and kicked the coffee table.

'Maybe they're waiting in the car,' offered Martie. MK had to stifle laughter.

'Bitches,' ranted Jackie. 'Hell is full of the cowardly whores of Satan.'

'Goodness,' muttered Martie, flustered.

'You're driving, auntie,' said Jackie, grabbing Martie by the arm.

'But,' blathered Martie, 'maybe this is a sign, Jackie.'

'The plan goes forward,' Jackie declared. 'Get moving.'

9

In-Flight Viewing

'OKAY, ALL CLEAR,' said David, giving Krissie a thumbs-up. A chill had crept into the air as Monday night gradually gave way to the wee hours of Tuesday morning, and Krissie shivered. She might have been surprised at the speed and ease with which they'd managed to secure a jet – and a private hangar with its own airstrip – but Krissie was accustomed to getting her way. She expected nothing less. Leaving the details to the two guys, she'd assumed her celebrity was what had clinched the deal. In fact, the request had been met with more resistance than she realised – until Mick had suggested that David attempt a bribe. This had worked like a charm, and now the three stood outside the hangar, waiting.

'What do you need me to do?' asked Mick.

'Nothing,' said the man, adjusting the shirt of the pilot's uniform he had just put on. 'Your job is done. You can go.'

'I'm not going anywhere,' replied Mick hotly. 'Not until MK is safe.'

'Who's MK?'

'Uh, Lisa. She's my best friend. I'm not going anywhere until I know she's okay.'

'Fine,' sighed David. 'Just hang back, out of sight.'

Mick moved over to Krissie, who was sitting on the ground watching the planes in the distance. She looked sleepy. Very sleepy.

'Are you all right?'

'Oh, yeah,' she said placidly. 'Whaduzzacappnsay?'

It took Mick a moment to decipher this: *What does the captain say?*

'He's going to check out the cockpit and get his bearings.' Krissie giggled at the word 'cockpit'. Mick, the father of a son who was quite fond of marijuana, squatted down and looked at her closely. 'Have you been smoking grass?'

'Izzat like pot?' she asked. He nodded. 'Oh, yeah've ya got some?'

'No,' he said. 'Have you had some already?'

'No,' said Krissie. 'Jussome wine anna pill.'

'What kind of a pill?'

'It's fine, mymom takesem allatime.'

'Oh God.' He stood back up and hurried towards the plane to inform the captain of the latest development. He was stopped in his tracks by the sound of Krissie's phone ringing.

'Fuckin' Britney Spears,' she mumbled, before answering the call. Mick held his breath. 'Hi, bay-beeeee,' she sang. 'Wheraryoo?'

Mick rushed onto the jet as fast as he could to call David.

A few minutes later, David came rushing out, followed at a distance by the panting Mick. Krissie was still on the phone.

'Oh, hang on,' she said, 'talk totha cappn.' She handed the phone to David. 'It's Frank. He wantsta know howda ged here.' David explained to Fahiem how to access the hangar. Mick took Krissie by the arms and pulled her up.

'Let's get you some water.'

'Omigod, my head jus todally wennaround wenyadid that.'

With very little help from Krissie, Mick dragged her towards the steps of the plane and sat her down on one of them. Better to get her closer now, in case she passed out in the next few minutes. David continued talking on the phone.

'Are you with an English guy?' he asked. 'Put him on... I'm psychic, just put him on, okay?'

'You drive like an old woman,' said MK. Martie threw her a miffed sideways glance. MK sat in the passenger seat.

'That's fine,' snapped Jackie from the back seat. 'We don't want to attract any attention. Besides, I don't want to get there too early.'

'I spy with my little eye...' said MK.

'Shut up!'

'Fine,' said MK peaceably, 'just trying to put some mental fun into fundamental.' She glanced in the rear-view mirror to see Jackie's bemused frown. She obviously didn't get it. 'Have you ever been in love, Jackie?'

'She told you to keep quiet,' said Martie primly.

'Love is for people who have nothing better to do,' replied Jackie shortly.

'I don't agree,' said Martie after some thought. 'Love is the reason why we're here. It changes your life.'

'Like it changed yours?' sneered Jackie. 'With your black husband.'

'Love,' said Martie, a trifle upset, 'is a wonderful thing. It makes you strive to be a better person. And these days, we need more of it. What's wrong with finding happiness in a world that's often so trying and dark?'

'Please shoot her with the tranquiliser gun,' MK begged Jackie. To her surprise, Jackie laughed. MK wasn't sure how she felt about that. The thought that they could agree on anything was disturbing. 'Martie, you're just saying that because you've been raised to find a man. It's your life's goal.'

'You know nothing about me!' cried Martie, wounded.

'That's enough!' Jackie slammed her free hand into the seat. 'Silence.'

Silence was all that greeted Gift and Jeremiah when they entered the deserted home of Jackie de la Rey. Gift noticed with alarm that Jeremiah had produced a gun. This alarm intensified when he saw the extensive cache of weapons piled in the middle of the lounge. Also the placed looked... vandalised. Or like some kind of violent scuffle had taken place there. Gift's heart sank. He looked up to see Jeremiah returning from the back of the house.

'Empty,' he declared. 'But it definitely looks like something went down here. You should see the bathroom.'

'Well, where have they gone?' asked Gift.

'Gift,' said Jeremiah, frowning, 'how could they have known anything about Miss Kwa Kwa? What was she doing in Cape Town?'

'I didn't even know she was in Cape Town. We don't keep in touch.'

'You know she was photographed on the town with Krissie Blaine...'

'Yes,' Gift admitted grudgingly, 'I kept the papers away from Martie.'

'What if Martie knew?' Jeremiah raised a suspicious eyebrow.

'What if she did?' demanded Gift.

'She could've alerted this group to her.'

'I don't know what you're implying, Jerry,' growled Gift, 'but my wife had no idea that Miss bloody Kwa Kwa was in town, and she is certainly not involved in whatever madness is going on here!' All the fire went out of Gift when he spotted Martie's purse on the floor near the couch. Numbly he walked over and picked it up.

'That's hers,' guessed Jeremiah, not asking.

'Yes,' said Gift. 'I think she could be in terrible trouble.' He glanced at the skeptical look on Jeremiah's face, and glowered dangerously. Jeremiah waved a hand of surrender in the air, opting to keep quiet. 'We have to find them,' said Gift.

'We agree on that much,' sighed Jeremiah.

'Martie's car isn't outside,' said Gift, 'so either they've taken that or it's been stolen...' He rifled through Martie's purse but came up empty-handed. 'The keys aren't in here...'

'We'll have to wait for further communication from them.'

'No,' answered Gift. 'The car is fitted with a tracking device. If the cops won't do anything, maybe the tracker will. But we'll call the police anyway. Maybe these weapons will prompt them into some kind of action.'

'I don't think we should call the police,' said Jeremiah. 'If we involve the authorities it could interfere with our investigation of these people.'

'Your investigation?' asked Gift sarcastically. 'You mean you don't want the government interfering in your activities, which are probably just as fanatical and illegal as this!'

'Nonsense,' replied Jeremiah. 'We want South Africa to belong to South Africans, that's all.'

'Right,' sneered Gift. 'It already does. But if you had your way, all the whites would be driven out! Including my wife.'

'Don't be silly,' laughed Jeremiah. 'We're not forcing them out. We just want to encourage them to see that it would be better for them to leave – of their own free will. Look at what these people are doing. We can't just do nothing.'

'Whatever,' snapped Gift, not keen to get into the details. 'We don't have time for a political argument. I'm calling the tracker company.' Gift hurried out the front door. Jeremiah followed. Gift got into the driver's seat as he reported his wife's missing car. Jeremiah grimaced, knowing that the authorities would soon become involved. For now, he would have to be a passenger – he needed to get hold of the De la Rey woman, and Gift was his only link at this point.

But if Jeremiah got hold of her first, well, then he'd see...

When Jackie saw Krissie in Fahiem's arms her blood boiled to temperatures hitherto unattained. They stood on the tarmac outside a large hangar, near the jet that was presumably now Jackie's. She ordered Martie to pull over to the side of the service road. With a quick, furtive look in all directions for concealed security personnel, Jackie stuck her rifle between the two front seats meaningfully.

'Remember,' she urged, 'casual, calm. If you scream or run, or even just walk in a way I don't like, everybody goes down in a hail of bullets.'

'Okay,' whimpered a fraught Martie.

'Come on, Martie,' said MK encouragingly. 'You must have some acting ability – you were married to Pieter Dippenaar for so many years.'

'Move,' said Jackie.

They got out of the car, and waited as Jackie concealed her rifle beneath a large coat. In a shoulder holster she carried a smaller handgun, and her pockets were filled with grenades, all of which she'd hurriedly collected before leaving the house. It had seemed a moment of such finality that Martie trembled just thinking about it.

Jackie kept the rifle under her coat and armed her free hand with the handgun, which she kept trained on the other two as she followed behind them. They walked over to the hangar amidst the thunderous sounds of the airport. MK noted with shock that behind Fahiem and Krissie stood Mick. What the hell was he doing here? How had he even come into contact with any of these people? Well, the board was certainly peopled with an interesting assortment of players. How the game played out remained to be seen. Mick smiled at her weakly. She threw him a helpless look in response. As unfortunate as it was for him, MK felt heartened at having someone she cared about present. With a jarring jolt, MK realised she loved Mick. He was her only true friend, and the only person she had actually loved since her parents died all those years ago.

Urgh, she thought, *of all the times to be having an emotional breakthrough. I suppose confronting your mortality will do that to you.*

Superstardom Lesson No. 53: Superstardom comes at a price. Some people will want to take you down. And one of the best defences against this is a true friend. And maybe a team of bodyguards.

When they neared the others, Jackie pushed ahead and pointed her weapon at the two lovers, who flew apart. For a heart-stopping moment MK thought she would open fire. Instead she did so verbally.

'You!' she hissed at Fahiem. 'What is he doing here?'

'Jackie,' he shouted, 'what are you doing?'

'You can join us,' she replied. 'I've got a black – a coloured will really help make my point. And if I need to eliminate a hostage, I'll have one extra.'

Krissie wailed and Mick put his arm around her. Jackie turned to him. 'Who are you?' Mick stammered. 'Answer me, fatty!'

'That's Krissie's personal stylist,' put in MK quickly.

'He looks the type,' grunted Jackie. Mick looked offended but kept quiet. 'Let's get going. We need to go, now. Where's the pilot?'

'He's on the plane already,' replied Mick. 'He doesn't know anything.'

'He'd better not,' warned Jackie. She then pointed the gun at MK, Krissie and Fahiem. 'You three, come.' She glanced at Martie and Mick. 'You two, help me secure these others. Move.'

Jackie hustled the five ahead of her onto the aeroplane steps. As Martie reached the entrance to the aircraft, a figure lunged out at her. She screamed as he pinned her against the rail. A deafening shot rang out, and the attacker yelled in pain. MK saw that Jackie had fired the tranquiliser gun into his backside. He stumbled a few steps then flopped down into the plane.

'Bring him down here,' screeched Jackie, 'now!'

Mick and Fahiem snapped to attention and dragged the groaning perpetrator down the steps onto the tarmac below.

'She shot him!' cried Krissie.

'It's just a tranquiliser gun,' said MK quietly. 'He'll be fine.'

'You shits!' shouted Jackie. She glared down at the sunburned man at her feet. 'Hell, where are his eyebrows?' She studied the word on his forehead with distaste. 'Whose idea was this?' Nobody answered. Jackie cocked her handgun and trained it at Link's head.

'Mine,' said Mick quickly.

'Any more surprises?' Jackie demanded. The others shook their heads.

'Omigod,' cried Krissie wretchedly, 'now whaddarwe gonna do?' Jackie smiled triumphantly at this. The sunburned assailant had to be the extent of their grand plan – this bimbo wasn't that good an actress.

MK's heart sank. This couldn't be it. Where were the snipers? The police? Anybody capable of bringing this twisted nightmare to an end? Obviously, the unconscious twit lying on the ground was meant to have tackled Jackie, not Martie, but surely that couldn't be the only plan these people had made. Please.

'Martie,' barked Jackie, 'you and the moffie are staying here.' She gestured with her gun for Mick and Martie to get away from the plane and join the prostrate Link. They did so quickly. 'Now, you two make sure the people get on their headphones and listen when I start talking from the plane.' MK felt hope circling the bowl... until the pilot appeared in the doorway. It was David.

What the hell...?

'What's going on here?' he asked.

'Who else is on that plane?' shouted Jackie.

'No one,' he said, raising his hands at the sight of her armour.

Jackie rushed the steps. Grabbing Krissie by the hair along the way.

'Jackie,' called Fahiem. 'Don't do this!'

Before anything else could be said, however, Jackie had herded the happy couple, the black princess and the pilot onto the plane. From the ground, Mick and Martie watched powerlessly as the door was closed. Martie's hands flew to her lips, and Mick put his arms around her protectively. The situation had now, quite literally, reached another level, and was entirely out of their hands.

Once the door was securely closed, Jackie used the deadly end of her pistol to compel her travelling companions into seats, with the exception of Krissie. Keeping her at gunpoint, Jackie dragged the heiress through the cabin and forced her to check every conceivable space so that she could reassure herself that there were indeed no more hidden parties. Satisfied, Jackie then ordered MK to tie up Krissie and Fahiem while she watched. Next, the pilot was ordered to restrain MK.

He tied her hands behind her back and waited while Jackie inspected his handiwork. When Jackie nodded her approval, he helped MK back into her seat with her hands behind her. As she plonked down, he winked at her once. MK's face registered no reaction, although inwardly she felt a flicker of hope ignite. She hoped it was not like the Joburg blackouts, where the return of lights didn't guarantee that they'd stay on.

'Now,' said Jackie, 'you people behave yourselves. Make conversation. The captain and I will be preparing for takeoff. If I hear anything I don't like, I'll shoot him, and we'll all go down faster than you can say 'De la Rey'. Got it?' Sombre nods all round. Jackie let David go first and followed after him, gun to the back of his head.

'We seriously outnumber her,' said Fahiem quietly when the cockpit door closed. 'Let's do something.'

'Don't be stupid,' hissed MK. 'She's armed to the teeth. Do you know what a bullet can do when it's fired inside an aeroplane?' Fahiem shook his head. 'Well, me neither,' she said, 'but I gather it's not good.'

'My father told me not to come to South Africa,' moaned Krissie.

'Oh, please,' snapped MK, 'like this could never happen in the US.'

'She's upset,' said Fahiem, defending her gallantly.

'We're all upset,' MK pointed out. 'But we need to stay calm if we're going to make it out of here in one piece.'

'You're so brave,' sobbed Krissie pathetically.

'Shhh,' cooed MK, trying to sound soothing, 'I need to think.'

By the time Gift and Jeremiah reached the hangar, the plane was already ascending into the night sky like a giant bullet, flying in slow motion towards the blackness and some unknown target beyond.

Gift had pressed the tracking company to give him the car's location, even citing his position in the government (not that it was active at this time, but they didn't need to know that). Once the operator had revealed the location of Martie's car, she had informed him that a chopper could not be sent into the airspace of the airport, but assured him that ground staff had been notified, as well as the police.

As Gift drove around the maze of the airport structure, scanning for Martie's car, his cellphone sounded and, although he didn't recognise the number, he answered at once. Relief and gratitude flooded through him at the sound of Martie's voice. Close to hysteria, she handed the phone over to a male voice that directed them to the private airstrip nearby. Screeching to a halt at the sight of his apparently unharmed wife, Gift fled the car and raced into her arms. Jeremiah followed.

After several minutes where Gift inquired after his darling fat-cakes, and inspected her body for visual confirmation that she was unharmed, Martie turned and noticed Jeremiah standing there.

'What are *you* doing here?' she shrieked shrilly. 'I don't have any plates for you to break! And I've already spent the whole night dealing with one political pitbull – I don't need to deal with another!' Gift took her flapping hands in his own.

'It's all right, dear,' he said, 'Jerry sort of helped me find you.'

'Where's your partner?' asked Jeremiah abrasively, glaring at the stunned Martie. 'Jackie de la Rey. Where is she?'

Martie's lower lip quavered and the others thought she would certainly burst into tears. Instead she punched Jeremiah with all the strength she could muster, which wasn't much, but the gesture was adequately effective. Jeremiah staggered backwards, helpless fingers pawing at his nose, which had started gushing bright blood. Gift laughed. He couldn't contain it.

'Gift,' said the guy who'd been standing next to Martie when they arrived, 'that head-case has hijacked that plane. There are four innocent people onboard. You have to do something. She wants to speak to someone in government.'

'Uh,' said Gift, taking a moment to recognise the man from the good old days – and one particular fateful night – of Studio 94. The name came back to him. 'Mick? What are you doing here?'

'Long story,' said Mick. 'We need to act. Now.'

'I'm retired from politics,' said Gift reluctantly. 'Who is this?' he asked, pointing at the unconscious Link.

'I actually don't know,' answered Mick. 'He knows the American guy.'

'American guy?'

'I think he's some kind of secret agent. I know that sounds crazy.'

'Not much could surprise me at this point,' muttered Gift.

'We have to help Miss Kwa Kwa and the others,' pleaded Martie.

'Miss Kwa Kwa?' asked Gift, who had clearly underestimated his capacity for surprise. 'What the hell is she doing mixed up in this mess? She's probably the cause of it, if her past adventures are anything to go by.'

'No,' said Martie gravely. 'She's a victim.'

'I got the impression from that young woman,' said Gift, 'that she's the last person who'd ever be the victim of anything.'

Onboard the night flight that as yet had no destination – and certainly not a happy one – MK worked the knot around her wrists. To her surprise it took only a moment of wriggling to free her hands. Obviously her new love interest, David (if that was his name), had a few nifty tricks up his sleeve. Krissie was clearly very out of it, so all MK had been able to get out of her was that he had pitched up at her hotel door – as if from nowhere – at exactly the right moment. She also said he worked for the US government, which would explain the false knot he had tied around MK's wrists. MK felt momentarily betrayed at the way he had misled her. In some cruel way, it seemed typical that she would meet a man who proclaimed to be a Hollywood producer but then turned out to be some kind of law enforcer type. Typical.

She gazed around the luxurious interior of the cabin. It was gorgeous. And again, just so unbelievably typical that her first voyage on such a spectacular vehicle of opulence should be under these filthy conditions. Keeping her hands behind her back, MK looked at the other two. Krissie's head lolled about like a bladder on a stick; beside her Fahiem kept bumping her.

'Stay awake,' he urged worriedly. 'Stay awake.' Krissie groaned irritably, her eyelids batting with all the energy of a butterfly in mud.

'She's probably used to it,' said MK with a sigh.

'What if she passes out?' he asked.

'It wouldn't be the first time.'

'What are we going to do?' asked Fahiem disconsolately.

'Stay calm, Frank,' she replied. 'This isn't the first time I've survived a homicidal maniac. Apparently, it's a calling.' She ignored the confusion on his face and returned her considerable mental prowess to coming up with a solution. Ever since they had taken off, she'd been feeling peculiar. It was an unsettling feeling, much like the way she had felt on the beach – only more potent this time. Trying to push it aside, she forced herself to think.

In the cockpit, Jackie racked her own, less remarkable brain. Now that they were airborne, the holes in her plan were becoming plainly apparent, and were widening until only tenuous, stringy bits of a plan remained. Ever since those spineless bitches had deserted her, she had been moving on autopilot (as it were), in full fight-or-flight mode. Well, they were now in flight – as for the fight... time would tell.

To make matters more taxing, ground control had begun radioing the pilot, but each time they did, Jackie ordered him to ignore them. She wasn't quite sure what to demand yet. As requested, the authorities were now ready to hear Jackie de la Rey... but she hadn't the faintest idea what to say.

'Where am I going, ma'am?' asked the pilot.

'Just... fly around. Shut up.' He nodded agreeably.

Jackie was beginning to experience an emotion very familiar to one who has been raised under the threat of fire and brimstone. Shame. She felt humiliated. This was not how things were supposed to go. This was ineptitude. This was the way the bloody Africans did things. She had lost her cool. She had lost her head, and was now suffering the consequences. All because of that stupid American slut, because she couldn't keep her manicured little claws out of... South African things she had no business meddling with.

Jackie seethed.

In the cabin, MK tried to decide if she should get up and take a look around for anything that could prove useful. If Jackie emerged and saw that she was out of her seat – with free hands – everything could go very pear-shaped. In a brief but bizarre sidebar thought, MK wondered if there wasn't some other, more violently shaped fruit that would do that expression more justice. As quickly as it had appeared, the thought was gone, and MK was back at possibly the most important decision she'd ever make. Time was of the essence here. Every moment she waited only increased the chances that Jackie de la Wreck would come bursting forth, eyes – and guns – ablaze.

She felt cold sweat on her forehead, cooled by the overhead fan. Her palms were soaked and her hands felt a desperate need to fly free and *do something*, but MK kept them firmly behind her. Her breathing had deepened. It felt as if she needed big gulps of air to keep herself steady. Her foot tapped rapidly on the floor. There was never to going to be a Right Moment, whatever that was. She needed to move.

The private hangar had lost whatever privacy it may once have had: it was now crawling with police and airport officials. Gift, Martie, Mick and Jeremiah had been escorted into a control tower, where they watched silently as the controller tried repeatedly to make contact with the errant jet – to no avail. Every now and then they would see it pass overheard. It appeared to be flying aimlessly around in large circles.

'Where's the British guy?' asked Mick.

'Hospital,' replied Gift.

'Gift,' said Jeremiah thickly, nursing his swollen nose. 'When she finally agrees to talk, you're going to answer. Play the politician, if you can remember how.'

'What do I say?' asked Gift.

'Whatever it takes to get them down from there,' said Mick.

'Don't make any promises,' Jeremiah put in. 'We don't negotiate with terrorists.'

'Oh, please,' said Mick, 'you've been watching too much television. Who are you anyway? I didn't get your name.' Jeremiah scowled at him malevolently.

'This is Jerry,' said Gift. 'He seems to know your friend.'

'What do you know about MK?'

'That's none of your business, whitey.'

'Did you have something to do with her disappearance?' asked Mick suddenly. Jeremiah looked genuinely surprised. 'In Joburg. For a week...'

'Eish,' grunted Jeremiah. 'That's not good.'

'What are you talking about?' demanded Mick. Jeremiah resolutely ignored the question. Gift turned to Jeremiah with a fed-up huff.

'Jerry,' he said, 'start talking. This is no time for secrets.' Jeremiah resisted, glowering at Mick. He sighed and turned away, but Gift took him firmly by the arm and spoke in fiercely emphatic tones: 'We need to know *everything*...' Jeremiah sighed again but looked like he might buckle.

'I wonder what's going on on that plane...' whispered Martie, gazing out at the lights sailing through the night sky. There followed a moment of awful silence as everybody considered this, then Gift turned back to Jeremiah with an expectant look.

The cockpit door flew open, and a rifle appeared. Jackie stood there, as if she'd been expecting to be ambushed. She stepped into the cabin, content to note that the three prisoners were still in their seats.

MK recovered from the biggest fright of her life: she had just been about to stand up when Jackie had reappeared. Thank God she hadn't. Next concern: not to let Jackie discover that her hands were free. But Jackie didn't seem very interested in her. Instead, she approached Fahiem and Krissie. Krissie's head lay on Fahiem's shoulder. She was out cold, drool pooling at the corner of her slack jaw. She felt something poke into her forehead and opened her eyes to the horrific picture of a rifle pointing at her head. Only a small sigh escaped her lips.

Jackie grinned and sat down on the seat facing the other two.

'Hi, lovebirds.'

'H-hi,' stammered Krissie.

'Jackie, please...' began Fahiem.

'I've made a very important decision,' said Jackie, cutting him off. 'I'm going to go back in there and make a statement on the radio...' The way she trailed off smacked of an implied finality that made MK's skin crawl. Jackie stood and picked up her rolled-up tapestry. Once she had found something to hang it on, she attached it and let the giant work unroll. Krissie gasped.

'What is that?' she asked.

'It's my answer,' said Jackie. With a final haunting smile she made her way back into the cockpit and closed the door behind her.

'It looks like a poster for *Saw* or something,' said Krissie in horror.

MK jumped to her feet and brought her finger to her lips. Krissie and Fahiem stared, dumbstruck, but kept quiet. MK went straight to the overhead compartment at the front of the cabin, where she had seen medical supplies earlier. Carefully she pulled down the defibrillator machine. She wondered what the shock of it would do to someone not suffering cardiac arrest. Next she moved on to Krissie's Louis Vuitton bag. She emptied its contents onto the floor.

'What are you doing?' hissed a frightened Fahiem. 'If she catches you, we'll be in huge trouble.'

'You moron,' muttered MK. 'She's planning to kill us all. Didn't you get that when she was just here? She pointed to that thing and called it her answer. She's going to make her political statement and then martyr herself. And that means us too. I thought she was too self-absorbed to do something like that, but obviously I was wrong. She's crazier than I thought.'

'What do you mean, martyr herself? What would that achieve?'

'I think she's hoping it will inspire people.'

'Why would it do that?'

'Historically, martyrdom is an effective means of popularising a point,' rambled MK. Then, glancing at the tapestry: 'Or haven't you heard of Jesus?'

'That's Jesus?' asked Krissie. 'Oh my God.'

'Indeed,' said MK. She pulled a small pill bottle from the contents of Krissie's purse. 'What are these?'

'Oh, sleeping pills. I had one or two earlier,' she added guiltily. 'But I'm feeling quite sober right now. Oh, hey,' she exclaimed happily, pointing at the perfume bottle near MK. It looked like a grenade. 'That's Terror by Tommy Gofigure.'

'Really,' said MK irritably. 'I don't much feel like talking about fragrances right now, Krissie.'

'No, no,' said Krissie, 'it's this new, big thing in the States. If you slip it in someone's drink, it'll knock them out. Or if you spray it in their eyes, it's like pepper spray. Some people back home are freaking out about it, and trying to get it taken off the market, but...'

'Fine, got it,' said MK, pocketing the bottle. 'Krissie, listen carefully, I've been thinking about something, but I'm going to need your help. You're going to have to be brave...'

'I'm listening,' said Krissie. For once she meant it.

'We saw Miss Kwa Kwa on that TV show she did,' said Jeremiah.

'*Kwa Kwa Konfidential?*' asked Mick. 'You saw that?'

'Anyway,' continued Jeremiah, ignoring Mick and focusing on Gift, 'she's not very clever. Actually she's quite stupid.' Jeremiah didn't notice the disbelief on the faces of Mick, Martie and Gift, who all knew better. They waited for him to go on. 'But she's very charming, very likeable. Watch-able. We decided we could use someone like her...'

'Who's "we"?' asked Mick suspiciously. 'Who are you?'

'What do you mean?' Gift interjected. 'Use her for what?'

'To further our goals,' stated Jeremiah cryptically.

'What goals?' asked Mick, his voice rising.

'How did you propose to do that?' asked Gift quietly. He had a pretty good idea of the extreme leftist goals that Jeremiah and his cronies in their renegade group aspired to. 'What makes you think she would help you?'

'That's why we chose her,' said Jeremiah. 'She's stupid. Easy to train.'

'You mean brainwash,' corrected Gift.

'Easy to train,' repeated Jeremiah.

'Brainwash?' asked Mick. 'What the hell is this?'

'So what did you do?' asked Gift, raising a hand in Mick's direction to quieten him. Jeremiah grimaced.

'Nothing,' he said.

'You kidnapped her, didn't you?' squawked Mick.

'No,' said Jeremiah, still addressing only Gift. 'That's just it. Her show was cancelled very quickly, before we could get someone to start keeping track of her. Next thing we know, she's in the papers with that American girl, here in Cape Town.'

'Oh,' sighed Gift with a small smile. 'You *seriously* underestimated your mark. Miss Kwa Kwa is not as stupid as she looks. Miss Kwa Kwa is smarter on her worst day than you are on your best day, my friend.'

'How did you know about W.I.T.?' asked Martie suddenly.

'That was a separate matter,' explained Jeremiah. 'They were just one of several right-wing groups we'd been watching. We had no idea they had any relation to Miss Kwa Kwa. Or you, Mrs Yeni. I flew to Cape Town yesterday to track Miss Kwa Kwa. The first time I heard that she was being held by W.I.T. was tonight.'

'So if you didn't kidnap MK in Joburg, who did?' asked Mick.

The conjecture was halted by a crackling voice coming in over the radio.

'Come in, tower,' it said in a male American accent. The controller answered. 'I have Miss Jackie de la Rey here. She wants to know if the authorities have been called as requested.' The controller replied that they had. 'Please put them on – she's ready to make a statement.' The controller turned to the police officer standing nearby. Before he could respond, Jeremiah stepped in and took him aside. To the others it looked like Jeremiah was issuing an ominous threat. The police officer stepped back. Jeremiah looked at Gift.

'Go on, my love,' said Martie. 'Make this right.'

In what seemed like another lifetime, Gift had been a corrupt politician married to an insatiable Lady Macbeth. Although he'd always been a decent man, he'd allowed himself to become complicit in some shady situations. But although he'd resigned before the consequences could catch him, married the wonderful, righteous Martie, and tried in many ways to atone, his past activities still haunted him. At this particular moment, he felt he had no choice but to step up. Perhaps this was his chance at true redemption.

He stepped forward and took a seat at the desk.

'This is De la Rey,' said Jackie with a touch of grandiosity. 'To whom am I addressing at the present moment?' Beside her, the pilot kept a poker face. While he knew that Americans were frequently challenged for their alleged ignorance and so-called bastardisation of the English language, even he could recognise Jackie's failure in this regard.

'My name is Gift Yeni,' said the voice.

'Who are you?'

'Er, I'm an MP in the government. How can I help you, ma'am?'

'You can start by not patronising me, Mr Yeni,' she said. 'I know you couldn't care less about me, or any other decent white folk, and that's fine – I feel the same way about your kind.' Naturally,

Jackie could not have been aware of the look that was exchanged between Gift and Jeremiah. 'I have something to declare,' she said, 'and I want someone from the press in there to hear it. An Afrikaner. Quickly. You understand, boy?' After a moment of silence, came a reply.

'Of course.'

'I'm waiting. Hurry up.' She sat back, victorious.

'Where would you like me to go, ma'am?' asked the pilot.

'Just keep circling around, fool.'

Jackie spun around sharply at the sound of knocking at the cockpit door.

'Get a journalist in here,' said Mick.

'No way,' barked Jeremiah. 'We cannot get the press in on this.'

'We don't have a choice,' argued Gift.

'I think even the President would agree with me on this one,' spat Jeremiah. 'Just get someone from around here, man. Anyone who sounds Afrikaans.' All eyes fell on Martie – evidently the only Afrikaner in the village.

'She'll know it's me!'

'Wait,' called Mick. 'I know someone – an actress.'

'How fast can she get here?'

'I don't know,' gabbled Mick, trying to calculate. 'Fifteen minutes?'

'Start dialling.'

Jackie entered the cabin in the same door-kicking, gun-toting manner as before. Fahiem recoiled, tripping and falling backwards onto the floor. The black girl and the bimbo were still in their seats.

'It's okay!' he called, startled. 'I was just trying to call you.'

'Why?'

'I need to talk,' he said.

Jackie licked the corners of her mouth. She had twenty minutes to kill. Once she had kicked him back towards his seat, she sat back down opposite them and dug in her coat. The others tensed, afraid of what would appear, but it was only a mangled pack of cigarettes. Jackie lit one, relishing the first hit of nicotine.

'You can't smoke on a plane,' said Krissie.

'I can do whatever I flippin' like,' sputtered Jackie. 'Whore of Lucifer.'

'Okay,' said Krissie, steeling herself. From her seat, MK tried to send waves of strength and encouragement.

'Like you,' said Jackie. 'You just do whatever you want...' She shot a swift sideways glance at Fahiem. 'But now I'm the queen of the bloody world.'

The only sound in the cabin for the next ten minutes was the loud drone of the engines and the occasional puffing of Jackie smoking her cigarette. When the first was finished, she lit another and stood.

'I need to pray,' she said, apparently to herself. 'And practise my speech.' For the next few minutes, she paced around mouthing words, only a few of which were audible... *nation... the black plague... white pride...*

During this intense monologue, MK and Krissie exchanged many looks. Krissie would look at MK helplessly, and MK would stare back urgently. Krissie would plead with her eyes, and MK would insist back with her own. This went on, back and forth, until one phrase escaped Jackie's lips that the others heard clearly: *I'll die so that others will wake up.* MK took a chance and mouthed to Krissie: *Now.* Krissie nodded, once, minutely, and cleared her throat.

'Well,' murmured Krissie to Jackie, voice trembling, 'jealousy makes you nasty, I guess.' MK cocked her head, thinking: *Okay, so not the most original line ever, but it'll do.* Jackie responded just as anticipated: she puffed up with fury.

'You think I'm jealous of you? Everyone here knows you're a spoiled little brat. Even your coloured boyfriend here, and this darkie princess. She agrees with me – she told me so.' Krissie looked over at MK, her eyes pleading, saying: *I can't.* MK's eyes burned back. *You have to. Remember what I said: imagine it's Lindsay.*

'Well,' said Krissie, trying her best to conjure the evil Miss Lohan, 'you're just jealous that *I got him...* when you wanted him.' Jackie's jaw bulged ominously.

'What?'

'He told me all about you two,' said Krissie, gaining momentum. 'In the closet, because you were so ashamed. You're obviously not a very good racist if you were sleeping with Frank. It's sad.' Krissie fought the low-grade fear in her gut – of course her wine–pill cocktail helped in this regard. MK cheered mentally. As long as Jackie didn't shoot anyone, this was going precisely according to plan.

'You slept with *him*?' MK asked Jackie, feigning complete shock. 'You slept with a coloured guy?' she added, overlaying disgust. She was pleased to see Jackie's colour turn to deep scarlet. Here comes the NG Kerk guilt, and the shame of the racist caught sinning with the inferior races.

'I...' Jackie floundered. Her worst fear had come true.

'But he came running to me,' said Krissie. 'And he loved every second.' She threw a hesitant look at MK, who widened her eyes pointedly. 'Um... and I did it because... I'm Krissie Blaine, and I get what I want!'

'You make me sick,' shouted MK. Jackie turned, expecting this to be aimed at her, but she saw that the black girl was talking to the Yankee Doodle Candy. MK felt Jackie's surprise but didn't acknowledge it; instead she continued her disgusted rant at Krissie: 'You little tramp. I hate you. You've probably never worked a day in your life; you spend all your time faffing around like you own the world and then you come here and do the same thing in our country? You make me sick.'

Silence descended as Jackie's arm straightened at Krissie, the gun leading the way.

'Wait!' called MK. 'You can't shoot her.'

'Why not? You're right.'

'But you haven't made your statement yet,' said MK slowly. 'And besides, don't give her the pleasure of such a quick ending. Let's punish her.'

'*Huh?*' Jackie stared at MK, taken aback at her venom.

'She deserves it,' said MK. 'Look at her smug face. Punish her.'

Jackie looked at Krissie, who responded by nuzzling into Fahiem's neck, afraid. This last move was not for show, but it had just the right effect nonetheless. Jackie grabbed her by the hair and yanked her out of her seat. Krissie screamed. MK forced herself to stay put – for now – but Fahiem instinctively launched out of his seat at Jackie. Shoving Krissie aside, Jackie brought the handle of her gun crashing onto his head. With a thin moan, Fahiem collapsed back into his seat. Jackie turned back to Krissie with all the furious hatred of a hormonal Harpy. She flung herself at Krissie, who turned the other way at the last second. Jackie slammed into the side of the cabin, but spun back around with supernatural speed and kneed Krissie in the leg. It was a clumsy attempt, not very hard, but it caught Krissie off balance. She fell to the floor, hands still tied behind her back.

Jackie fell on top of her, straddling her useless arms between her legs. Krissie howled as her hands were mashed beneath their combined weight. In a heated moment, Jackie tossed aside her gun in favour of a more intimate approach and slapped Krissie through the face, a punishment she meted out with psychotic satisfaction.

MK lurched forward in her seat but did not rise. She had to wait for just the right moment. She couldn't risk Jackie regaining control. She gasped audibly when she witnessed Krissie buck her hips up into the air violently, with enough strength to topple the unprepared Jackie. Jackie flopped to the side, her face mashed into a seat.

'That's called Pilates, bitch,' roared Krissie. Hands still bound behind her, Krissie struggled up onto her knees and flung herself on top of Jackie, sinking her teeth into Jackie's ear. Jackie's scream was muffled by a mouthful of plane seat. MK cheered.

Until she noticed that Jackie's hand had found the gun.

MK pounced without another thought.

'May-day, may-day!' called the pilot's voice on the radio.

Mick, Martie, Gift and Jeremiah all froze. Their eyes drifted from each other to the radio.

'Something is going on back there. I'm going to have to take a look.'

'But who'll be flying the plane?' squealed Martie.

'Autopilot,' said Mick numbly. He wasn't even sure if there was such a thing on this aircraft. In fact he had absolutely no idea what he was talking about. But he hoped he was right.

MK landed with her full weight on Jackie and grabbed for the gun. She tried desperately to pry Jackie's fingers off but they held on like a vice. Following Krissie's example, MK bit Jackie's hand. It tasted like cigarette smoke. The gun fell to the floor, but before there could be a moment of gratitude from the good guys, Jackie's body pitched upwards, suddenly and forcefully. Her arms wrenched free and sought the air.

MK was pushed backwards. Krissie, knocked by one of Jackie's arms, bit her tongue. She cried out in pain. Jackie used the temporary distraction to clamber over them, trying to kick free her legs. MK felt the sickening thud of Jackie's savage kick to her chest and groaned. What was happening? A moment ago they'd had her, but now it looked as though the tables were turning. MK struggled to draw breath and saw Krissie spit out a mouthful of blood.

Suddenly Jackie was standing over them, grinning.

'Ha!' she roared. Her hand clutched a grenade. Her gaze shot down on them, like the hostile beams of an alien craft. 'You stupid, stupid, stupid little cows. Get up.' MK stood and helped Krissie to her feet.

'What's going on?' said David behind Jackie.

Jackie snapped around to place the voice. MK knew it when she saw it: the Right Moment. She leaped at Jackie, tackling her to the ground. In a final moment of rage, Jackie pulled the pin. An array of unpleasant things crossed Jackie's face when the grenade did not explode, bewilderment chief among them.

Suddenly David had Jackie's hands behind her and in a pair of handcuffs. She fought with everything she had but he was stronger. MK untied Krissie's hands and then picked up the discarded grenade. She waved it in front of Jackie's face.

'You're the stupid, stupid, stupid little cow,' she said hoarsely. 'This is perfume.'

'Here,' said Krissie. She marched over, snatched the bottle and sprayed it into Jackie's eyes. Jackie screamed in agony. 'You fucking psycho bitch.' Krissie then picked up Jackie's cigarettes and lit one.

'Well,' said David, disarming the subdued but groaning Jackie with practised skill, 'I'm not one to use that kind of language, missy, but I have to say I agree wholeheartedly with the sentiment.'

'Shouldn't you be flying the plane?' asked MK warily.

'Right,' he said with a smile. There was so much he wanted to say to her, and he could sense that she wanted some explanation but there was no time for that now. 'Tie her up, good and tight.'

'With pleasure,' said MK. David put Jackie into a seat and hurried back into the cockpit. MK took on the task of tying up Jackie with unfettered gusto. She used every conceivable thing she could find in the cabin to ensure that the only way Jackie would be able to get out was with very sharp scissors and a lot of patience – neither of which she possessed. Krissie smoked as she watched, but halfway through the cigarette she stubbed it out and headed to the front.

'We need champagne,' she declared, searching the supply

locker.

MK worked on until Jackie de la Rey resembled a latter-day mummy. Jackie, with eyes tightly shut but streaming, hurled abuse at her throughout the operation. MK's head felt weirder than ever and her patience was short.

'I don't suppose we have any cotton wool onboard?' she asked. Krissie shrugged, opening some bubbly before taking a thirsty swig straight from the bottle. MK considered other gag options for a moment. Finally she picked up Krissie's pill bottle and counted out three. With a deft move that would've made a veterinarian proud, she forced Jackie's mouth open, dropped the pills into the back of her throat and held her neck until she swallowed. 'Here, drink this,' she ordered firmly, and poured some of the champagne into Jackie's mouth. This seemed to shut her up. Pretty soon she'd be out for the count.

MK slumped into a seat, utterly exhausted. The ordeal had apparently had the opposite effect on Krissie Blaine, who danced around the cabin jubilantly, drinking the bubbly and wishing out loud that they had some music.

'Excuse me?' asked Saartjie Williams bluntly. First Mick had woken her in the middle of the night and demanded her immediate presence at the airport (which she'd eventually agreed to on condition that she be paid her full three months salary if the sitcom was cancelled, or received a substantial raise if it went ahead), then she'd been ushered up here into this tower, upon which Mick had in three minutes ranted a story so complex and far-fetched it could not be true. 'Come again,' she said.

'We don't have time!' he groaned. 'Just pretend you're an Afrikaans journalist, that's it. A *white* one – that's critical.' She raised an eyebrow. 'You'll pretty much just be listening anyway. Sit, sit.'

Saartjie sat down at the desk. Silence.

'Well?' she said. 'I thought we were in a big hurry.'

'She'll radio when she's ready,' Mick said.

'Fine,' said Saartjie, an imposing figure when tired and without makeup. 'Just get me a cup of coffee, someone. Black, one sugar.'

'I'll go,' volunteered Martie. She recognised Saartjie from the television and was star-struck. She was always in funny, feel-good shows, and Martie appreciated that. 'It would be my pleasure.' Saartjie donned a fake smile and Martie hurried off.

'Houston,' said the pilot from the radio. 'Everything is under control, repeat: everything is under control. The suspect has been contained. The threat has been neutralised and nobody is hurt. We'll be coming around to land now. Out.'

'Hmm,' said Saartjie in response to the American accent and the melodramatic dialogue, 'I appear to have walked into an American cop show.'

'Thank God,' sighed Mick. Gift looked similarly relieved.

'So, what?' asked Saartjie, peeved. 'You don't need me now?'

Mick smiled apologetically and offered to buy her breakfast.

Unfortunately they were all wrong. Saartjie would still be needed, because the situation was not over.

SICK OF ENDLESS AD BREAKS?

USING BRAND NEW TECHNOLOGY, IT'S THE PRODUCT YOU'VE BEEN WAITING FOR. ONCE INSTALLED, AD-GO ELIMINATES COMMERCIALS FROM YOUR TV – AND YOUR LIFE! ALL FOR THE LOW MONTHLY COST OF R5 000. ORDER NOW AND WE'LL INCLUDE A MONTHLY SUPPLY OF COCA-COLA, McDONALDS AND A SUBSCRIPTION TO *OIL & AUTO* MAGAZINE.

AD-GO is a registered trademark owned in partnership by several interested corporations working under the ethos: 'Too much choice is just overwhelming. Better to have no choice.'

10

It's All about Advertising

THE PLANE HAD a brand name on it. The airport was plastered with brand names. Screens around the airport, and indeed in countless homes around the globe, flashed brand names. Billboards outside the terminal and across the city, every city, carried glad tidings of brands. The shops in the terminal building carried brightly coloured shelves full of brands. Brands adorned the watches people wore, the things they carried, their underwear, their mail, their newspapers, their magazines and even the buildings where they worked. Brands were what they saw when they looked at their internet pages and the clothes of their children. Everything was selling something.

One of the few places one might look and see no brand is the moon, but with Richard Branson promising commercial space travel, the day may yet arrive when one will gaze into the night sky only to see the word 'Virgin' splashed across its silvery surface.

Television, for example, is driven solely by advertising. Spots during hit shows command higher fees for advertisers and so make the broadcasters more money. Even when people believe they are simply enjoying a relaxing bit of entertainment, they are being manipulated according to the bottomless hunger that is advertising. Americans cottoned onto this years ago, to the extent that today pharmaceutical companies pay broadcasters to include 'news' segments on their products during national news broadcasts. So if current events are too depressing, you're likely to see 'news' about a pill that can numb the pain.

In the advertising onslaught that constitutes our daily lives, competition for attention heats up. If you want to be heard over the din, you'd better be doing something mighty spectacular; something that's never been done before... which is perhaps why terrorists choose such radical measures. What is a cause, after all, but something begging to be bought?

One person who knew all about the evils of advertising was Mick Emmott. He'd worked in television long enough to know his true master. Of course, like so many others, he'd been so conditioned by the endless attack of selling that he did not perceive advertising as potentially harmful in any way; rather, it was simply a fact of life to be tolerated, like taxes or crime. However, Mick had yet to encounter the terrible intersection between advertising and politics...

Equally unaware of this imminent clash, Krissie flounced around the cabin of the jet in high spirits. How could she know that the book's actual dramatic climax was yet to come? She lorded over the drowsy, bound Jackie.

'Ladies and gentlemen,' she announced playfully, 'welcome aboard. We are about to take off. Please ensure that your seats are in the upright position and your tray tables are securely fastened,' she giggled. She did not notice MK's eyes close.

MK felt something happen inside her head... a moment. It felt nothing like a Right Moment, however – in fact it felt very, very Wrong. As though a switch had been flicked when Krissie had started doing the airhostess bit.

'Oh, and make sure your seatbelts are buckled,' sang Krissie in her best airhostess voice. It must've been pretty good because it was having the effect on MK that had been programmed into her mind, during her lost week in Johannesburg. If she'd been in Johannesburg at all...

Things had certainly been programmed into MK's mind, things, as you may recall, that were waiting for just the right trigger. Well, the trigger had been pulled. MK's eyes reopened. Had Krissie looked closely, she would have noticed that they appeared oddly vacant. They were colder, as if some tiny but vital sparkplug had burnt out. Krissie did not notice; she was too busy relaxing in her seat, sucking on her NBF, the champagne. MK stood, her exhaustion apparently gone, and with quiet purpose bent and picked up one of Jackie's guns. She walked to the cockpit and entered quietly.

'Hey, you,' said the pilot with an awkward grin. This faded when MK pointed the gun at him.

'Put me in touch with the ground,' she intoned.

'Oh, ha ha,' he said, 'I get it. Very funny.'

'Do it now,' she said with a dreadful calm that was totally unlike the raving mania of Jackie de la Rey, and yet all the more disturbing for it.

The man stared at her for a second longer. He'd seen that look before, on the kind of face that meant business. Bad business.

'Uh, ground control,' said the pilot from the radio. 'We have a situation. A new one...' Initially the happy chatter in the room continued. It was only once the controller had called their attention to the radio that it stopped. 'I have a lady who wants to make a statement...'

Everyone tensed. Mick gestured for Saartjie to sit back down, expecting to hear Jackie speak. He was astounded to hear MK's voice instead, although it sounded a little strange. Unfamiliar.

'*I have a message for the people of South Africa,*' she droned.

'Palesa?' asked Saartjie.

'Shhh,' hissed Mick.

'Go ahead,' said Gift, leaning in.

'We see the way the world is going and it displeases us...' The stunned listeners listened, stunned. 'We have seen what the endless consumerism has done to the United States of America. We see it happening here at home.'

'Who's we?' asked Saartjie without thinking.

'We are CAMRA,' said the voice.

'Camera?' muttered Jeremiah. 'Never heard of them.' This was the same thought that struck the pilot as he watched the messenger beside him.

'Citizens Against Mindless Repetitive Advertising...'

It took a good long while for this to sink in for everyone standing around the radio. They exchanged looks of confusion, incredulity, hopeful amusement.

'Are you joking?' asked Mick into the receiver.

'No. We are dead serious.'

'What's going on, Lisa?' asked the man, but it was as if she didn't hear him.

'We have noted, with dismay, that while children today are largely ignorant of truly important things, and display a greater and greater aversion to books, they could probably recite the slogan for any product you could care to name. We seek a guarantee from a government representative that advertising be strictly reduced and regulated.'

The man stared at her, wide-eyed. He'd heard his fair share of crackpot causes in his life, but this took the cake. He touched Lisa's arm gently, but retracted it hastily when she brought the gun closer to his head.

'Uhhh...' said an uncertain voice on the controller's radio. Some part of MK's mind – one that felt paralysed – called out that she knew this voice. 'Okay, hang on...'

The man thought he could make out the faint sounds of arguing in the background static, but presently a male voice came on. The man recognised it as the same guy that had come on to speak to Jackie... Gift Someone.

'Hi,' he said, wondering if this was for real or just another scam by Miss Kwa Kwa. Mick had insisted he play along with whatever she said, however. 'I'm from the government.'

'That was quick,' MK spoke into the radio.

'Well,' he stammered. 'I was here already... for another matter.'

'I want a member of the press too,' stated MK, newest spokesperson of CAMRA. Another moment of silence, interspersed with very distant whispering.

'Hi,' grunted an unfriendly female voice, 'I'm a journalist.'

'That was quick,' repeated MK in her new drone.

'What do you want?' asked the woman, a touch impatiently. This was followed by what sounded to the man like recriminations in the background.

'You must guarantee,' instructed MK, 'that you will print our demands on the front page of your publication tomorrow. Or, if you're in television, in every news broadcast. Or repeated every hour on the hour, if you're on the wireless.'

In the control tower, Mick blinked. *The wireless?* That was the second time in the last two days he'd heard the radio referred to by this archaic term. Strands started pulling together in his mind: MK's lost week in Joburg; her neighbour there, Mrs Siegl; their neighbour *here*, Mrs Siegl; Mrs Siegl talking about the wireless; Mrs Siegl always complaining about the volume of the television... The strands wrapped around each other, interwove and tied together to form a very clear picture. A tapestry (perhaps not quite as unsightly as Jackie's, but distressing nonetheless).

'No,' he said aloud. 'I know who's done this to her.'

'Fine,' complained Gift, 'but right now, that information isn't helping defuse the situation.' Mick grabbed the microphone.

'Pilot, listen,' he said, 'she's been brainwashed or something. I know it sounds insane...'

'Yeah, yeah,' interrupted the pilot. 'I got that much. We need the deactivation. It's usually a word or a phrase.'

'Er...' Mick racked his brain. He barely knew Mrs Siegl, much less the bloody deactivation word or whatever it was that would stop his best friend from doing something stupid. *Could this night get any more bizarre?* Mick handed the microphone back to Saartjie. 'Keep her talking. Listen to her demands, whatever. I need to make a call.' He hurried away from the radio to try to phone Mrs Siegl, when he was stopped dead by the terrible realisation that he didn't have her number. Well, he did, but it was in his phonebook at the flat.

'Goddammit!' he roared.

Even Martie was too enthralled by the drama to reproach him for his blasphemy.

'Okay,' said the female journalist's voice. 'I promise. It'll be put in the press tomorrow. What else do you want?'

David turned to MK, waiting for her to answer, but she appeared to have shut down completely. Her eyes were open but there was nothing in them. Porch lights on but no one home, as they said in the States. He waved a hand in front of her face. Still nothing.

'Lisa?'

She sat there, a statue of coffee-coloured marble. David found himself becoming quite upset by this. The stillness of her exterior, however, contrasted sharply with the turmoil raging inside her head. MK, the true MK, with the mental capacities of several genius men, wrestled with the icy stranger who had seized control of her mind. It made the tussle with Jackie earlier seem like a schoolyard scrap in comparison. This was war. The war for her sanity.

Oblivious to all this, David reached across to take the gun, but was taken aback when her free hand shot up and grabbed his wrist and pushed it away. The gun in her other hand remained firmly trained on him.

'Do not take this lightly,' she warned. 'I am trained to take any action necessary to achieve our goals. If I must sacrifice myself in the name of our cause, then so be it. People must reject advertising altogether. The global economy must be brought to its knees.'

'Okay,' said David, 'they heard you. You hear me? They got it.'

'Okay,' said MK. Suddenly her face crumpled into an expression of pain and torment. She leaned forward and cried out, putting her forehead in her hand.

'Lisa?' He panicked. In his years with the agency, the man had heard stories about plants – people that underwent some kind of mental reprogramming – that just mentally wigged out. With a sick feeling in his stomach he realised that Lisa was the plant in South Africa that he had heard about – the person placed by some unknown terror group. CAMRA. He cursed his stupidity for ever suspecting Krissie Blaine. She was probably back there in the cabin right now, getting wasted like the dumb kid she was. (He was right about that.) Now here he was, in the cockpit of an ill-fated airplane (American spelling) with the woman he loved, and the woman he had to take down so as to save everyone involved, including her. It was like a Greek tragedy. (The man knew very little about Greek tragedy, but he felt certain this qualified.)

'Oh, Lisa,' he moaned. The sweet agony of forbidden love.

MK screamed, clutching desperately at her head. The gun dropped to the floor in the process, but that had ceased to be a consideration for the man who, for a while, had only worn island shirts. His new mission was clear: he needed to save the woman he loved from almost-certain mental collapse.

But without the deactivation key, he felt powerless. In a moment of sheer inspiration, he sang. This scenario was so much like the movies anyway – maybe love would be enough. He sang the song he had written for her – 'Star-Spangled Lady'.

'Oh, us at the beach!' he sang to a tune closely resembling that of The Star-Spangled Banner, 'by the dusk's golden light! That so sweetly we watched as we nibbled on ice cream!'

'It sounds like the US national anthem,' said Gift to the others, who were now packed around the radio, struggling to hear.

'Great,' remarked Saartjie, 'now the pilot's lost his flipping mind too.'

To his delight, the man noticed that his serenade seemed to be calming Lisa down. She had stopped groaning and her hands had dropped away from her head. He responded by singing even louder, finishing the end of the only verse he had penned with a grand flourish.

'And the star-spangled lady sweet ki-i-sses sha-all giiiive... In the land where we are free and the hooome wheeeere we'll liiiiiiiiiiive! Badda-boom!'

She looked at him with a slightly strange expression, but it was definitely her. The CAMRA-bot was gone and Lisa was back. He threw his arms around her joyfully. MK allowed herself to be hugged for a moment while she got her bearings back, but then extricated herself from his bear-like embrace.

'Fly the plane, captain,' she said dully. 'It's time to land.'

'Yes, ma'am,' he chirped brightly, sitting back down in his seat and preparing to do just that. 'Oh, Lisa,' he sighed, 'you don't how happy I am that you're okay...' He realised that he was alone when the cockpit door closed behind her. *Oh. Well, she's obviously gone to tell the others the good news.*

MK hurried into the restroom to be alone for a moment. She stared at herself at the mirror and was pleased to see only herself in her eyes. Whatever had just happened, it was over, and she looked forward to getting her feet back on solid ground. This was one instance where she preferred to be as far away from the stars as gravity would allow.

When she returned to the cabin, both Krissie Blaine and Jackie de la Rey were unconscious. Fahiem stared out the window dejectedly. They said nothing to each other. MK chose the seat farthest from the others and buckled up. Then, she opened up Krissie's makeup bag, which she'd collected from the floor, and began putting on her face. Despite what may have gone on during the last hellish night, she intended to be ready to face the public when she disembarked.

Superstardom Lesson No. 85: There is no excuse for being seen without makeup. Believe me, I should know.

When the plane touched down safely and the steps were put in place, MK was the first to appear. Mick's heart sang at the sight of her. She looked as gorgeous as ever, and took the steps with the beaming wave of royalty. He ran over to meet her and kissed her on both cheeks.

'Please, sweetie,' she drawled in her best Palesa voice. 'I've just put my face on.'

'And you look divine,' he said, bowing.

'Thank yoo, thank yoo,' she sang.

'Good news,' he said, 'Mrs Siegl has been arrested.' MK could not conceal her surprise. 'Turns out she's the local head of some terror cell that operates internationally. Citizens Against Mindless Repetitive Advertising, in case you don't remember.'

'It's coming back to me in bits and pieces. Hmm. If she hadn't abducted me, she might have had a supporter in me,' observed MK wryly.

'She and her gang are the ones who abducted you in Joburg. When they saw you on TV, they thought you were the perfect candidate for brainwashing. Evidently they, like many others,

261

don't give your brain much credit.'

'I see.'

'Ever consider hanging up the dumb routine?'

'I am considering it,' she said.

'How did you snap out of it?' he asked curiously.

'Hmm,' said MK. 'Sheer force of will.'

The fact of the matter was that Mrs Siegl had made the deactivation key the melody of 'Star-Spangled Banner' – assuming that the chances of an American being onboard would be very slim, much less that said American would start singing it.

So much for the redemptive power of love.

The man who'd spent his time in Cape Town wearing only island shirts never got a chance to address the matter of his love for the mysterious Lisa: no sooner had he set foot off the plane than he was nabbed by two men in black suits. They barrelled him into a waiting (black) car and revealed themselves to be agents of the very organisation that the man himself had belonged to, and more recently fled.

With this revelation, he panicked, fearing that they had come to arrest him. He was relieved – thrilled actually – to hear that he was being hailed as the hero who'd brought down the South African arm of the international terror threat, CAMRA. He was to be put back on duty with immediate effect and whisked across to International Departures, where they would soon be boarding a flight bound for home. It was a mixed blessing. On the one hand, he felt redeemed and excited to be going back to the US, but on the other he would be leaving Lisa behind without a word of farewell.

He gazed out of the tinted car window, wondering if he would ever see her again.

Jackie de la Rey was arrested, insofar as an unconscious person can be arrested. Let's just say that she was carried off by the police, who planned to officially arrest her as soon as she awoke.

The police also carried Krissie Blaine off the plane, although she was not arrested, but rather escorted back to her hotel. As she lay unconscious in the back seat of the police car, the officers posed with her and took photographs with their cellphone cameras.

Fahiem Abdul returned home to the warmth and love of the family he had taken for granted so often before in his life. He swore never to date an American girl again. He also swore never to date an Afrikaans girl again, or to get involved with anyone at his place of work. When he was done swearing, he curled up in front of the TV and fell asleep to the pleasant, innocuous jingles of commercials.

Lincoln Thomas awoke in a hospital with a stabbing pain in the arse (British spelling). He was relieved to learn that he had not been shot with an actual bullet, but apparently by something more commonly used on wildlife. He was informed of this by the lovely nurse who came in to put cream on what she called his 'chronic sunburn'. Her name was Lorenza, which he found very exotic, and she was what he supposed was called 'coloured' around here. She was gorgeous.

'So,' she said in her charming accent, '*are* you?' Link didn't make the connection until he realised that she was applying cream to his forehead.

'No,' he said emphatically. 'I'm not gay. I like birds. A lot. I've slept with hundreds, at least.' She considered him skeptically and laughed. 'You're a right fit bird, luv.'

'Thanks,' she said. Link blushed. He'd expected her to slap him across the face, or tell him where to get off, or scream for help. Those were the reactions he usually elicited. But Lorenza just smiled at him indulgently with a look that said she had his number, but was perhaps prepared to overlook it.

'How old are you?' he asked.

'You really know nothing about women, do you?'

'Nah,' he admitted. 'Not really. Want to teach me?'

She said something he didn't quite understand – sounded like: yo mah sa poos – but he caught the gist.

Lorenza married him a month later. Someone had to.

After a day of R 'n' R – rest and recovery – some of the crisis survivors gathered at the Hotel Shmotel at the invitation of Krissie Blaine. In a private area of the grounds, the staff had set up what she called a barbecue, but her guests sniffed out as a braai. In attendance were Mick, MK, a reluctant Saartjie and an even more reluctant Gift and Martie.

Krissie announced that she would be leaving the next day, returning to Los Angeles to shoot an ad campaign for Tommy Gofigure's Terror. The concept had a dark, brooding Arab man, dressed in traditional gear succumbing to the enchantment of the all-American, Terror-drenched Krissie. The others nodded politely as she explained it, deciding it would be in poor taste to critique their hostess. Let the American press take care of that.

At one point Martie noticed that MK was a short distance away, alone, looking out at the sea. Martie joined her.

'Hello,' she said awkwardly.

'Hi, Martie.'

An immensely uncomfortable silence followed.

'It's so big,' said Martie eventually. 'The sea,' she added when MK's face creased. 'The sea. It's hard to believe there's a whole world out there.'

'Have you been overseas?' MK asked.

'No,' laughed Martie.

'Do you ever want to?'

'Maybe,' said Martie, shrugging. 'But I'm happy here.'

MK nodded, letting this knock around her head for a moment.

'Thank you,' she said.

'For what?' asked Martie.

'For whatever you were doing at the airport,' said MK. 'It was nice to know you were there. You're a nice lady.'

'Well,' said Martie, blushing. 'It seems like there must be some reason we keep bumping into each other.' MK hmmed in agreement. 'Perhaps some greater plan...' finished Martie, her eyes drifting skyward.

'Anyway,' said MK amiably. She held up her glass. Martie clinked her own against it. 'To the sea.'

'To the sea.' Martie wandered off back to Gift. MK's eyes drifted back to the sea, the horizon. A flat line. MK remembered the defibrillator from the aeroplane, and decided that if anyone could shake up that line and jolt some life into it, it was her. The mountains reminded her of her one date with the man who had called himself David. Well, that had ended abruptly. Probably just as well – the man clearly had issues. Still, she wondered what might have happened if the right wing hadn't intervened so dramatically...

With a heavy sigh, she made her way over to the braai. Krissie was playing with Wiggy and Mick was chatting to Saartjie. Saartjie smiled benevolently at MK.

'We were just talking about the show,' she said. 'Such a pity you won't be staying on, my dear. We so loved having you.'

'How can such a good actress be such a bad liar?' asked MK sweetly. Saartjie gaped, trying to decide if this was a compliment or an insult. Opting for compliment, she smiled gracefully. Mick chuckled to himself. Pleased as punch because he'd managed to replace MK with a promising young thing here in Cape Town. Production would not be delayed as long as he'd expected. MK had decided Saartjie's ultimatum for Mick by resigning from the show. Life was too short to squander her talents on sitcom. Even temporary poverty was preferable. Not really poverty – yet... Mick had generously paid her a month's notice, insisting he would take care of the channel's objections to paying an actress who had worked so little. MK looked forward to hanging around in Cape Town for a while, and experiencing the city without all the other chaos going on.

A hand slung itself over MK's shoulder. Krissie.

'That kitty is soooo cute! Can I have him?'

'No, sweetie.'

'I can't wait to get home and see Lord Poopington.' She was referring to the mouse-sized dog that was almost as famous as she was. 'I love that smell,' she said, changing gear.

'Ah, yes,' said Mick. 'The smell of the braai. That always says summer for me. That, and the raging thunderstorms.'

'Yes,' said MK, 'something to look forward to when I eventually get back to Jozi.'

'Well, I hope you know that you can come visit me any time,' said Krissie.

'Thanks. But I think it'll be a while before I can set foot on a plane again.'

'Yeah,' sighed Krissie. 'I've just bought a new jet. The vibes on the old one would just be, like, too intense. Like that potato salad! My God, don't touch it – it's disgusting. I'll have to tell the manager.'

'I made it,' Martie said quietly.

'Oh,' said Krissie. 'Thanks, gorgeous.'

MK was the only one who laughed in the awkward silence.

'What will you do now?' Saartjie asked MK suddenly.

MK smiled secretively.

'What I always do,' she purred. 'Shine.'

Superstardom Lesson No. 100: People always think they want to know what's going to happen next, but they don't, really. Keep them guessing. It's what cliffhangers are made of.

Epilogue

Jeremiah was denied his prize of capturing Jackie de la Rey. He consoled himself with the knowledge that there were others just like her out there, and put all his energy back into the insidious activities of his group.

On the other wing of the metaphorical bird, Wilhelmina turned ninety. She celebrated her birthday in her new hometown of Orania, around their prized Koeksuster Monument. She abandoned political intrigues, certain that other, younger people would continue the new Struggle.

Their efforts, like Jeremiah's, have thus far not amounted to anything.

Jackie de la Rey was, for the most part, unpopular in prison. Throughout the lengthy wait for her case to be heard, she maintained an unyielding silence. She ignored requests to appear in adverts for bleach, and refused to talk to the press.

Surrounded by many other women in the overcrowded prison, but always alone in her head, Jackie had a lot of time to think. Fantasies of escape gripped her constantly, and she longed for the day she could run free. Prison changed one aspect of her: she no longer wished for the eradication of all blacks...

Only one.

Mere days after Krissie Blaine's departure, the staff of the Hotel Shmotel broke into the safe she'd left locked. In it they found a cellphone. On that they found pictures of a weird sunburned guy posing beside a sleeping Krissie. These pictures never made it into the media – too dull.

About a month later, far juicier pictures hit the press: Krissie had been snapped smooching a married Hollywood actor. Before you could say cha-ching, the two were starring in a reality show about their new romance.

When Mrs Siegl was finally interrogated, she admitted that she and her operatives had taken MK into the Kalahari Desert to be reprogrammed among the Khoisan. This was not for any particular reason other than it was remote and nobody ever listened to what the Khoisan had to say anyway.

Her message was vaguely reported in the press and inspired something of an email sensation: an online community of supporters sprung up and faithfully tried to carry the message about advertising.

Their efforts were unsuccessful.

And so ends the second book of the one and only MK, not with a bang (although it was close)... but a full-stop.

Acknowledgements

FIRSTLY, I MUST offer deepest, humblest, profoundest thanks to Jo Watson, who spent hours and hours with me helping me get this thing straight in my head (well, as straight as either my head or hers will ever be), and for slapping me around when I gave in to maudlin floor-crawling. I honestly could not have done it without you.

To my mother, father and Sharon for not disowning me when I retreated almost entirely from the world to get the book done. Ditto for the friends I avoided at around the same time... your names escape me right now...

As for the motley Jacana crew, one couldn't ask for a nicer bunch of people. Your support and encouragement (and work) is greatly appreciated. Ditto to Bronwyn, my editor (right now, she's probably questioning my repeated use of 'ditto').

Stephen Simm

As ever, I couldn't pass up an opportunity to smooch in black and white my extended family: the Empangeni clan, mi London Twin, Red Muffin, Simoon and the kidlets, the Zoids (welcome, Ben!), the Barnes Trio, Lady Death, Lady Laila, Kevin Costnay, Didi, Carms, and the rest of the Jozi bunch.

Finally, I wish to thank everyone out there who has embraced this crazy world of MK and its little army of inhabitants. It is, of course, for you.

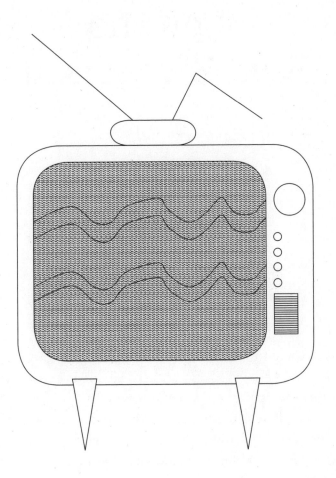

Join the
Kwa Kwa Klan!

THE KWA KWA KLAN, or KKK, is a meeting of minds that are enquiring and perhaps a little twisted. We are not to be confused with a certain right-wing American group who, as grown men, have decided there is honour in wearing white dresses and pointy hats. Our ideology differs in the following ways: 1. We abhor racism, and 2. We prefer men in kangas. Oops, did we just use the new K-word?

The main thing you need to know about the KKK is that nothing is sacred and nowhere is off-limits. Feel free to join us in pointing the finger (the only condition is that it may get pointed at you too... or us). We don't tickle funny bones... We break 'em.

So if you wish to receive our madcap monthly newsletter, drop us a line at misskwakwa@gmail.com to join the mailing list.

You can also check us out online at www.stephensimm.com, on Facebook (a group called KWA KWA KLAN), or read the author's blog at www.stephensimm.book.co.za.

Keep watch for special events! If you're lucky you may meet Miss Kwa Kwa herself and get her to sign your autograph box below.

I met Miss Kwa Kwa!

Thank yoo, thank yoo xxx

Other fiction titles by Jacana

Coconut
by Kopano Matlwa

Death in the New Republic
by David Dison

End
by Barbara Adair

Miss Kwa Kwa
by Stephen Simm

Seven Steps to Heaven
by Fred Khumalo

Six Fang Marks and a Tetanus Shot
by Richard de Nooy